CW00395035

v|b|z
ZAGREB

istrosbooks

NA MARGINI
ON THE MARGINS

BOOK SERIES
NA MARGINI / ON THE MARGINS

book no. 4

EDITOR-IN-CHIEF:
Drago Glamuzina

MANAGING EDITOR:
Sandra Ukalović

Marina Šur Puhlovski
Wild Woman

PUBLISHER:
V.B.Z. d.o.o., Zagreb
10010 Zagreb, Dračevička 12
tel.: 01/6235-419, fa: 01/6235-418
e-mail: info@vbz.hr
www.vbz.hr

FOR CO-PUBLISHER:
Istros Books
Conway Hall, 25 Red Lion Square,
London, WC1R 4RL
e-mail: info@istrosbooks.com

FOR PUBLISHER:
Mladen Zatezalo

EDITOR:
Susan Curtis

PROOFREADER:
Charles Phillips

LAYOUT:
V.B.Z. studio, Zagreb

PRINTED IN:
Znanje d.o.o., Zagreb
July 2019

This project has been funded with support from
the European Commission.
This publication reflects the views only of the author,
and the Commission cannot be held responsible for
any use which may be made of the information contained therein.

Marina Šur Puhlovski

Wild Woman

Translated by
Christina Pribichevich-Zorić

v|b|z ZAGREB
2019.

BOOK SERIES
NA MARGINI / ON THE MARGINS

book no. 4

ORIGINAL TITLE
Marina Šur Puhlovski
Divljakuša

This book has been published with support from
the Ministry of Culture of the Republic of Croatia.

ISBN-13: 978-1912545216

For my daughter Mirta Puhlovski

I.

THIS IS the third day that I haven't left the house, except to take the dog out, early in the morning, as soon as it's light, and again late at night, when it's dark, it's out and back in, no walking, no running, he just does his business and it's back to our refuge before anybody can see us. Because I look a wreck in my faded track suit with its sagging knees, unwashed, my cheeks practically ashen because I haven't eaten a thing in three days, except for the cubes of toasted stale bread that my mother left in the oven for breadcrumbs before she took off. I dip them in the pan with what remains of the pork drippings from this winter; we already ate all the crackling.

You can buy ready-made breadcrumbs in the store for nothing, you don't have to bother making them, but it's a sin to throw bread away, says my mother, the memory of poverty always close to the surface, so, she grumbles, since we have no chickens to feed, she makes breadcrumbs. But you've never kept chickens, I remind my mother, who was born in a town, in the city centre actually, two tram stops away from the main square, like me, like her mother and her mother's mother; chickens are not part of our family lore, you can't cite them, not even when talking about being thrifty.

But being thrifty has proven to be useful to your daughter, I say to my mother, who isn't here, as if she were still sitting at the kitchen table playing Patience, which she started doing when she retired, when life stopped before it had even begun – to the daughter who is incapable of going to the local shop let alone cooking, but there are always your breadcrumbs, I smile, and my mother understands, even though she's absent, even though she ran away from the horror of my marriage, she hears everything even when she's not here; you can count on her as if she were here. The secret of breadcrumbs.

I give Tanga the cooked giblets that I froze. Thank God we've got reserves, you won't starve, I say aloud, thinking that without them even the dog would starve, she'd be on a diet of toasted bread cubes, because her mistress is incapable of doing anything – except drinking wine – my mother corrects me with concern but without reproach; because this mother doesn't do reproach.

It's red wine, Dalmatian Pharos, twelve-and-a-half per cent alcohol, says the label, but it doesn't get me drunk, it's as if the alcohol turns into water in my mouth, every drunk's nightmare.

I've switched on the TV, hoping that it will bring me out of myself, but it's no use, I can't follow, I can't connect one scene with the next, nothing makes sense, even sleep doesn't seem to want me, although I occasionally snap out of the doldrums, not knowing where I am, as if I had dozed off.

At one point somebody rang the doorbell, it's a terrible moment, an assault, I went rigid in my chair, who's that breaking in, and Tanga runs off barking to chase away the intruder, but it's no use, violence has taken hold of the bell so I open the door, foaming at the mouth.

And standing at the door is a girl, barely eighteen, I figure, barely of age, or maybe not even, and she's in tears, trembling, saying she's lost, she has no place to go, she doesn't know anybody here, not a soul, she says, and I wonder what that's got to do with me, why me, how did she wind up at my door, and then I learn from her confused talk that she's been in this flat before, even slept here, last summer, she says (where was I then? at the seaside, I decide), when she came to Zagreb with the amateur theatre of Pula that Aunt Višnja runs; aha, Aunt Višnja, my mother's "client", so she's the connection with this poor girl whom I can't take in, not into the flat or into my heart, such are the times.

As soon as Tanga sees how miserable and tearful she is, she runs up to her, sniffing, wagging her tail, saying "Come in", because we like visitors, says the tail, but not me, I keep my distance, I don't move, I stand there at the door as immutable as a rock.

Can't you see what I'm dealing with here, what's around me, I tell her in my mind, but she keeps sniffling, gazing at me, her eyes full of hope, which I will have to kill, so I look around to make her look around, because she's obviously blinded by fear, she doesn't notice that I'm standing on sheets of newspaper streaked with paint and dirt from my slippers, because we've started painting the place, started and stopped when my husband walked out of the house, slamming the door, never to return, never to save me from myself.

But she doesn't see the sheets of newspaper or the rubbish or the can of paint that I shoved into the hall, she doesn't see the paint rollers and paintbrushes, she just sees her own problem, she doesn't care about mine, we're human, that's just how we are, we won't hold it against her but we won't take her in either, I'm clear on that. Although I'm not exactly happy that I have to turn her away when she's so miserable, lost in a strange city, and I know that my mother, when she hears about it, will criticise me, how could you send the poor thing away, she chides me in advance; I could do it, I say to myself, because I'm not you, I'm not a constant shoulder for the homeless, the disenfranchised, the betrayed to lean on, I don't sacrifice myself, I mind my own business, it's not my fault that she was unlucky enough to come not upon you but upon somebody like me, who will let her down …

Which I do instantly: I'm sorry, I say, but you can't come in, you can't, I'm a mess, I shake my head, slowly closing the door in her face, because I don't want to be unkind, and because I'm wondering hypocritically where she'll go, who's going to help her, I feel sorry for her already, and guilty, but not to the extent that I want to run after her, bring her back to this mess of a flat, and of me, falling apart at the age of twenty-six and not knowing why.

As for Aunt Višnja, she's been in my bad books for a long time, I think to myself, as if such thoughts are any justification before the all-knowing and all-seeing, maybe he records everything in the mysterious memory of the Universe – that Aunt Višnja of ours would give the leading roles to the children of important, politically powerful parents and leave the bit parts for the rest of us when putting on plays at the theatre she once ran, where my mother wound up at a certain point in her life, with me, of course.

Oh, she's not that bad, my mother said when I complained, the poor thing has been through a lot, and when I grew up I learned what "the poor thing" had been through, which was that at the age of sixteen she had run away from home with an actor she had fallen in love with and who had literally gambled her away in a card game when he ran out of money. And then she passed from hand to hand, became an actress and, when she got old, a drama teacher, which is how she came with the children from Pula to Zagreb and stayed with us, where she had a free bed and room service.

But you've never been fair, I tell her, the thorn of her injustice still in my heart; as if that justifies the inhumane way I treated the girl.

To hell with her, too, I say to myself, disposing of the ballast that landed on me, as if I don't have enough problems of my own, and I open the door to the space between the bathroom and the two rooms, a space that is a room in itself, except with no window overlooking the street – it does have a window, but it looks out in to the elevator shaft, which is always dark because it's a ground-floor flat – and I step onto the carpet just long enough for the insects nestling inside it to jump out and take possession of my ankle.

Get off of me, I shout, shaking them off my leg, pushing away the hovering dog; what do you want, you stupid thing, I say, showing her my bite-pocked leg, which these guys go for when they've got nothing better around to nibble, and I close off the "prohibited zone", as I've called the rooms ever since they started breeding there and the dog and I escaped to the other side, to the dining room with the small kitchen and little maid's room, the only refuge we've got left. For now.

Luckily, the insects haven't made it into the hall, where the toilet is, but they've occupied the bathroom, and the cupboards; I unplugged the phone, and at the last minute moved the television into the dining room so that at least I'd have something to break the silence, even if I didn't watch it, so I'd know I'm alive because that's not how I feel.

m as alive as a zombie. As the living dead. And I have no idea how it happened – how I became a zombie – when only three days ago I was literally dancing with joy around the house, happy that the bastard had finally left; forever, I even sang, because we had thought it would be forever.

You and I are going to solve this, I tell my canine adviser curled up on the chair, who, hearing my words, raises her head and pricks up her ears, actually the top part of her ears, the bit next to her head, because she's a cocker spaniel and her ears hang down to her neck so she can't really prick them up, only to immediately sink back into her chair. Yes we will, I say, though I don't know how because to know how you have to know what's happening to you in the first place. And I don't, life has caught me off-guard, it's as if I was possessed by demons the moment he walked out of the flat, slamming the door behind him, when I thought I was so strong, when I did a victory dance around the space still uncontaminated by insects.

Hey-ho, I danced on the corpse of my marriage, the dog at my heels, twirling my twenty-six-year-old body down the hall, into the bedroom, and then into my mother's room, as if to make sure that he wasn't hiding there.

My mother's room is a mess, with rolled up carpet leaning against the wall, the furniture pushed into the middle of the room, the paintbrushes, buckets and paint tins that I will later move into the hall, who knows why, probably to have a reason to stretch my muscles, as if that would help. And then hey-ho, it was back again to the dining room for the wine, because you always have to drink to victories, to make them bigger, and to defeats, to make them smaller, and then with the bottle back again into the hall, where we keep the bottle opener handily on a tray on the table and just as I grabbed it I fell onto the floor, as if mown down. And the bottle dropped out of my hand, quietly rolling until it came to a stop under the table.

It wasn't that I tripped, no, I literally collapsed onto the carpet, as if my legs had given way, the same legs that had danced their way here, stockingless, in brown cork sandals with four-inch heels, legs as white as a naked corpse on the carpet, I suppose, because I'd never seen a corpse on the carpet, dressed or otherwise, legs that didn't seem to belong to me, that were huge, they'd always been too strong, at least in my opinion, because there were also other opinions, legs that the dog immediately proceeded to sniff, maybe she knew something that we have long since lost.

So what if I collapsed, I tell myself, getting to my feet pretty easily, because I'm elastic, I have no trouble assuming a lotus position, doing cartwheels or a bridge, but I already know that I fell not because I wasn't paying attention but because I had a blow to the head, an internal not an external blow, and it wasn't my blood vessels that had decided to burst, as they had with him. No, the blow came to my head from my stomach, from my solar plexus where the third chakra is located, I read that somewhere but forget what it means except that it's something vague and connected to your whole being, something that comes to life or collapses, that masters life or is mastered by it, as in my poor case.

The fact that I could stand on my legs and move them again was of no help at all, because while the machine worked externally, internally it was experiencing a permanent, endless breakdown. Early this morning I crept out of the house, waited for the poor dog to poo, trying not to impatient because she was taking so long to sniff out a ,ood spot, and feeling guilty because that's all I can offer her now, she's being deprived of the long walks she enjoys as if her life is unimportant, and it isn't, so, keeping my head down, I ran back into the house and the realm of insects.

Until recently, there were no fleas at all, except for two or three on the dog, which are good for it and should be left there, say the experts, but after I collapsed on the floor they reproduced at the speed of light, as if they were unable to reproduce while I was strong, but the loss of my strength was a signal for them to breed, for a population explosion in my flat, miraculously arrested at the door to the hall.

At first I tried to exterminate them individually, one by one, since I couldn't go out to get something from the pharmacy, and I listened to the blood-bloated insects crack, satiated to death, I thought to myself, as if that was any consolation. It wasn't, I didn't empathise with the parasites, I even drowned them in the sink, but to no effect. They came out of the water just as alive and hungry as before, so I gave up. I preferred taking the dog and retreating to the uncontaminated zone, even if I was bitten all over. And there I waited for who knows what, because it's a known fact that fleas can go hungry for a long time, they can go without food for a year, they're biblically tough. The dog and I aren't.

And so I finished up on the southern, warm, sunny side of the world, where the balcony overlooks the courtyard with an apricot tree, its fruits scooped up into a bucket a long time ago by the neighbour who lives in the basement. I don't know if she gave them to the other neighbours, but she certainly didn't give them to me. The neighbour from the apartment above ours, on the first floor, had planted the tree when she was a child, accidentally, when she was playing in the courtyard and buried the pit of an apricot she'd just eaten in the ground.

It's a miracle that apricot tree grew at all, my mother would say, because nobody took care of it, gave it compost, watered or weeded it, it simply sprouted up out of the ground and grew into a sturdy tree and in springtime its broad treetop would blossom with a whiteness you could never get enough of.

I usually prefer the south, warmth and lots of light, but not now. Now I could do with the other side of the world, with the north and its perpetual cold and dusk, its connection to Hades where I landed when I collapsed on the floor and clearly died. Died as the wife of my husband, as his partner, died along with love, faithfulness, loyalty and everything that goes with it, all shattered by the broken vow of "forever", now nothing but an empty word. Because nothing is "forever", not the dog, not me, not the damned insects or this apartment or this building or this tree or this town or this planet or the Milky Way and the Universe with it, everything changes, and so do words, which are basically always a matter of politics, in other words, a bitch.

To Hades what's dead, to life what survives, I tell myself rationally, but I don't go out, I'm still down there, looking down on my corpse as if I want to bring it back to life, although I don't. And I can't. Because you can't revive the dead, the dead stay dead and should be buried or cremated so that we don't look at them anymore, so that we can part ways because they don't belong to us anymore, nor do we to them. We belong only in our thoughts – me now and me once upon a time – and in photos, and these photos keep us together like Siamese twins attached at the head, making it impossible to separate the two. Except with a knife. When one of us will drop away.

II.

FINALLY SOMETHING I can wear, I say to my mother seven years earlier, meaning the latest fashion pictured in the women's magazine *Žena*, aimed at women of all ages, but especially mine – an age group that doesn't know anything yet, that has just an inkling, an idea – offering fashion trends and advice on how to catch a man and keep him, nothing about how to get rid of him, I notice now but don't then, no I don't – my mind then is on the craze for maxis, as compared to minis, which I can't wear ... I'm a bit chunky for a girl of nineteen, with narrow hips and broad shoulders, but strong thighs and calves, and legs that are neither short nor long, but definitely not made for mini skirts, which is what all the girls are wearing when I'm in secondary school ... The vogue is for willowy girls with no curves, for girls built like boys, something I will never be unless I starve myself, and not even then. Because even when I starve myself, the curves remain, I am still chubby, I'd have to starve myself to death for my flesh to melt down to the bone, I'd have to waste away, I realised later, when I lost a drastic amount of weight, though still not enough to wear a mini, with all its damned demands.

In school, it never occurs to me to lose weight, I have no idea that you can lose weight, not even theoretically, for some things I am just stupid, even when they are obvious, I just schlep around in dresses and knee-length skirts like some old bag. The boys in my class give me a "C" for my legs, those little idiots graded us, a "B" for my face, and an "A" for my body, so my average is a "B" and I feel doomed and unhappy; I drag myself through life like a downtrodden cat, casting morose looks at people right and left, which nobody finds attractive, and if somebody does, then I don't find them attractive. Whatever happened to that attractive thirteen-year-old girl, I wonder miserably, when three love-lorn boys used to stand under my balcony, the fourth pining for me in the school corridors, tossing me little packets of foreign chocolates and sweets, hoping to impress me ... I ate the sweets with the brazenness of a vamp who takes but gives nothing in return, and even laughs at him. So now you try being the one who is invisible when she walks by, despised in advance, looking enviously at the other girls' long, slim legs, because even trousers don't look good on you, watching them you smile at the magic encircling them but that locks you out a hundred times over. So you stop even smiling and all you can do is nurse your contempt for the girls who leaf through fashion magazines that offer pointers about clothes and make-up, colour-coordinated brand-name shoes and handbags, and, to make matters worse, the sluts are rich, which you are not, and they revel in the luxury of all that fashionable plumage whereas you have already opted for black, dark blue and dark brown, colours that make you look thinner and taller because they hide your shortcomings. Your superiority comes from the inside, you tell yourself, because you see how shallow it is to view fashion as fundamental to life, to prattle about hairstyles and eye shadow and mascara and shaping your brows to look arched, to admire skeletal women who five foot ten inches tall and weigh less than eight stone but since everybody is crazy about them then you have to be, too, and how much it will cost you to work on your body instead of your mind, which is the only thing worth the effort.

And then I start uni, and the fashion changed, not by ditching the mini but by introducing the maxi, the skirt that goes down almost to your ankles; maxis had been in, then they disappeared, and then they had a comeback just at the right moment, as if somebody heard me secretly calling out for something that those of us with fuller figures could wear, and so I ran to my mother's cousin Julia, a dressmaker who made all our clothes for us, with a fabric that I loved – dark brown, studded with details in the same colour – my eyebrows already plucked and pencilled into an arch, my mousy brown hair bleached, I just need that maxi to be trendy, too, rather than one of the herd taking the early morning tram to work, I think to myself, overjoyed.

I even found a pattern for a dress, with an A-line skirt and a long-sleeved button-up top – I'll have the buttons covered in the same brown fabric – and with a belt to emphasise the waist, I chatter away, telling poor Julia what I want. She does her sewing in the kitchen, which is crammed with all sorts of things, and where all six of them congregate – her husband, three daughters and son, the neighbours often joining them, all of them sitting around, huddling like birds, filling the room with their warmth. There is always a pot of coffee on the stove, not the real thing, chicory, a coffee substitute, with everybody helping out, chatting, joking, laughing, even the two older sisters' boyfriends join in, and miraculously, with all the comings and goings, everyone manages to fit into that kitchen; I love all the babble, which I don't have at home because I am an only child, always alone.

I ask Julia when I can have the first fitting and she says the following week, but that is too long for me to wait because I want to wear the dress that minute, on the catwalk, in the street, at uni, my lectures have just started, and so has the flirting, and I want to present myself in the best possible light as soon as possible, because first impressions are crucial. So I ask for the fitting to be on Thursday, in two days' time, and I want to be able to wear the dress on Monday, because tomorrow I'm going to have the buttons covered. And I can come for the dress on Sunday, even if it's in the evening, I say, pestering her, I don't care that I'm making the woman work on a Sunday, not giving her a moment's rest, even though I know she suffers from constant headaches because of all the pressure she has, from her family, from her clients, and that she always has a little packet of headache powder in her pocket, which she takes whenever she feels she needs it, as she's doing now, while I'm pestering her; her childlike little hand dips into her pocket, takes out the packet, opens it and, using the paper like a funnel, she pours the powder into her mouth, while her son, already well trained in these matters, brings her a glass of water.

Julia is almost a midget, she's always been grey, with a face like a raisin, round and soft like a puff of cotton, placed on this earth as if she's always been crushed, though maybe she hasn't, maybe that's just how I saw her; mind you, I would be crushed, too, if I had to deal with the pressure of the five of them, no matter how much I loved them. And when you are crushed you don't know how to defend yourself, not even from a squirt who is barely nineteen, who is breathing down your neck, who is young and big and on your back – two of you can fit into one of her – because all she can see is Monday when she'll be fitted into that brown fabric, the one she brought, and it will shape her figure, highlighting the difference between her and the rest of the world, launching her into the starry heights of beauty, or at least attractiveness, making her feel important, feel like somebody, because in her mind she is nobody. Who am I, nothing and nobody, the words keep reverberating in her head; she has no idea that she will remain nothing even when he tells her that she is something, because in his mind he is nothing as well, but she is supposed to reassure him that he is something; what a farce ...

We don't live far from one another, our parents and us, it is a ten-minute leisurely walk under the autumn chestnut trees whose fruits, when they fall to the ground, burst open and little, shiny brown conkers roll out, inedible though, because these are wild chestnuts, but nice to look at, to hold in your hand, to make patterns with and then attach with toothpicks, or at least imagine what you can do with them if you keep them, since they are so lovely.

It is Sunday, early evening, and I am running to pick up my maxi dress, I'm prepared to wait for it until midnight if it turns out it isn't finished yet, even if it means Julia dropping dead; I'd soften up by the age of twenty-six, but at nineteen I am still hard-nosed, the only thing I've experienced is my father's illness, with no tragic outcome so far, and though I can sense my own selfishness, I'm not fighting it because I haven't yet dug myself a well into which I can toss in the truth and leave it there to die a slow death.

Luckily, the dress is ready, there are just the buttons to sew on, and I've brought them, along with a pair of suede high heels, a nice brown to go with the dress, so that I can have a dress rehearsal in front of witnesses before my debut to the universe the next day, which is how I see this snippet of life I've plunged into. As soon as the buttons are sewn on, I disappear into Julia's bedroom, where the fittings are done, and dive into the dress as if into a new life, which this remake will give me, because even Cinderella found her prince and became a queen only after she had her dress (and shoes and carriage), not before, that's what the fairy tale taught me.

Ah, that bedroom of Julia's, with its jumble of fabrics, double beds and eiderdowns, all puffed up and white as if one sleeps in the clouds, and on the walls souvenirs of bygone faces in ornate gilded frames, ribbons, threads, fashion magazines and dress patterns tossed on the table and chairs, clothes hanging from the wardrobes waiting for fittings, skirts, blouses, dresses, coats, and then the dressing table with its triple mirror in which clients can look at themselves from all angles, from the front, in profile, left and right, and over their shoulder at the back.

I put on the shoes and twirl in front of the mirror, posing like a model, fixing the expression on my face as soon as I catch sight of myself in the mirror, something I do even in shop windows, I am always so surprised that what I see in the reflection is me, I mean you don't live with your face, a face you can't see, so of course it comes as a surprise. And I decide that I'm satisfied with what I see there, the dress is exactly what I wanted, striking, unique, because maxis are still new on the street, they aren't seen everywhere and never will be because women like to show off their legs, as I'll come to understand soon enough. I still have to try it out on the people behind that door, in the kitchen, especially on my younger and middle cousins and their brother, whose response to everything is to joke, so that when I'm with him I always feel I've been pecked by parrots – my eldest cousin left to meet up with her fiancé as soon as I walked in, because they are about to get married – so I throw open the door, stop, and say, What do you think?

Oh, beautiful, it looks great on you, my cousins say in unison, both carbon copies of their mother, but prettier, in fact the younger one is gorgeous, they wanted her in the movies, but she wasn't interested, their brother makes some crack that I've forgotten because it isn't worth remembering, and laughs to himself; the middle cousin says I remind her of Marilyn Monroe, she's exaggerating, of course, because I'm not pretty, I have an ordinary face,with a jutting chin and suspicious dip to my nose, thin hair, I have to tease it to give it volume, I have charm, not beauty, the only thing that breaks the mold of this perfect mediocrity are my eyes, big, heavy-lidded, piercing, I'm all about the eyes. But I enjoy being Marilyn Monroe for a second in that dingy kitchen with its Singer sewing machine and smell of chicory coffee; the whole point of that dress is to be who you're not, to create an image, not be a person.

Standing by the bed with the elderdowns, I take off the dress, so that it doesn't age by the time I get home, and can hardly wait for daybreak to put it back on again and walk to uni in my heels, my maxi billowing around my legs, straight-backed, fast, with a magnificent walk, as some people later said, my skirt probably carrying the smell of my little dog which was in heat. And what I want to happen happens, the skirt does its job, it sweeps, it collects, it drags some thoughts underneath it, adopts them, imprisons them. I have no idea that from then on I will be imprisoned myself, that the game is over.

III.

I'D ALREADY noticed him, he'd already caught my eye at the first lecture, in the huge lecture hall, the college amphitheatre, with its semicircular rows of benches, and down below, in the middle, a table called a lectern, and behind the lectern a green board to write on. I noticed him when I briefly turned around to see who was sitting behind me, I always turn around, because I can, and he was leaning against the wall by the door, tall, thin, all bones, nice looking but nothing special, I decided, glued to my bench as I turned back to face the lectern. The lecture hadn't started yet, the students were still settling down in their seats. So I turned around again to get a better view, and he was still there, leaning against the wall by the door, exceedingly fair-skinned, which I didn't like, his hair thin and lank, like mine, which I didn't like either, the only thing I did like was that he had dark hair, but standing next to him now was another guy of the same height but much healthier-looking, he was more the athletic type, he didn't look tired, or melancholic, or tubercular as they used to say before tuberculosis was eradicated, with thick fair hair that had no intention of falling out, but for who knows what reason I rated less attractive than the first one.

They gave no sign of wanting to sit down, like the rest of us, they doggedly stood their ground by the door, as if intending to run off, because I could envisage them opening their mouths, waving their arms, nodding, laughing, as if they knew each other from before (and, as I was later to find out, they did, they went to the same high school, there was a two-year age difference), and I was slightly jealous that they had each other, compared to me, I knew nobody there, everybody was a stranger, and I was one of those people who didn't know how to bridge the gulf between two bodies with the ease of a smile, I'd accept a smile but wouldn't give one, and as a result I was the person always sitting on a chair in the corner whom nobody approached.

Admittedly, one student did approach me, all fair and blond and bearded, he introduced himself as Adam, but two girls, smiling ear to ear, immediately dragged him away, as if they owned him, and as there was nothing for it, he shrugged his shoulders and disappeared.

Meanwhile, the double act disappeared as well – I saw that when I turned around again, at the end of the lecture, and I decided that they were rude. That they had some nerve. That they had no respect. They had come to study something wonderful and lofty like literature, not technology, economics, medicine or law – so boring you wanted to die, just thinking of the syllabus was enough to make you go numb, but they had scuttled out like rats caught stealing. I wrote them off right away, but they reappeared on the evening of the same day, and stayed. And so I felt more kindly disposed. Amazingly, they kept coming regularly, in the morning and in the evening, with the other one taking notes, like me; but my guy didn't, he didn't even carry a notebook with him, ignoramus, I thought, but I didn't hold it against him.

I usually went to classes with Flora, my neighbour and childhood friend, who was studying English and History, and we often waited for each other after lectures; we talked about boys, and soon also about the double act, because she had noticed them, too, especially him. I also got to know two or three other girls, one of them, Petra from Kutina, ambushed me on the tram, I think you're the most interesting person at uni, she said out of the blue, and would I like to hang out with her? Of course, I answered, what else could I say, flattered, but also surprised by her manner, by the way she belittled herself, I'd never do that, I thought to myself.

I met the other one first; Filip: he introduced himself before a lecture, my guy wasn't there and I was with Petra, who immediately glued herself to him, and I thought, never mind, I'm not interested in him anyway.

***

For a while I vacillated, yes I do want him, no I don't, some things attracted me, others put me off; his eyes were big and blue, like forget-me-nots, but when you looked into them they weren't warm, they were cold, like blue ice; you're going to melt that ice, I said to myself, always stupidly believing in my own power to change things, as I know now but didn't then; his regular features gave him a beautiful profile, but when you looked at him *en face*, one side of his face seemed to overshadow the other, like bad over good, or the other way round; his legs were too short for his body, but at least he had no fat on him, I didn't like them chubby, and then there was that odd walk, tottering, sluggish, he shuffled along like a sixty-year-old, his shoulders stooped, all he needed was a tail like the Pink Panther, I thought, checking him out in the university corridors, in the café, outside, on the way home, in those wonderful days before anything happened.

Inwardly, I was attracted by the very things that put me off, the look that needed softening, the smile that needed coercing, and then the weariness, especially the weariness, with its hint of something tragic, of the predetermined downfall of the novel's hero, he exuded an unhappiness that needed soothing, a pain that needed easing, a wound that needed healing, it was all written there in his eyes and on his brow, especially on his pale, high brow ... Suddenly he became gorgeous.

Outwardly, nothing had happened, except that our eyes would meet, collide, avoid each other, underestimate each other, overestimate each other, working surreptitiously, spinning a web that you'd be caught in, and weren't counting on. That day I was powerful, prancing around in a new dress, a striking maxi, and offered a choice, which one do you want, this one or that one, but by tomorrow I'd be helpless, everything would be slipping out of my hands, as if the previous day had never happened.

If you don't want him, I do, Flora says as we walk home together one day, it's so out of the blue that I'm startled, the kiss of death to my power, but I'm also stung, because, what the hell, somebody is prepared to snatch him away, just waiting for you to take your paws off him so that she can pounce; so he has to be protected, and that from somebody who, when you were kids, became your blood sister as a proof of everlasting friendship; even if you hadn't wanted him, you do now, you don't want him snatched away from you, you're not generous, you're selfish, and that's something you'll have to pay for, starting with valuing him more than he deserves. And that immediately sharpens your senses, you see something you may not have noticed in your previous role as queen, which is that suddenly his mind is elsewhere, he's in a hurry, ignoring you with a bleak look as he rushes off, he doesn't even come to the lectures anymore … Disaster, horror; what's happened, you ask your rival of only yesterday who shrugs her shoulders, no idea, she says; so it's true, you tremble inwardly, because you were expecting her to try to persuade you otherwise. She finds it odd, too, she says, still cutting you with her knife; all that interest I showed in him and nothing, he never even approached me – she tells me indifferently, not realising that she's hurting me – nothing except for that something in the corner of his departing eye, I say to myself, but not aloud, because it's pathetic to grasp at such straws when somebody is ignoring you.

Well, now you're in a position to grasp at what's allegedly been caught, which upsets you and keeps you awake, you wait day and night for the moment when you'll see him again and catch that something in the corner of his departing eye, your stomach knots when you unexpectedly run into him in your neighbourhood, and you immediately think it's no accident, you are the reason why he's here, although it's a busy street, and so an ordinary hello becomes an event of universal magnitude that you take to bed with you and all atremble dissect it down to the smallest detail, looking for hidden messages that work in your favour, what he said, how he looked at you, was he flustered, did he turn around to look at you, and by morning you've gone completely crazy, your chemical make-up has changed, you're incapable of judging, of separating the wheat from the chaff, ready to eat the chaff as if it were wheat, until it poisons you to death. That's what happens if you fall in love with love, with the possibility of love, with the perfect setting, the kind found in books that men don't read, like in *The Witch of Grič*, for instance, whose instalments I still keep in the storage compartment of the sofa, if you fall in love with the unreal, which will never be confirmed by reality, because it can't be. Because it doesn't belong to it.

There's also the other side of things, hidden behind the visible, the other story, which unfolds before your eyes, the other one's story, which you don't know, because you know only your own story, you imagine the other's only in relation to your own, beyond that the other's is empty and you imagine yourself filling that void, just as I imagined it when I ran into him in my neighbourhood and he was flustered. He even blushed as if he had been caught on a secret assignment, following me, as if we didn't see each other at uni, where we could have settled everything, but didn't, as if he hadn't simply said hello and moved on, but rather had taken advantage of the opportunity.

He's shy, the nineteen-year-old idiot decided, dancing home to dream of the future, while he rushed off to a small afternoon party at a nearby flat, to his thirty-five-year-old mistress, he later confessed, who had a tail at the end of her rump, a stunted tail; imagine, she's got a tail several inches long, he said with a mocking laugh, taking demonic pleasure in somebody else's deformity, I should have left him as soon as he said that, it was so indiscreet, and he loved it.

But I didn't. Something inside me prickled, something went dark, something shrank and went cold, and then finished up with a sheet thrown over it, like unused furniture that's covered to protect it from the dust. I started building my room for the unspoken, un-discussed comments I kept to myself, afraid that talking about them would force me to draw conclusions. And then to act accordingly, which was the hardest to do, which was why these comment rooms were created in the first place, so as not to have to act. Until the room filled to bursting point, and life boiled down to one single comment, ending with the word: enough!

At that time, we were still only sending signals, it was all still innocent, I was at home going crazy, my tonsils inflamed and I had to stay in bed, feverish, sweating, aching, taking caramelised sugar for my sore throat, our next encounter at uni ruined, an encounter that would resolve everything, I felt sure, after that encounter in the street, when he had blushed to the roots of his hair. I've been dying for two days, feeling more and more miserable, more and more desperate, with only books to keep me company, and then Flora appeared, my blood sister; there's a party at Ria's tomorrow night, she says (Ria and she attended the same courses), he's been invited, too, she says, it's Ria's doing, she says, she's being generous because she's given him up. And, anyway, she's interested in somebody else who's coming, she says ... Ah, Ria, that red-headed, scrawny witch with the imposing nose, dragging around some pretty-boy whose eyes can't get enough of her and she doesn't know what to do with him because the pretty-boy is dumb, and even his good looks don't help; plus, she has a strange brother who's already been in prison, and he isn't even eighteen yet, I mused; it gives me the chills just to think about the future that's descending on me; I'm a mess.

That was three o'clock now, and I had to get better by seven, I decided; a bath, do my hair, make-up, I had my work cut out for me, I jumped out of bed with a temperature of thirty-eight, by the evening it dropped a whole degree; I never recovered so quickly in my life as I did that day when I had to worry about my own ruination, I muse now, seeing myself in the dining room all those seven years ago, when it was still a kitchen, before I moved the kitchen to the pantry, and traded in the kitchen cabinet for two rustic-style cupboards – ready to go to the bash. In my brown maxi dress, with its patterned details in the same colour, tailored to flatter me, not the opposite, as it eventually transpired, you'd think the devil had personally stepped into the story ...

Everything worked out well, as I had imagined, the dancing, the groping, the gazing into each other's eyes, time stopped. At eleven in the evening he walked me home, that was my curfew, and on the way it started to snow. Out of the blue, after a warm day, so early, we were surprised by the big wet flakes of snow that melted as soon as they touched the ground, and I looked up at the sky, shielding my eyes with my hand; I didn't see anything around me anymore, it was quiet, solemn, taking me outside of the world, to a place where everything was possible, where miracles happened. He took off his jacket and put it around my shoulders, because anyway I had a cold and had forgotten my cardigan at Ria's, I was just in my dress. At the door he kissed me, a wet kiss, I could smell his saliva, and I didn't mind. I died of happiness.

IV.

THERE'S SOMETHING wrong with that boy, my mother said, worried, two months after I had brought him home to introduce him to my parents so that he could come to the house and visit me. He isn't just my boyfriend, he's a colleague from uni, we have the same interests, books, the same plans for life, I explained to my mother, my feet weren't on the ground, I was on cloud nine, thrilled to have found a soulmate, with whom I was in love, because there were plenty of guys around for the physical part, but to find a kindred soul, mused the virgin who had yet to be penetrated and whose sexual life was therefore a matter of fantasy.

Her body was still untouched, there was just a bit of groping, he was not in a hurry, he said, and I even less, I was afraid of being deflowered, which, they said, hurts, tears you until you bleed, they said, so what kind of pleasure was that, I secretly wondered, to be torn and bleed; others had already tried it on with me, but to no avail, each time I'd run away. Actually, one time I did set out to get it done, the deflowering, just to get it over with, like an operation, I'd heard that the best for that were slightly older guys, who were well-worn, rather than young guys bursting with energy and wanting to explode inside you ... God help me!

And I found just such a forty-year-old, with a square head streaked with grey, good-looking in a way that meant nothing to me, because I didn't care, but tall, straight-backed, a good body, a tennis player, an oil expert who'd travelled the world, a picture of experience. He literally offered me his services like a surgeon, he would do it so that it didn't hurt, he said, there was nothing to worry about, he'd done it before. And it would be in a wonderful setting, at his friend's villa in the woods, with a fine meal, drinks, then the bedroom, everything nice and gentle and civilised, like in a fairy tale, though fairy tales didn't include that part, except metaphorically, and it meant nothing to the body for the simple reason that you couldn't eat or drink a metaphor, you couldn't seek refuge in it. And once we've finished with that first part, you can't imagine the pleasure that awaits you, he promised, oh yes I can, I thought, because I'd tried it on myself when I entered puberty; we know what's what, I mused, but obviously kept it to myself, it was private, I was the object and he was the instrument that would work on it, that's all. If I was satisfied, he could continue to provide his services, he said, nuzzling me like a cat, it was the first time that I noticed the cat in him, one that would make short work of you if you were a mouse, but since I wasn't, he played up to me. And he told me about a student he had serviced when she was at uni, and it calmed her, he said, liberated her from any kind of drama with her peers; it's you I have to thank for graduating, she told him when they parted, my jaw literally dropped listening to him talk about this robotic idyll as the ultimate consolation, and I discarded it in advance.

Still, I went with him to the villa, it belonged to a lawyer friend of his who looked sick, floundering in a mouse-grey suit that was too big for him, his face like a crumpled sock, white as wax, stretching a smile that seemed servile, especially as he kept agreeing with everything you said, you were always right, and it was with that smile that he walked us to the room upstairs, raising the glass in his hand as if toasting us, and when we came back downstairs he was there waiting for us, nodding at a job well done, except it had been a fiasco … I had undressed and laid down on the bed, he had undressed and laid down next to me – when I saw all that hair on his chest and arms and the signs of fat on his body, I didn't let my eyes stray any further – and he started to massage my breasts to help me relax, because I was all tense, and then he pressed his hairy body against mine and I cringed. I can't, I won't, help, I'm leaving, I screamed my head off, I sat up, hugging my knees, closing myself off. He hovered over me, Just try it, you'll see you'll enjoy it, we're already half-way there, he said, trying to reason with me and, as I later came to understand, for my own good, but it didn't work because I just wanted him to disappear, to evaporate, to not be there, to never see him again, not even casually in the street.

Because a few years later – during which he disappeared as if wiped off the face of the earth – his lawyer friend, standing at Republic Square, at the place where Zagreb's trendy sophistos hang out from noon till two, and where you can inspect them like cattle at a fair, informed me with that same stretched smile that he had died, a heart attack, they said, and he said, I didn't know he had a heart problem, he never mentioned it. It's possible it was something else, he stressed … And then added something that shocked me, that he'd been a spy, a Russian spy, which was discovered only after his death, just so I knew. He suddenly turned serious when he said these last words, there was no smile.

He looked even sicker and more miserable, floundering in that mouse-grey suit of his.

I didn't understand why I needed to know that, or even what I had learned except that it was something from another planet, from another part of the universe, outside my own reality, which I believed to be the only reality, strong and indestructible from the outside, destroyable only from within, following clearly set rules. So I left that particular story outside somewhere, and locked the door. Because spies didn't walk around my world and people weren't killed like in the movies and books, in my world you looked out into the radiant distance, where a miracle would happen and the expectation of that miracle remained strong, even when the ground under my feet turned into quicksand.

V.

WHAT'S WRONG with him, what, I accost my mother because her words are eating away at me, I want her to say that everything is fine, that she gives me her blessing for the person I think is the one, the person I've been saving myself for, because somebody had drummed that into my head – that there is that one and only you have to save yourself for – somebody, maybe her, books, the church, no, not the church, because I don't go to church, we aren't allowed to go to church, but the church still inhabits my mother, she went to church for years, she had virtually lived in the church before she got married, before the war, and I guess she spontaneously absorbed its ideas, one of which was to save yourself for the right one, in other words for your husband, because only he can be the right one. And from the church, through my mother, this idea spilled over into me.

I sing his praises to my mother, he's polite, he's a gentleman, he holds my coat for me and pulls out the chair, if he sees me shivering from the cold he'll take off his jacket and give it to me, leaving him to freeze, he always chats with her in the kitchen before we retreat to my room, and I remind her that he is somebody I can study with, that we are interested in the same things, the same books, that we've been together for three months now and he still hasn't touched me, he's waiting for me to be ready, that's how much he cares about me, I want to tell her, but I don't, I don't want to embarrass either of us, not her or me.

I still don't know about the woman with the tail, he'll tell me about her later, about the radio journalist whose needs he satisfies, I realise, whom he's met through Leon, another journalist, a family friend, I still believe that I'm the only one. At least since the girl he'd been with before me, the girl who left him, Dunja, her father died while they were together, he said, and her father was all she had because her mother had died long before. He went with her to visit her father in the hospital, practically every day, they brought him lunch because the hospital food was terrible. Then one day her father's bed was empty; awful, that bed, already made up for the next patient while her father was lying in the refrigerator down there in the basement, he said, she didn't even cry or go to see him, she couldn't, but when they left she threw his lunch into the bushes, he said, pretending to throw something, obviously impressed by the gesture. After the funeral she moved in with him and his family, because she was afraid to be alone in her flat, he said, but their place was cramped, I had already seen that for myself, a living room, bedroom and kitchen, you could barely call it three rooms, so it was a tight squeeze. That was in the spring, and in the summer she went to the seaside, but he stayed behind, he had to study so he could get his high school diploma in the autumn, because he had failed the summer term; she had passed. During her summer vacation she fell in love with a musician at a dance, confessed everything to him when she got back, all tanned and happy; he was a guitarist and singer and she immediately married him, he said wistfully, but not unhappily, it didn't surprise him. Guys like that are attractive, he said, especially at the seaside, in the summer, he said, when it's all about the body, I thought to myself.

But the odd thing is, he said, that now he again has a girlfriend with a dying father, I thought it was odd, too, although my father has been at death's door forever, and even odder, I found, was that his own father was retired, like mine, but on a disability pension, not an old age pension like my father, and it was so little that it was hardly worth mentioning, so his mother had to hold down two jobs, like mine.

My mother is an office worker during the day, and types at night. His is also an office worker during the day, but she sews at night. She isn't a seamstress, but she makes things for whoever needs something, colleagues, neighbours. The only work the husbands can manage is household stuff. And even then, only shopping and cooking, not ironing or cleaning, that's beyond them. Both help the wives with their work, my father puts carbon paper with the typing paper before she rolls it into the typewriter, and then sorts out the number of typed copies for delivery, and his father hems the clothes, and both are pitiful.

That's what I was thinking when I saw his father Frane hunched over in the living room armchair, cross-stitching some of the clothes – that he was pitiful. My father didn't look so pitiful to me because I was angry with him, I fought with him and hated him and told him it was his fault that he was sick because he drank, but when I saw his father, I realised that mine was pitiful, too. But I didn't ask myself what I was doing in this house which was just like mine, where the mothers slaved away and the husbands were sick, whether it was their fault or their fate didn't matter, and where you felt bad so you got out; no, I felt at home, I was glad we were so alike and I saw this similarity as an argument to use against my mother – the man I chose was the right person.

She had already met them, Danica and Frane, and she liked them, they are good people, our kind, they were struggling like us and had nothing, she said, she had no complaints about them, they were fine – but their son wasn't.

Why not, I jumped on my mother, I wanted to hear her arguments, so that I could knock them down, because every argument can be knocked down, and my mother knew it, so she didn't give me any, because that would have been the end. Because what she knew, what she sensed, what the angels had whispered in her ear, would turn into fear, into a foreboding, a constant worry, a desire to protect her daughter from anybody who could take her away, into her own bad experience that she'd passed on to her daughter, it would be anything but the truth she felt in her heart – that this man was going to destroy me. Or at least would try to.

But like all stupid twenty-year-olds I had decided to get my way, because you're indescribably stupid when you're barely twenty and haven't yet experienced anything except in your imagination, based on the stories you've read in books which you see as real, though they're not, and you project yourself into the story as if it's going to be yours, but you haven't had life's robotic principles instilled in you for some sort of protection, principles based on logic, on controlling bad karma, bad karma can't be avoided but its blade can be blunted if it is not too extreme, so I extract my mother's arguments out of her like a dentist pulling teeth, which he will then throw away.

It's not normal to flunk every single grade in high school and then pass them all privately, says my mother, embarking on a battle she has lost before she started, so she doesn't wage it openly, face to face, loud and clear, no, she does it in passing, while doing something else, she tosses the words out in passing, over her back, in the kitchen, the heart of the house, where, as usual, we're talking, she throws them into her daughter's gaping jaw because the daughter is now a beast – and it's also not normal to study for two years and not pass a single exam, I'd think about that if I were you, she says, already defeated by the resistance she's meeting.

The daughter is shocked, they had told her mother these things half-jokingly, as something completely unimportant; did he finish high school, yes, did he enrol in university, yes, did he travel around Italy for two years, yes, so how was he supposed to pass his exams if he was travelling in Italy, he's still young, he'll catch up, anyway you were the best student in your school and look at how you wound up, a clerk and a typist, I don't spare my mother a thing, look at how many geniuses flunked their year and were the worst students in their school, it takes talent to resist established thought – where did I pick up these stupid phrases, I wonder today, when I have to pay the price for them – now that he's with me you can be sure he'll pass his exams, we're already working on it, I reel off the words in defence of the man who is right for me, the man I haven't slept with yet, he's not yet my lion, but I'm defending him like a lioness.

At the same time, I remember, it occurs to me that he never told me anything about his time in Italy except that he stayed with a cousin from Split, who lives in Rome, not a word about all the wonderful things he saw, about the amazing architecture, about the paintings and museums, about Michelangelo or the pope, that's ancient history, he said putting an end to the conversation, and I guess he hugged me and said I was beautiful so who needed Italy? I admire him for having travelled at all, when I haven't, for having seen things, when I haven't, for having experienced things, when I haven't. I don't even have a passport. The other thing that went through my mind was how it was strange that he couldn't speak a word of Italian even though he spent two years in Rome and other places in the country, and that Leon, whom I'd already met, with his goatee, eagle-eyes and mocking smile, had said to me: if he saw Italy, then I'm the pope, to which I took mortal offence and went on the attack, saying what kind of a friend tells such lies. That's Leon, he said, he likes to provoke.

He didn't learn the language, what he did was look, he said, Italy is for looking, for getting drunk on culture, not for wasting time on learning the language, and if I had any doubts they were quashed by his parents, Danica and Frane, who confirmed those two lost years there, two serious people crushed by life who certainly wouldn't lie. And later it was also confirmed by Renata, his married cousin from Rome, when she briefly visited Zagreb and stayed for lunch. A beautiful, elegant woman, obviously rich, and wearing designer clothes.

Now, when I remember them talking about Italy in that cramped living room, crammed with furniture, where the sofa bed was pulled out for the son at night, and then folded back again in the morning, where the father sewed the hems, coughed and watched television, and the mother worked the sewing machine, like my cousin Julia, or peered smilingly from the kitchen where she cut clothes using *Burda* patterns – I see that they were stiff, that they exchanged confused glances, that they were constrained, and that they used few words because they hadn't been taught how to lie or how to deceive people, they are the ones who had been deceived, but they did it all the same, they did it because they had to, because they were forced to by their one and only son, of whom there were both afraid.

VI.

His parents will leave the apartment so that what has to be done can be done, he has seen to that. I don't ask him anything, I've got my own problems, my own fears of all sorts of things, I wish I could call the whole thing off. But it's too late now.

We arrive at the flat while they're still packing, searching for this and that, and everybody feels awkward. Except, maybe, him. He's irritated that they're still there, scowling as he sits in father's armchair and lights a cigarette. His father is asthmatic, so smoking is confined to the balcony, but not now, now he's the boss. He's pretending to browse through the newspaper. I'm sitting on the sofa with the green slipcovers that still haven't lost their shape. I'm sitting there all tense, my legs pressed together under the maxi that had sealed my fate. At least this part of it. I hear them moving around the apartment, in the hall, the bedroom, the bathroom, talking softly, whispering, I can sense a growing fear, but I don't understand it because they're in their own house.

They never go anywhere, as if they were stranded in this flat, on some kind of rock, up on the third floor with no elevator, his father can barely gasp his way up, he wheezes so loudly that you know he's coming even before he reaches the door. And when he walks in, he coughs for a long time, in the cramped hall. Everything in the place is cramped, all the rooms, even the balcony, where you can't even fit a chair. The bedroom would be spacious if it weren't stuffed with furniture, a huge double bed with an ottoman at the end where they sit to put on their shoes, along with walnut wardrobes, heavy and dark, as if designed to make life difficult, to cast a pall over it, even in your own flat. As if life outside weren't hard enough, with all its demands, shake-ups indignities, political pressures and constant evil. In nice weather even this dark room would be brighter if you could open the window, but you can't. Nearby is a leather factory and it stinks of carcasses, of skinned animals, the smell is enough to make you faint. The two of them sleep here at night as if they were in a prison, and the son sleeps here during the day, when he takes an afternoon nap. I will not let myself be led into that room, the execution will take place in the living room, on the sofa.

His mother, looking distraught, bursts into the room, saying she's looking for her brooch, she left it somewhere, and slowly she moves around on her square legs. She's one of those women with broad hips but narrow, drooping shoulders, and she's still pretty, although in a doll-like way, and although she's old, she's already in her forties. I draw that kind of heart-shaped face on scrap paper when I'm on the phone and the conversation is boring. It's always faces, in profile or *en face,* with the eyes, nose, mouth and hair, finishing with the neck. I rarely draw bodies, and if I do they are slim, like a model's. Her nose is exactly like the ones I draw – small and straight. And her mouth is like what I draw, too – full, the lip-line heart-shaped, not too big. She's got high cheek bones, which is what makes for her regular features. Her eyes are big and blue, the deep blue of a summer sky, which her son has inherited, and with their dark lashes they look fabulous, they don't need any make-up. Her dark hair contrasts with her milky white skin, skin like her son's. It really is milky white, like in books, but I don't really like that. For instance, I'm blond and olive-skinned – that's a better combination. She looks surprised, like a three-year-old who doesn't understand why everybody is searching for him. That surprised look is heightened by the freckles on her nose and cheeks; her son has them, too. But his nose is bigger than hers, he's bigger in every way, a head taller than she is, scrawny, angular, built like his father.

She's all red from searching for the misplaced brooch, she's looked on the bookshelf, in the tin box of threads, in the shell-studded box on the television stand, in the kitchen, where on earth did I put it, she asks herself, her eyes flitting like a bouncing table-tennis ball from the kitchen to her son in the armchair and back again. I offer to help her look, but she decides to stop, I can do without the brooch, she says, though I see that she needs it to close the brown woollen jacket she's wearing over a light blue blouse. Maybe it's in your room, I say, but she waves away the idea with her white, freckled, plump hand, saying she's already looked there, and smiles at me dolefully as she walks out, as if paying her condolences.

She was supposed to live in a villa in a leafy suburb, as the wife of an officer, but instead of a life of good fortune and plenty, the war came, changing everybody's plans, mostly for the worse, which was her case because the officer died of typhoid at the very outset of the war, although some fared better, like those who lazed around the villas confiscated after the war. She didn't tell me the story of the officer, her son did, and according to him he was the one who lost out, who was short-changed, as if he'd have been born with a silver spoon in his mouth if she'd married the officer, as if he'd been created in that never-achieved marriage, and then mistakenly wound up with this poor excuse of a father, who wouldn't even let him smoke in his presence. And whose coughing pierced his ears all night long. He didn't say it as crudely as that, but I got the point, that he'd been robbed of the wealth that should have been his. And in which he had revelled in advance. And so now, though he couldn't even afford a little Zastava 500 car, he saw himself sitting behind the wheel of a silver Lincoln Continental, wearing a custom-made suit, with a Rolex on his wrist, in New York, of course. These stories of his made me explode with laughter, I dubbed him Lincoln Continental, but he just nodded, swinging his crossed leg – it was never still – saying, you'll see. And he'd light another cigarette on the ember of the old one. But when I asked him when he was going to earn all that money for a life that would give him a Lincoln Continental and a Rolex, he'd just repeat that I'd see, and nod at the wealthy future he already saw as his. Then his father came into the room with his shiny bald head, his hat in his hand, his dark green loden coat dancing around him, saying that he would be back in two or three hours and we should take care. The son jumped up and almost pushed him out of the room, closing the door behind them, and they began arguing in the hallway. I heard their voices but not the words, and I didn't feel like listening. There was the sound of the front door finally closing and he came back into the room.

It was nothing like what Steve - the forty-year-old I had chosen to deflower me – had promised: tender and painless and afterwards lovely, no, it was painful and bloody and anything but lovely, but at least it was over and done with.

VII.

WE LIVE now like two butterflies flying over a meadow of flowers, fluttering here, there and everywhere ... Lectures at uni in the morning, and once or twice a week the cinema in the afternoon, usually the one near my house that shows art films, Bergman, Godard, Truffaut, then we'd see friends from uni, couples like Petra and Filip, or just people like Adam, who had joined our crowd. We see each other every day after lectures, there are endless conversations in pubs – when you become a world-famous writer which, of course, you will – we philosophise, laugh, drink, all in clouds of smoke, because we all smoke a lot, we are together everywhere, in his apartment, in mine, holding hands, arm in arm, embracing, darling, sweetheart, honey, a kiss on the eye, on the cheek, on the mouth, on the chin, under the chin.

In the street we run into a poet, he's our age, wearing a black, broad-brimmed Bohemian hat, with a black beard that I scan for any remains of food, it's so thick it's bound to get some stuck in it, I say to myself, he's grown it because he's going bald. He stops us, he wants to read us a poem that he pulls out of his pocket, alright, says my beloved, as long as it's not long. He reads the poem as if he's on stage, performing in front of an audience, full of himself, and we smirk, it's good, old man, says my one and only, patting him on the back, while the poet looks at me goggle-eyed, as if he wants to grab me.

There's a lot of flirting going on. Adam flirts with me, too; strange that people from the Podrava region should call their son Adam, I think when I learn that he's from there, a rural boy, that his father is a tailor and mother a midwife, that they moved to Zagreb from Bjelovar five years ago so that he and his brother could get an education, and that they're still building a house to which we'll be invited once it's finished. Whenever he gets a chance, he puts his hand on my knee, and I immediately remove it. I don't get angry, I giggle, I like being twenty years old, having a boyfriend and an admirer, and I get along better with Adam than with the others, sometimes better even than with my own darling, whom I love more than anything ... And from talking I move on to just enjoying his presence, his mere existence, being together, without any demands except that he be with me. And so in the evening I often doze off on his lap, I lie down on the sofa, my head on his lap, and drift off to sleep.

He'll wake me up before he leaves, because we're at my place, in my little room next to the kitchen, where I moved from the bigger room next to my parents', because my father is in there dying, and it makes me feel uncomfortable. Anyway it suits me to have so much space separating me from them, the kitchen, the hall, it's like being on the other side of the world. Of course, they come into the kitchen, shuffle around in their slippers, creak open the door, take glasses and dishes from the kitchen cabinets, pour water, say something to each other, but then they leave and we're on our own again. Mind you, not for long enough that we can do anything, they're too close by for that and you never know when they'll burst into the kitchen, maybe even say something through the closed door, usually it's to ask if we need anything, if we're going to eat after all that studying, my mother has been known to come in with lemonade as a pick-me-up, though she does knock first, just in case, but we're not really up to anything, we're happy the way we are.

When he leaves, when I walk him out, laughing, kissing his mouth, his nose, his eyes and his ears, so that he can feel my kisses all over, I pull out the sofa, make my bed and go to sleep, all happy. At night I fly over my city, I simply leap off the pavement and fly. It's wonderful to soar over the houses, the roofs, waving my arms like wings, my heart almost bursts with the joy of it, it's better than flying on a magic carpet, like in Scheherazade, which I imagined when I was a child, better than anything I've ever known, even if it is only in my dreams, because, honestly, what's the difference?

The only thing it's not better than is being in the heavenly forest I dream about before the wedding. At first I'm somewhere down below, above there's a clearing, greener than any green I've ever seen, sunnier than any sun I've ever seen, emanating something that makes me feel as if my lungs are expanding, a feeling I've never had before, it's like some kind of magical breathing, and it's all here laid out for me, it's all mine, it's all waiting to embrace me, and it's merely the road to something even more perfect, to the woods at the end of that clearing, to the heavenly forest.

As soon as I enter it, I know it's heavenly, it tells me so, there's no doubt about what kind of a forest this is, it's incorporeal, and yet with a body, with the bodies of the trees, the bushes, the grass, but there's nothing hard, nothing sharp, nothing to prick you, nothing to hurt you, the way there otherwise is in nature, which is magnificent to look at, but don't lie down because it will attack you.

When we're not at my place then we're at his, lounging on his living-room sofa after lunch. His father Frane nods off in the armchair, which is where he does everything anyway, reads the newspaper, hems, coughs, drinks his coffee, watches television, whatever's on, he likes the news, we're not interested in that, or in politics generally, we don't even read the newspaper, except for the last page, for its humorous column, but his mother never sleeps, she sits down for a bit, washes the dishes and then tackles the sewing, because the clients will be coming later in the day.

We don't sleep either, we just enjoy lying next to each other, side by side. Standing on the table are glasses of red wine with the wedges of peach inside, and when they soak up the wine we eat them with a fork as a treat; only soft, ripe peaches are good, they dissolve in your mouth, and we move to the balcony, where we can smoke, to finish the wine. We'll stand next to each other, our elbows resting on the railing, and look down below, or off into the distance, feeling full, languid, floating through life like a cottonwool cloud, and he'll tell me how a sparrow once fell off the balcony, the little bird hadn't learned to fly yet, and down below was a cat waiting for it with open jaws, and it polished it off in a second.

In the evening we'll go to the cinema. Or to a nearby restaurant, on the edge of town, where he lives, where his local friends go, where I don't really like going, I'd rather be with our friends from uni; his crowd is too mixed for my taste, and they're all men, one is hunchbacked, he always sits on the arm of the chair otherwise you can't see him, he works at the telephone exchange, another is some sort of former football star, a dubious character, they call him

Blacky, the third is an actor who's never sober and tried, unsuccessfully, to make an actor out of my darling, because he's supposedly talented, and because when you're an actor you can earn enough money to buy yourself a Lincoln Continental, but he flunked the entrance exam, so that was the end of that. And he could have also been a painter, his mother Danica told me when we were discussing all of her son's talents, showing me a watercolour he did when he was ten and they had framed.

Then it's summer and we go to the seaside for a week, to Omišalj, the two of us, with Flora and her boyfriend Boris, whom she'd picked up at Ria's, but she mysteriously vanishes, probably because she's busy being a sorceress and casting her spell, I now think, but at the time I'm amazed that she can disappear like that, people here don't just disappear, except when they die. The lads are in tents down below and us two girls are in the little hilltop town above, staying with a friend of my mother's in a narrow, stone house. The friend's mother, dressed all in black, her braided hair wreathed around her head, makes sheep cheese in the cellar, then puts the yellow rounds of cheese on the shelf to dry, they smell to high heaven, and she sleeps in the adjoining space. My mother's friend and her daughter sleep in the room above that, and we're in the room above theirs, which has a double bed, a wardrobe, a chest, and everything is ancient, huge, the room is so full you can barely move in it, but we love it.

The village is on a hill, and after dancing at the seaside hotel down below every night, my darling walks me back up to the house. On the way, we always stop and sit on the bench to make out, which we did that night, too, when I took off my sandals because they were pinching me, and when we finished, we continued on our way, with me barefoot, which I didn't notice until I got to my room, even though I'd been walking on an unpaved road laid with stones.

What now, I panic, those are the only sandals I've got, except for the flip-flops I have for the beach, my boyfriend has gone back, and Flora's not around to help me look for them. Never mind, I tell myself, collapsing onto my side of the bed, onto the damp sheets, my feet dirty, I'm sure I'll find them in the morning, I tell myself, falling asleep before I know it. But my poor brand-new blue sandals are gone by the morning, somebody took them. I'm devastated, because, of course, that means no more dancing, so I run to the post office to phone my mother and tell her my tale of woe, she isn't far away, she's in Pula, staying with Aunt Višnja. My father was feeling better, his brother and his wife had come to stay for a week and so my mother had given herself some time off; I'm barefoot, I sob, as if they'd cut off my legs, and my mother says: come to Pula, you can buy yourself some sandals, I've just won the lottery! Auntie Višnja isn't here, she's gone to the hot springs in Serbia.

And it's in Pula, where I immediately buy myself a pair of sandals like the ones I lost, blue with webbed straps, each one with a nickel-coloured clasp, that I first experience what is to become the rule of my life, until I extricate myself, though it still has a hold on me – my darling vanishes.

That happens on our third day there, he goes out to buy a pack of cigarettes and doesn't come back. Like that joke about the man who went to the newsstand and disappeared forever. I wait for him and his cigarettes for five minutes, ten, then, after going to the corner newsstand to buy cigarettes, furious, obviously, I wait just for him, I wait half an hour, an hour, two, becoming more and more worried, where is he, where can he be, I pester my mother, maybe something's happened, I lean out the window, stretching my neck to see better, firing nasty looks at passers-by for not being him, I go out into the street and stand there like a mad woman, spinning around, as if looking for a child who's hiding. We were supposed to go for a swim, then come back for lunch and now everything is ruined. And that's the least of it!

After waiting for two hours, I go looking for him, it's noon already. Auntie Višnja doesn't live far from the centre of town, which is small anyway, you just have to walk down the long dusty street, past the dilapidated houses neglected since the war, and you're in the centre of town, near the ancient Arena, and the café garden, where I decide to look for him.

I find him immediately, as if I'd conjured him, sitting by himself at the table, under a sunshade, his legs crossed, with that thoughtful, hard expression on his face that sometimes escapes him. There's a glass of brandy glowing on the table like amber, a cigarette between his long, slender fingers, virtuoso pianists have fingers like that but so do schizophrenics, I later learn; the smoke rises straight up like a candle's, because there is no wind, his gaze is intense, the café is packed and I can't see what he's looking at, I don't think he's looking at anybody, he's just looking, because he's sitting, because he's alone, because he's got eyes and it's natural to look.

And I'm livid, just livid watching him, I dig my nails into the palms of my hands, I could kill him, gouge his eyes out, pull his hair out, break his fingers, throw the brandy in his face, yank that cigarette out of his hand and crush it with my brand new sandals; there he is, leaning back, enjoying himself, while I'm at home waiting for him, worrying, despairing, how can this be happening, it can't be happening, it's not part of the agreement, it's beyond logic, its madness, it's not reality, it's the end of the world and you can't do anything about it because it's the end and because it's beyond comprehension; because it's beyond you.

I know what I should do, I should leave without his seeing me and return to Auntie Višnja's house, pack up his things and send him back home on the bus that same afternoon, no arguing, no discussion, that's what I've decided to do and that's it. I especially need to avoid any discussion, I know and I understand that, I'm enough of an adult, after all, so no discussion, that's basically just mirrors and smoke, it doesn't let you move on because you don't know where you're going, because the different sides of the world have disappeared and you're happy just to see any object that belongs to this world and will show you the way, even though you don't know where it leads: into the abyss, to salvation or to something else, neither here nor there … to something that's maybe worse.

And though I know what I know, I reliably know, and though everything is as clear as day, I do not head for Auntie Višnja's flat to finish what I started, no, I slip my feet into the new blue sandals that my mother won at lotto – it's the first time she ever won anything and she's been playing for years, working out the odds of probability, on the basis of which she writes down the numbers, because she's mathematically gifted – and let them take me to the table where he's sitting under the sunshade, none the wiser yet, and where they come to a stop. I wait for him to notice me, for him to slowly stand up, hesitate, his hand leaning on the table for support, the expression on his face changing from guilt and contrition to fear as it turns red, until, with a sigh, he slumps, as if life were too heavy a burden.

Because, having dropped the idea of not saying anything, or of sending him straight home, which would have been the end of it, I, understandably, want to know why, why, why. I want an explanation that I can accept, even though I know there isn't any, why did he come here in the first place, and then stay, knowing that I was waiting for him at home, that I was sure to be going out of my mind, was it possible that he didn't give me even a minute's thought, or remember that we were here with my mother, who would be asking questions as well, even if she didn't say anything, who would be unhappy that her daughter had to suffer such a lack of consideration, and for no reason? How could we continue our relationship after I'd seen what he was capable of doing, what I could expect? What does he want, anyway, to be alone, OK then, so be alone, let's break up and be done with it, we each go our own way, I shout in front of everyone in the café garden, as if they're not there, because for me they don't exist. For me, the only things that exist are the two of us and the unresolved matter of him having gone out to buy cigarettes and ending up here. I continue shouting as we leave, and all the way home, beside myself that he has no explanation, that he says he doesn't know. What do you mean you don't know, I yell, shaking my splayed fingers in front of me, are you insane, if you don't know then go to an insane asylum and leave me alone, I start repeating myself, I'm getting tired of myself, of my own voice which is beginning to crack, and of my futile questions which get no answers, just an attempt to calm me down, as if it's me who's crazy not him. And that only makes me even more furious; if I'm crazy then there must be a reason, it didn't come out of the blue, we were supposed to go for a swim, and in the evening to the cinema at the Arena, and now it's ruined. No it's not, he says, we can still go to the cinema, if I just calm down, if I forgive him, if I realise that he didn't mean to, he just felt like it, he has no idea why, he went into town for a glass of brandy and simply got lost.

And then I suppose he hugged me, and kissed me, and begged me to forgive him and said he would never do it again, that I shouldn't be upset because he loves me, because he can't live without me and that we need to calm down before we get home because my mother will be there, we have to think up some story for her, for instance that he ran into somebody and they got talking and he lost all sense of time, and we'll have lunch, and a rest and then go to the cinema, at the Arena, just as planned.

***

When I think now about how I was heading towards certain disaster, towards him, not away from him, against all reason, I have an image of a solitary table, in an empty street, with not even a car, as if the table is in some kind of square, and a man is sitting at that solitary table, a table for one, as the song goes, the song comes to me with the image – because this is the century of songs, not of poetry but songs, which are played constantly, which are the omnipresent sound of this century – a nice song, melodic, sad, it says that all of us are alone, that's our fate, a song full of profound forgiveness for this lonely being who can't survive, he will die alone – and in my mind he and that song join forces against the facts, against the obvious, against the possibility of my recognising the wolf in sheep's clothing who wants to gobble me up.

The wolf grinned at me, his eyeteeth gleaming, and then, like a phantom, disappeared, leaving me with just the poor sheep, bleating as it was being chased away from its young.

VIII.

His parents leave on a five-day trip to Dubrovnik, his father's home town, hurray, I mentally dance with joy, an empty apartment just for the two of us, to play at being married. I'll have to sleep at home, though, because that's only right, an unmarried girl can't sleep at her boyfriend's even though she's already slept with him. Which my father knows, because he asked me and I told him, I don't know how to lie, and it appears I'm brave to boot.

We're sitting at the kitchen table when he asks me, both of us are serious, it's a serious question, especially when asked by a father who doesn't want yes for an answer, he can't take yes for an answer, but he asks because he suspects it, because he's upset. He smokes Herzegovina unfiltered, and he knows that I'm also a smoker because I lit my first cigarette in front of him, when I came of age, I saw it as my right. On the table is a raspberry soda, mixed, exceptionally, with two fingers of wine, because of the importance of the occasion, because otherwise he isn't allowed, not even one finger of wine, because his liver is disintegrating. His eyes are a murky yellow, the pupils strangely dirty and his face already has a dark tone to it, as if he's been in the sun, which he hasn't, it's dark because he's sick; he's half-bald and the little that's left of his plastered down hair is grey, only his Hitlerite moustache is black, because he dyes it. When he hears my answer, he immediately reaches for his glass, his face looking even deader than usual, which seems impossible until it happens, it literally collapses. And he's breathing heavily, through his nose, in and out; he doesn't say anything, but it's hit him hard, to the very depths of his fatherhood. He shouldn't have asked.

I can't spend the night with the man I've already slept with, that would only confirm something that mustn't be confirmed, it has to be covered up, denied, the exact opposite has to be proved, as if I had just been joking. Never mind, I think, the coming days are worth more than the nights, days when we'll be alone from morning till night, something I've been dreaming of for a long time. The market, stalls with vegetables, yellow, red, orange, green and purple, you pick them carefully, I like wild lettuce, but his family eats butterhead lettuce, we'll have to choose, and I like a salad of grated carrots, with garlic, which they don't eat because it upsets Frane's stomach, salads without garlic have no taste, I say. A bit of haggling over the price is a must, for the pure fun of it; cheese and single cream for breakfast, the peasant woman will take the cheese out of the cheesecloth and scoop the cream out of the tub with a ladle, it will all be delicious. We'll buy the hard cheese at the shop, along with the cold cuts, some roast ham, some aromatic *kulen* sausage links, smoked in pork intestines, that come from Slavonia and which he loves. And for our first lunch we'll have fish, say mackerel, which he will bake, because his father bakes them. At our house we only eat sardines, which my mother prepares and cooks. And in our shopping bag there'll also be peaches for the wine, tradition is tradition, I think happily as we see Danica and Frane off. They're taking two pre-war leather suitcases with them on the train. They're calf leather, but you can see that they are old, they're scuffed, especially along the edges, and grimy somehow, like their once-gilded clasps that are now dotted with light spots. The suitcases would join the junk up in the attic if they had the money to buy new ones.

It's the first time Danica and Frane are going anywhere – at least since I've known them – the first time they are visiting the town where his father grew up, as a gentleman, a gentleman, his son keeps repeating, never having forgiven him for being a gentleman, well-born, upper-crust, with an ancestry and money and a mansion and power, somebody who wasn't a nameless face in the crowd, part of the amorphous mob, only to become a nobody in this town, and to pass that on to his son, as if to mock him.

Frane left Dubrovnik around the age of thirty, trained to work as a hotel manager in Zagreb, and for a few glorious years was the assistant director of the Hotel Esplanade, and he married a pretty woman ten years his junior who worked for a lawyer, the world was open to him even if there was a war on, because there are those, you know, who navigate their way through war as if it didn't exist, they don't take sides and they don't get involved. The Esplanade's guests were no longer kings, or princes, or dukes, or exotic maharajas, they were no longer famous actresses, dancers, singers, writers or shoe moguls now they wore the officer uniforms of the Wehrmacht, the Gestapo, occupiers to some, allies to others, depending on how you looked at it; they took over the hotel, along with the personnel. The hotel offered its services to those who could pay for them, and that now meant these people in uniform: welcome to our hotel … And then the war was over, the uniforms discarded, those still in uniform were killed, imprisoned or banished, and those who had once welcomed them, received them, tended to them, cleaned for them, cooked for them and along the way chatted with them and even had a drink with them, would now pay the price for having provided their services to the occupiers – because they were no longer allies – even though that had been part of their job description and they described themselves as being neutral. But there is no being neutral in wartime, there is no doing things halfway … It didn't help if you gave some money to support the partisans, like Frane, or felt compassion for the weak and persecuted, you should have picked up a weapon and not played the fool, kowtowing to criminals. Now, deputy director, you will see what it's like to be out in the street, said the authorities, and be grateful that we didn't hang, execute or banish you, be grateful that you can even stay here. True, he was left with nothing, except his life, which was the greatest favour that those interesting times could render; as the Chinese famously said: God forbid you should live in interesting times.

Meanwhile, in Dubrovnik, his younger brother was executed in the clamour to find people to blame for all that had happened, which some used to settle personal matters, like the jealous neighbour who could not forgive the executed man for being an upper-crust gentleman when he himself wasn't and never would be, so it was onto the rubbish heap with the upper-crust gentleman, as prescribed by all wars.

Frane's response to all this was bronchial asthma, because that's the easiest, you languish, everybody runs around pampering and nursing you, feeling guilty about the good health they enjoy that you had been denied, so that in the end your illness is the only problem you have left, and it takes priority over everything else. I realised this last part watching my father die for over ten years, poor man, poor thing, such bad luck, such a pity, and still young, everybody felt sorry for him, although he slept as much as he wanted, got up when he wanted, did what he wanted, read detective stories and westerns while my mother was killing herself with work, the entire burden of life on her shoulders, but she wasn't a poor thing, a poor woman, they weren't sorry for her – because she was healthy.

This is what I am thinking as I see Danica and Frane off on their trip to Dubrovnik, with their battered suitcases and hand-made tote bag, made of bast fibre, bought from the blind, packed with breaded chicken, tomatoes and layer cake, which they're taking with them on the train because it's a long trip. Their last words of warning before they leave is, the gas, don't forget to turn off the gas, and of course the light, don't leave the light on all night, and also be careful not to burn anything, set fire to anything, or leave the door open when you go out, or forget the keys and have to force open the lock. As if we are children or feeble-minded; we roll our eyes but we nod yes to everything they say. After we kiss them goodbye and wave at them from the balcony until the taxi arrives, and then, laughing like crazy, return to the kitchen where breaded chicken, tomatoes and layer cake are waiting for us and I start talking about all the things we're going to do over the next five days and what fun we're going to have now that we're finally alone, from cooking at home to going out, and we'll go to the zoo and look at the animals, because I've wanted to do that for a long time, and the zoo is not far from the flat – I learn that actually we're not going to be on our own because that same evening the daughter of his mother's cousin is coming from the provinces to stay with us, somebody named Rafka, short for Rafaela I suppose, twenty-three years old, she's coming for some medical check-ups and will be staying for three days ... Almost until they come back!

If he'd punched me in the face it wouldn't have hurt as much as the news about the relative coming to stay, disturbing our five days, which I'd already planned in my mind, like an annoying fly trapped in a room with you, and there wasn't an inch of room for her, let alone for her stay overlapping with our five days, and nights, when I won't be here. The days, OK, she'll be a pain, but the nights, now that's a betrayal, I think to myself, in defiance of all logic – why would it bother me for his relative to sleep here? – but it isn't just bothering me, it's killing me, I literally go icy cold, as if it's minus a hundred degrees both outside and in, I gasp like a fish tossed onto the quayside where it's destined to die. I don't even touch the drumstick he left, because he likes only white meat, or the tomatoes or the layer cake, which I love. I just drink my red wine, which I still drink even today, and smoke and run my fingers through my hair and sulk so that I stop laughing, and wonder why his parents hadn't mentioned this relative before they left, not a word, I note, despite all the instructions they had for us. And you knew, too, but you kept quiet about it, I say. Then I'm told that his parents didn't know about it, the cousin announced her daughter's arrival out of the blue, when they were packing, and they couldn't say no, and he was caught off guard, he forgot to tell me, and they probably guessed that having the girl stay would be a bother so they avoided saying anything. Blah, blah, blah … But as far as I'm concerned, all my plans have gone down the drain.

The day that started like a joyous song has turned into the hush of a funeral and just before its end the girl appears, tubby, the white flesh quivering under her chin and forearms, with stocky legs but in a mini, she's got no shame, I say to myself, and a biggish hawk nose, eyes close together, a bird woman, especially with her hair pulled tightly back into a ponytail, leaving her face completely exposed. She's wearing gold earrings with red glass chips in the shape of a flower, they're not rubies, they're ordinary paste, I notice, I don't wear earrings at all. I haven't even had my ears pierced. Strangely enough, she hasn't dyed her hair though it's a forgettable brown, her almond-shaped eyes shoot all over the place, but sneakily somehow, as if she's looking for things to steal from the flat, and she's constantly grinning, but she's not relaxed, she's on guard. I don't understand a thing. She's got a great appetite, even though she's supposed to be unwell, it's her thyroid, she says, polishing off the layer cake, I'm surprised she even knows what a thyroid is because she looks uneducated somehow, actually she looks awkward, that's the word that best describes her, awkward in her body, in her thoughts and in her speech, and this awkwardness somehow fills the flat, rising and expanding like baker's yeast, pushing me out of the room. I can hardly wait to leave.

The next day they're having coffee in the kitchen, I can hear the laughter even before I ring the doorbell, it's convulsive, too loud, mocking, the kind in which every mouth opens wide, and I don't like walking into a house where there's that kind of laughter, as if it's directed at me. She's all ready to go out in her denim mini and green top with blue polka dots to match the denim, the top so tight that it reveals rolls of fat, topped off by black platform sandals. He's in his pyjamas.

She says she was waiting to say hello to me before leaving, no need for that, I think, but I'm polite and it's not her fault that she showed up at the wrong moment, and sick to boot.

After she leaves I say it's strange that she came just when his parents went on a trip, that she didn't know they were going when she announced her arrival, just where did she think she would sleep if they were still in the house, with them in their room? Yes, on the ottoman, my one and only says from his bed, in a fit of coughing, and I think to myself, this is all so pathetic. She returns in the afternoon, he fries some mackerel and we lunch together, talking about nothing in particular, and then she goes to lie down. I notice that she has a strange way of eating, leaning into her plate as if about to fall into it, and then putting her arms around it as if afraid somebody would snatch it from her. In the evening, we take her to the cinema and then for a drink and I'm so angry I could kill him.

She leaves in the morning, just before his parents are due back, unobtrusively, like a serpent, like the daughter-in-law who turns into a snake in the fairy tale "Stribor's Forest", she simply vanishes. We didn't even say goodbye to each other. When I arrive at the flat he tells me he took her to the train station early that morning, that her medical results were not good so she was in a hurry to go home. He's already shaved, has patted on some 4711 cologne, which his parents adore, and can't stop yawning. I tell him he looks as if he's had a sleepless night, I've got my suspicions, but the kind that you don't want to believe, so you're happy when they persuade you otherwise.

But I keep thinking about the other day, when I saw him lean down to her yellowish-white, bullish neck, as if wanting to inhale her scent, and she giggled, threw back her head, making the gold earrings with their red glass chips in the shape of a flower swing, and opened out her arms as if to stretch, which lifted her breasts, they were quite literally bursting, probably full of milk because she had just had a baby, and the expression on his face was the same as when he was telling me about his mistress's tail, satanic, as if they half disgusted and half excited him.

IX.

WE ARE playing strip poker at his school friend Kostja's, it's autumn again and the leaves are raining down, yellow and red, blanketing the streets, the street sweepers can't sweep them up fast enough, even though they are at it all day with their twig brooms. They are joined by Adam, who has been given a grey uniform saying "Sanitation", a broom that looks like a witch's, its twigs loosely tied together so that they stick out on all sides, and a grey bucket that he pushes in front of him as he collects the fallen leaves. He didn't take the exams he needed to enrol in the third year and his father had been pestering him to find a job, because he was not about to dole out money to a wastrel, he said, and so his son got a job with the Sanitation Department, and, to embarrass his father, he would park his wheelie in front of the house, which was still under construction, for the whole neighbourhood, tiered like a theatre, to see. And we all laughed, agreeing that this was his father's comeuppance.

My one and only and I have now been together for almost two years, an eternity, like a married couple, only without a place of our own, always staying with someone. Everybody lives like that, either with their parents, like the two of us, like Adam, and Filip, which means under constant supervision, or in a student dorm where you are two to a room that's too small for even one person and their things, and nobody is without things, or in a rented room, like Petra, where you're barely allowed any visitors, especially not of the opposite sex, and you aren't allowed to make any noise, in fact you aren't supposed to be heard at all, so again, supervision.

But his best friend Kostja has his own flat, it's still in the attic of his parents' house but it is separate, it has its own entrance, up the iron steps from the garden, so his parents can't even see that their son has a visitor unless they happen to be on that side of the garden at that very same moment. Here we are, finally free to enjoy ourselves without supervision, without anybody watching how much we've had to drink or complaining that we're drinking alcohol at all, and smoking like Turks. We are too young for all that, which we'll do when life tosses us a rope, stations itself behind us like a huge dislodged boulder, and lets these addictions help us pull it along, I guess.

Here our bodies are free to delight in themselves, because they are young and beautiful and desirable, that's what they want to know most, that they are desirable, because they themselves are full of desires, especially physical desires. You can't fight nature. So our visits to this flat, free of supervision, are physical in every possible way and our bodies make us happy, they make us laugh, they make us clever, we do what the body wants, give it to the body, give it all, the air quivers, and the body receives.

The response to this from my beloved's friend Konstantin - known as Kostja, because his father was of Russian origin, with imperial connections, when emperors still existed, until the Revolution brought some order, and tossed the emperors and their vassals into the same basket, shook it to make sure that the contents were all mixed up, and then, when it upended the basket, saw that what fell out were comrades – is to buy a projector and porno movies for this oasis and to invite us over to watch, the two of us and the girl he is currently dating, because he keeps changing them. So we watch, the guys loving it, and the two of us girls disgusted, although Kostja's current girlfriend pretends to enjoy it, because she wants to please him.

And please him she does, first of all because he's fantastically attractive, even though he is already bald and not particularly well-built, he doesn't have the ideal proportions and muscles of an Apollo, he's already acquired a little tummy, but the hypnotic way he looks at you leaves you weak in the knees. And he has blue eyes, more bluish-grey really, but in this case the colour doesn't matter because it's something else, beyond the eyes, something inside him, something powerful, that leaves you defenceless when you're with him, that makes you want what he wants, so that he can do whatever he wants with you and you will unconditionally submit to all his demands, and will be insanely happy in a way you never would be if he hadn't vanquished you.

I had experienced the same thing with him myself, so I knew. Nothing happened between us, no touching, but the possibility of it was there and that allowed me to imagine what it might have been like had something happened. As soon as my beloved introduced us, Kostja suggested that we meet up, just the two of us, of course, and I went to the meeting, because I couldn't resist, because he'd won me over on the spot, and at that meeting I protected myself from him by talking about my beloved, so he gave up. Something I have always regretted.

There's another reason why his current girlfriend caters to him – because of the flat he acquired at the age of twenty-two, a flat he built himself with money he earned from the neon commercial signs he made while a student, all of which was commendable.

He doesn't dream about owning a Lincoln Continental, he's already earning it, I say to my beloved, who helped him search around town for customers who wanted to advertise, without any particular success, though.

He's one of those technically minded types, is the response to my comment, implying there is something limited about such "types", they lack insight into the spiritual side of life, not that this means he's stupid, just that he's limited, with no talent for art. I might have agreed with that, though Kostja used to paint, there's a self-portrait on his wall that he made when he still had hair. But later he lost interest in painting.

He did up his flat in a slightly weird, almost morbid, way, because in the middle of the sitting area, a huge space with skylights as well as a window overlooking the garden, he hung a noose, who knows why. I never asked him. Or maybe I did, but I've forgotten what he said, it was irrelevant. I thought he did it as a stunt. There was a saloon door to the kitchen, you just had to push it open and it would swing shut by itself, as if wanting to hit you. And standing on the desk under the window overlooking the garden was a shiny white skull. The real thing, not plastic. I have no idea where he got it. He decorated the bedroom, which had a humongous bed and black sheets that must have been custom-made because I don't know where he could have bought them, with African masks decorated with all kinds of colours and with slits for the eyes. They hung on the wall, their faces elongated, with fat lips and horrible expressions that were enough to scare the daylights out of you. He was certainly clowning around with all this but it was also a show of power, so that you knew right away what you were in for.

That's the sort of person you want to and can please, there's a point to pretending that you like what you're being offered, as she did when watching that porno film which I'm sure made her sick. Just as it did me, because, generally speaking, women aren't keen on pornography, they don't enjoy gazing at a woman's reproductive organs, stripped back to the flesh and pubic hair, yuck, or at where you pee, or even do number two, yuck, at a woman's legs spread open like a frog's and the erect male organ with a shiny drop proudly glistening on top, yuck, at that rod savagely pushing into her sex when he lifts her legs, yuck, at the animal panting and grunting and at the gaping hole, yuck, they enjoy celestially merging with another soul who is always Zeus transformed into a cloud, always the Holy Spirit, always an experience. Or else they don't enjoy it at all ... They pretend to ... The current one is now pretending to enjoy the porno of some emaciated girl – all skin and bones, in black leather, her panties visible when she sits down, in heels that must be six inches high, with hair reaching halfway down her back, like a black fleece – jumping up and down in the leather armchair, clapping her hands, shouting *aaaaah,* looking at me every now and then, pouting at me with her bright red lips, matching the colour of her nail polish, signalling that we understand each other but will keep quiet about it.

The guys are already hot and bothered. Tense because their erect penises are bulging in their trousers, and their balls are screaming with pain, they're about to explode, but they can't screw the actress in the film whom they're hot for, they can only screw the two of us, they'd do it right now if they were emperors and we were ladies of the court – they'd even do it side by side, and then swap us – or if they were wild rapists, soldiers, say, but they're not. Our boys are home-grown, they have to suppress their urges, control themselves and be polite, even if they've gone wild inside.

So Kostja, the entertainment master, suggests a game of strip poker, and immediately produces a pack of cards and more to drink, whiskey, to bolster the nerves, although we're all already drunk, and we're already playing and stripping, just us two girls, because we're losing and they're winning, either they're lucky or they're cheating, it's all the same, because nobody cares about poker anyway. The tops go first, then the skirts, then the bras and lastly the panties, it's still warm so we're lightly dressed; we're sitting naked, still in our sandals, clinging together because we're not very happy, although we're drunk. Seeing us naked, exposed, for grabs, like in a brothel, they suddenly start losing, playing any old way just so they lose, and soon we're all naked and we're all in the bed with the black sheets, our sandals now on the floor, surrounded by colourful African masks with no eyes. I've already been groped all over though I don't know by whom, I close my eyes and surrender to the kind of pleasure I've never experienced with my beloved, though I won't admit that to myself, it's not him I want, it's Kostja, which I also don't want to admit to myself, I'm just waiting, with unimaginable excitement, to fuse with Kostja, with Kostja, when suddenly, Kostja, the entertainment master, sits down on the bed, his feet on the floor and says: We can't do this, we have to stop, and he takes his black plush dressing gown off the hook on the door and puts it on to seal his decision.

The three of us on the bed feel as if we've been doused with cold water, we even avoid looking at each other, we sit up, now what, now what, the words ring in my head, I grab the black sheet and wrap it around me, because nakedness is shameful now. I go into the living room for my things, they're strewn around the armchair where I was sitting, all of them black, the current girlfriend's underwear is red and lacy (mine is plain and cotton), so I easily find mine and dress in the bathroom, which is tiled also in black. And then it's let's go, let's go, let's go, we can't stay here anymore, I yank my beloved out of there as fast as I can, out of the flat where something awkward has happened, where I betrayed him, I don't think about how he also betrayed me, I'm the only one who matters to me, I don't understand myself, I disgust myself, and I feel humiliated, humiliated, I've got to go home right now.

A week later, my beloved and I come back to Kostja's, holding hands, smiling ear to ear, with plans exploding all around us like fireworks, and we inform him that we're getting married. And ask him if he would be our best man, and he says yes.

X.

My beloved was going on a trip, and I was going with him, a short business trip, but it was spring, spring, we were going to a small town where spring stretched out its arms extravagantly like a giant, not modestly like a dwarf, the way it did here in the city, and I was looking forward to it as I packed, clothes for both warm weather and cold, because spring was capricious, warm in the day and freezing at night; you wouldn't believe how many little things like that you had to think of.

As soon as he got up, he wanted to tell me about the dream he had. He remembered every last detail; great, so don't forget anything because I have to pack and can't listen to you now. I'll forget to take something, and then it'll be where is this, where is that, you can tell me about it later, when we're in the car, because we're driving. And I sent him off to brush his teeth so that I could pack his toothbrush; he wasn't happy about it but he did what he was told, maybe I'll forget it, he said, as if it was immensely important, oh come on, I cut him off like a meat-axe, we've got things to do and you're stopping me, and I was already in the kitchen making sandwiches for the trip, ham, cheese, pickles, a bit of mayonnaise ... And a thermos of coffee.

And then we hit the road, he was at the wheel, I was asleep, as soon as I sat down in the car I nodded off, I just passed out, my head dropped onto my chest, and he worried about my neck, that I'd break it ... I slept the whole way, and I was alone, he said, and when I woke up it was already dark, pitch black, but we left in the morning, have we been driving all day, I asked. And we still haven't arrived anywhere, I said, even more surprised; just a little longer and we're there, he said, pointing at the lights in the distance, which moved and jumped, becoming bigger and bigger, because, we realised, they were coming towards us.

And then suddenly, darkness everywhere, as if there were no lights in this part of the world, and silence, broken only by the sound of invisible crickets, so he stopped the car, and now those faraway lights were all around us, they were torches, we realised, like in olden times. These were country folk carrying them, you could tell from how they looked, not that they pay much attention to that, I said. Because they were unshaven, their hair uncut, their clothes ragged, even smelly, a miserable bunch, trust peasants, I commented. Still, they looked unfriendly and dangerous with those torches in the darkness of night, on the unlit road, especially the leader, with his long moustache and beard, thick shaggy brows and small eyes, like two slits. And a nose like an eagle.

It turned out that we had lost our way, that this wasn't the place we were looking for, that we had nowhere to spend the night, that we'd have to sleep in the car, but that we were welcome to join the festivities which had just started, it's the festival of the Wax Queen, their leader told us in a raspy voice. You're going to melt the Wax Queen, I asked somewhat ironically, with a laugh to match. Seeming not to notice, their leader said yes, we were welcome to join them, if we wanted to, he said, as we drove slowly behind the torches, unable to refuse. And then we were already in the village and it was something to behold, wooden huts everywhere, as if nobody here had ever heard of progress, and in the middle of the village a huge burning pyre, without which we wouldn't have been able to see those wooden huts, because the place was otherwise steeped in darkness. Encircling the pyre were women, all big and blond, their thick braids reaching down to their knees, you could almost climb up them, and when we got closer we saw that the women had blue eyes and dark lashes. They were all wearing the same white silk maxi dresses, the top part decorated with pearls and buttons covered in white, the belt on their waist is encrusted with pearls, he said with astonishing precision. But the men look ragged and I was surprised by the difference, which was so obvious, it's hard to understand, I said to him as we got out of the car, still side by side. But not for long, not for long, because he was already following the men while I stayed behind with the women. He saw where I was and what I was doing, as if he had eyes in the back of his head. I stood there, staring into the heart of the fire, we'd never seen anything like it before, he said.

Are you hot, one of the women asked as I looked around, still not realising that he had disappeared, or what was happening, two of them had already taken you off to one of the huts for a bath and dinner, he said, as if he'd been there, though he hadn't; firmly holding me under each arm, one on either side, they cuddled me, as if rocking me to sleep. The heat and voices made me feel languid; you gave in, he said, though you fought it; and then I was in the hut, it was plain, no decoration, like the one we saw in the village at Auntie Olga's, my mother's friend, at her neighbours up on the hill. In the hut was a black, carved, almost royal chest, and tossed over it was a white silk, extremely regal dress encrusted with pearls.

I couldn't resist stepping closer and closer to the dress, until I could touch it, I wanted to feel it, and just as I was tentatively reaching out my hand, a woman said: don't think twice about it, take it. The dress is yours!

What do you mean mine, I asked, both happy and scared.

It's yours, the woman assured me. You are the Wax Queen!

And before I knew it, they took hold of me, undressed me, bathed me, dressed me in the royal gown, while I tried to explain that I was just passing through, that I had come with my husband, that they were wrong, they had made a mistake, and what do you want with me anyway, I asked them, will you melt me like a candle?

And then I saw him at the head of the crowd of peasants, him, my husband, and the women stepped back so that he could come to the front, to me, to the pyre, to say goodbye, he said.

Tell them who I am, and then let's get out of here, I shouted, trying to grab hold of him, but it was no use, he ducked away.

He ducked away and I stood there stunned, I couldn't believe it.

You're with them, I said, as if the penny had suddenly dropped, and he nodded yes. Then I grasped at a straw, at that dream he had told me about that morning, well he hadn't really, because I wouldn't let him …

You were in your pyjamas when you mentioned the dream, I reminded him, and I said we didn't have time for dreams, you'd tell me about it later ... I had to pack our toothbrushes ...

And at that moment, two executioners stepped out of the crowd and grabbed me, they were faceless, as if somebody had erased their faces; as if they were robots, not humans, he said.

The dream, I screamed as they dragged me towards the pyre, tell me about the dream!

That was the dream I wanted to tell you about, he said, surprised that it had taken me so long to understand, and then he raised his right arm, as if to signal that they could bring the ritual to an end ...

And then I woke up, he said.

***

I dream of a heavenly forest, and you tell me about a pyre, I say after he's recounted his dream to me, and I'm laughing and kissing him on the eyes, on the nose, on the mouth, on the ear to make everything ring, and I think how handsome he is, how good and intelligent, how he is everything that I want from life, everything I will ever want, how lucky I am. And how we will never part again.

XI.

WHERE ARE we going to live when we get married, at his parents', at mine, the discussion goes back and forth; no, no, no, at Auntie Olga's in the countryside!

What an idea! Twelve miles outside of town, no car, only the bus to rely on, no money, a house where the only heating you get is from the kitchen stove, where the water in your glass is frozen solid when you wake up in the morning, so what's the problem? Our love will keep us warm, we'll keep each other warm, I dream on, pushing this insane idea all the way to Auntie Olga's in the countryside, and she agrees to it, because she knows that it's insane and that nothing will come of it, so why say no, why not keep on my good side. Sure, she says, come, you'll live in the library, and we're already packing our bags; my mother stares at me and comments by grimacing, because I had already turned a deaf ear to her doubts before, and I suppose she knows that the idea is crazy, it's unrealistic, so she leaves me be. And then the phone rings, Auntie Olga, of course, I'm sorry, can't be done, she says, Koraljka is threatening to hang herself if I take you in, we're told, but we're already at the door, our suitcases in hand, images of our new life suddenly aborted.

That crazy Koraljka, we say miserably, dropping our suitcases onto the floor, she's been crazy since the day she was born, crazy like her whore of a mother who drank like a fish and caught syphilis, and left her and her twin brother Juro in the hands of social services, because even their father didn't want them, just as he didn't want their mother, he wanted to enjoy life, and then that drunk of a woman shafted him with the kids, but since he didn't want to be bled dry, he decided to send them both off to an orphanage, where Auntie Olga, unlucky woman, found them.

This crazy story goes through my mind while I'm sitting, paralysed, at the dining-room table in my washed-out track suit, full even though I'm starving, sober even though I'm drunk, with the dog curled up on the other side of the table for company, a story to which I had wanted to add my own at the beginning of this marriage: I didn't want to be married in the house where my father was dying, so I invented somewhere else to go, to Olga's, to her freezing cold library, full of books that no longer existed, books that her husband had collected when they did exist, can it be, I asked myself the first time I saw them, these no longer existing books and no longer existing writers have been rendered senseless by time, that great unforgiving judge no one takes into account.

That was the end of the ideal life I'd imagined in Olga's black library of non-existent books, a warm life under a duvet in the freezing cold wintry room, because we'd married in November, a life of tramping through the snow to reach the bus station early in the morning in order to make it to our first class at uni; I didn't even think about what or where we would eat if we didn't go to our parents', I didn't ask myself what we would do; we were like birds who pecked at what they found and had no problem migrating, without a bus or a tram … What on earth was I thinking, I wonder today when everything is finally over, when I'm beside myself as to how that idea of mine ended, an ending I had worked on and prepared.

Because the end was the beginning.

Except it didn't finish even when it finished, it's still going on, that old life of mine still won't let me go, like an amputated limb that still hurts, as if it were there, but it isn't. What hurts is what you don't have. And it hurts, say the experts, because the brain won't accept that you no longer have what you once did, what it still remembers, and so it turns its absence into the pain of loss, which keeps going back to the beginning. That's my story, I guess. Because if it weren't, then I wouldn't be sitting here for three days now, incapable of extricating myself from it.

XII.

My mother offered us the smaller room next to theirs, my old bedroom, but I didn't want it, we'll stay in the little room, I said. It was a tight squeeze, though: it wasn't that cramped when he used to just drop by occasionally, but for two people to live in it was a nightmare, I realised it right away, but I didn't say anything, after all, to whom was I going to complain? In the room was a shelf and two storage compartments that were part of the three-seater sponge sofa bed, upholstered with a yellowish-green bouclé fabric. When you pulled it out, the back slid down into the seat, and you could keep your bed linen in the compartment behind. On the shelves were books and trinkets, once mine, and now also his. Everything fitted into the room, we saw that when we emptied the bag full of our things – books, silly presents from past birthdays and New Year's presents, which you couldn't toss out, a gilded four-inch-tall Eiffel Tower, a spoon with Big Ben painted on the handle, a long-stemmed coral red glass shaped like a flower, a thick glass globe with a fir-tree scene inside, which would snow when you turned it upside down and, most important of all, a silver model of a Lincoln Continental, a present from the cousin in Rome, which he put prominently in front, so that he could always see it.

There was no room for our clothes, so they were in the wardrobes in the other room, along with our underwear, our shoes were jammed into the little cupboard in the hallway and everything was crammed full. To dress, we either had to go to the room with the wardrobes or bring our clothes here, where we first had to fold the bed back into a sofa because when you pulled it out it reached the desk by the opposite wall, taking up all the space. We watched television in the hall, so it turned out that we used the whole apartment, but mostly we were in the kitchen. The kitchen hadn't changed since the middle of the war, when the house was built; the walls were covered in ancient white tiles, the stone floor was black, white and grey, as if somebody had scattered pebbles on it, there was the grey-green kitchen cupboard, a table and chairs, the table was old but sturdy, it had been through a lot but was still in one piece, the only thing that was new was the water pipe and the boiler that replaced the old iron one, the *wasserleiten* as we used to call it, and the built-in gas stove in lieu of the old wood stove, it was huge and white-tiled, like the walls. But at least we were on the southern side of the world, I told myself; when the sun was out it was nice even in the winter, whereas the other, northern, side, where my father was dying, was always dark.

He was still able to walk when we got married, the ceremony was at the town hall, with only the immediate family present, along with Kostja as best man, Flora as maid of honour, a few friends from uni, Adam, Filip, Petra, my high school friend Irena, and Leon; then, at our flat, a modest dinner, commensurate with our income. I wore a plain, light blue dress in which I looked terrible; I looked good in black, light blue was a killer, it turned me into somebody else, but I couldn't get married in black, everybody told me. Danica used a pattern from the German magazine *Burda* to make the dress and as soon as I saw it I knew I would wear it for the wedding and then never again, it would die a natural death in the wardrobe. Danica shoved a bouquet of white roses into my hands at the last minute, when she realised that we had forgotten to buy flowers at the market. Instead, we had bought some books from a second-hand dealer, the price was so reasonable we just couldn't resist; one of the books was Karl Marx's *Early Writings,* and we sang and jumped with joy because you couldn't find it anywhere anymore.

You can't get married without a bouquet of flowers, Danica said in horror when she saw us carrying only books, so she ran off to get the roses – I'm thinking back to those times that brought me to where I am today, to these three days of starving in a flat teeming with insects, with only my poor dog for company, three days of spacing out on toasted bread cubes, dripping, heavy wine and filter cigarettes, which I'm converting to disgusting butts in the ashtray, into a cemetery of smoked cigarettes, and I keep staring at it in the hope that it will make me feel even more disgusted, make me finish off that drink with a sting in its tail, as they used to say, and I empty the ashtray only when the ashes start flying all over the table, where I leave them. Let the mess spread, let it cover me all over, let it surround me, God forbid I should try to bring some order into the world and then decide that I'm OK, too, that I'd clean myself off if I sweep, wipe and wash, if I put things back in their place, as I did six years ago when my father was dying, and I went to scrub the kitchen cupboard, which tended to get unbelievably dirty, with yellow greasy dirt sticking to its greyish green paint, making it hard to clean, so I avoided washing it.

Facing the cupboard from his seat in the kitchen – where the dog was now curled up – my father always seemed to be just waiting to say: When are you going to scrub down that cupboard? He was prepared to keep saying it until it drove me crazy, so I'd throw down the dish towel or the ladle, or whatever it was I was holding – because my father and I took care of the shopping and cooking, due to the fact that my mother was working – and run to my room and scream into my pillow. But then I had to look at my mother's exhausted face when she came home from work and asked in a trembling voice: What's happened now? Because father and daughter couldn't live together without squabbling.

But that evening, when illness was making itself at home as if it had taken over, saturating the whole place with the smell of decay, so that it didn't even help to go out on the balcony for fresh air, although the cold outside was the kind that killed off smells, that evening, when my father was in his room, saying his farewells to his brothers, I was in the kitchen scrubbing down that bloody cupboard like a broken machine that had gone crazy. I used *Vim* and it ate away at my fingers, but I kept on scrubbing, the cupboard was enormous and complicated, with big and small drawers, a space for two shelves behind the two panes of glass, which had to be cleaned too, and so did the niche in the middle for bread, the bottom shelf, the legs and who knows what else, all of it neglected and greasier than it had ever been, because I was being battered by life and who could think of cupboards in such a situation, and death had been prowling around the house for weeks, waiting for a sign from heaven to say that his time was up – so I kept on scrubbing until dawn, until day broke, leaden and icy, which was when my father died.

My husband walked around the house like a ghost, trying to stay out of the way, because the house was full of mostly unfamiliar faces, who looked at him like an intruder, while they smoked and drank, waiting for the end when he would be the only man left, and that was not to be sneezed at, I know now, but all I saw then, as I was bending and stooping to clean the cupboard, was the sympathy and concerned looks wafting above me, that's assuming I could see anything at all from the damned cupboard that I was trying to scrape clean of my hatred for my father before he died, as if it were a place of reconciliation.

He did not die in the flat, he died in the hospital, where he was taken by ambulance, which had been called so that we would not be left with a corpse in the house and go crazy. But before that, while he was in the hallway, on the stretcher, my father asked for a shave, he wanted to spruce himself up for the hospital; he was yellow, black, desiccated like a mummy, a pile of ashes, reeking, soon he would flutter away from his body, but for the moment he was still holding on to it, still believing in it, still wanting some camouflage, to win people over, to have them confirm he existed, still frantically holding on to the transient, leaving the non-transient to its fate, as something of lesser importance …

Who was going to shave my dying father, who, who; two of the brothers had left, the third hung back, he would go with him to the hospital, but he wouldn't shave him, his expression and gestures made that clear, presumably he was afraid to, he literally rolled his bulging eyes, which had always been lifeless, and the orderlies wouldn't do it either, that was for sure, they were here to carry patients, not to shave them, especially not somebody who was falling apart, they didn't say so, they just their crossed arms on their chest and stood there like tombstones.

My mother? I looked at her but she couldn't do it either, I realised, she wasn't sleeping well, she was worn out, and her hands were shaking, she might cut him, and I couldn't do it either, he wasn't a kitchen cupboard, he was a living human being, and he was my father, and he was also horrible, and anyway I didn't know how to shave someone, I'd never done it before.

And so the only person left was my husband, who shaved every morning; we surrounded him and sent him to the bathroom to get my father's shaving kit, soap, a soap bowl and brush, and razor; he had it in him to shave a dying man, I realised later when I thought about it, when I deconstructed the scene in my mind, that scene and many others, like the one of him copulating with a body that had a tail, just because of the tail; he was a destructive person.

But not at the time, at the time I was just surprised that he agreed to it so quickly, yes he blushed, but with a smile, an ironic one but a smile, when he knelt down to lather my dying father's face, he kept nodding, as if talking to himself, I remember thinking. When he finished with the lathering, he placed the bowl on the floor, picked up the razor and started shaving, first his cheeks, then his chin, concentrating, clearing away the soap, without a nick. He didn't have to shave under his nose because my father had a moustache. Lastly, he wiped my father's face clean with a towel. My father thanked him in a barely audible whisper, and even tried to lift his arm, I still wonder what he meant to do with it, but his arm flopped back onto the bed. He closed his eyes.

Later my mother told me that a week earlier, realising that it was the end, that he was past saving, that he was falling apart, my father had told her he felt bad about having to leave her, because the two of us would destroy her.

They're not good people, he told her. Be careful.

They! – I exploded at the insolence of it, he wanted to destroy me as a daughter who adored her mother, not her father, whom she hated, a daughter who had always been her mother's child, who would sometimes toss and turn in bed at night, afraid that her mother would fall sick first and that her father would survive her, who would not let anyone touch her mother and who watched that slanderer destroy her mother with his drinking, illness and idling, day in and day out, for years.

That's what he said, my mother repeated, shrugging her shoulders and firmly closing her mouth, not showing whether she agreed or disagreed, but flickering somewhere deep underground was the sentence that something was wrong with that boy, a sentence uttered at the beginning of our relationship two years earlier, and that it was now pointless to repeat, because we were already married.

XIII.

MY TOOTH hurts, my tooth hurts, the moan drags itself through the house, it hurts, it hurts; it's the third day of the new year, which fell on a Friday, making it a long weekend, and this is Saturday when the dentist doesn't work, but the tooth hurts so badly it's driving him crazy. And he has a headache as well. Actually, he isn't sure exactly what hurts him, his tooth or his head, he decides it's the tooth, because aspirin doesn't help, and you can pull out a tooth, but not your head, I say to make him laugh, to ease the pain.

We got through the funeral, it was just the immediate family, my mother and the two of us, plus Adam who appeared, unannounced, around ten o'clock in the evening, he had no place else to go, he said, stamping his feet in front of the front door, without a bottle because he never brings anything, he drinks alone. Of course, come in, I said, you couldn't turn away somebody who said he has no place to go, even if you were in mourning.

Adam is a man with a beard, and my beloved is a man with a beard – he started growing it after my father's funeral. Whether because of that pre-death shave or for some other reason, I didn't know and I didn't ask. Like Adam, he also has a moustache, except Adam's is shaggy and his is wispy, and in tandem with his beard it provides a kind of facial adornment, as in the days of the French nobility (like in those historical movies). He no longer has to shave every day, but the beard has its own requirements, it has to be trimmed. Otherwise it might grow down to his navel and make him look like an oddball, which is not how he sees himself. He sees himself as good-looking and elegant, and a trimmed beard is a poetic touch. Maybe he grew his beard because he had started working part-time at the radio, it occurs to me when I think about it. Leon got him the job at the radio so that he could earn some money, because we don't have much. Being still a student, I am entitled to my father's pension, but it will take months for the paperwork to go through, so I'll just have to wait. His parents give him some money, but not enough, because they don't have much themselves, so we live off of my mother's salary, and she is about to retire. And as soon as she does, she plans to work part-time somewhere as an accountant, which is what she is, because she wants to build a headstone for my father's grave. The only thing there now is a brown varnished wooden board, with a five-pointed red star, his full name, years of birth and death, all in black letters, and embedded in a clay pot. The board with the five-pointed star declares that he was an atheist and a communist, although he was never a communist. He messed up somewhere, opened his big mouth, drank too much – they wouldn't let him join, and after that he always lived in fear. And that fear lasted right through to his death, because even though he burned all of my mother's religious books, prayer-books and brochures when he returned from the war, and wouldn't let her baptise me (so she had to do it in secret), and even though he never put a foot inside a church after they married, he told my mother before he died, just in case, that she could bring a priest to his grave, to send him off to the next world – with the

Bible, its stories, a recommendation and absolution, and with a few hymns. You never know what's waiting for you over there, if anything, so why risk retribution from that side now that everything is finished on this side, because they can't catch you anymore, he probably thought, clearly considering that he might be moving on to a place where there would be more questions, though of a different kind, and where there could be trouble if you came unprepared.

My mother gave him a send-off worthy of a man of importance (which is how he felt when he was drunk), though she had to borrow a black winter coat for the funeral because hers was black-and-grey check, and she couldn't afford a new one, and she gave him an equally worthy wake, using up every cent she had saved for such an occasion.

My father was left in his grave, and we were left in dire straits; our income was now minus his small but regular pension, and our expenses had increased because now we had my husband living with us, and he was used to his little treats, he couldn't imagine breakfast without cheese and ham, surely he wasn't expected to eat bread with jam, he said, and there had to be wine with lunch, and cigarettes, and he was not about to stop going out, so when he mentioned Leon and the chance of working at the radio, I said, well then go and earn some money, although he was also supposed to study. And attend classes. The woman with the tail also worked at the radio, which made me fume, because I didn't believe him anymore, not really. I did, and I didn't, depending on the moment, but I realised that I couldn't even believe myself too much anymore either; you had to accept life, you didn't have to believe it, especially not if your emotions were running amok.

Our wedding, my father's death, the funeral, and now seeing out the old year – all we can do is get drunk.

We all drink, it's practically a must, I don't know anybody who doesn't drink, except for my mother. His parents don't drink either, except for a glass of watered down wine at lunch, but my mother doesn't drink at all. She was at a tasting when she was young and got drunk on a liqueur, it was sweet and tasty, and it made her laugh and forget her shyness, it made her less shy, and allowed her to flirt a little, and then she vomited her guts out, was sick for three days, couldn't work and swore that she would never touch alcohol again, no matter what it was and no matter what the occasion. And she kept her promise, which I do and don't admire, because holding firm can also be bloody-mindedness, it can mean giving yourself too many rights and being unhealthily judgemental and cruel, as a reward for holding firm, in which case it is not worth a thing. But drinking is not the same thing as getting drunk, the two of us drink to feel better, to lift ourselves a little above the world and its burdens, but Adam gets drunk the way my father did, he is only alive when he is drunk; he is dead when he is sober. He doesn't leave until he has drunk every last drop in the house or passed out, calling it sleeping, but in truth he's unconscious.

Seeing in the New Year – with roast ham in a crust of bread and a piglet with crackling, the best part of the roast, as the kings of France knew, caring only about the outer crust and leaving the meat to the servants, along with a colourful Russian salad with home-made mayonnaise using only one egg, mustard and oil, Flora's grandmother's recipe, which was the best and never disappointed, and then *ajvar,* pickles and peppers stuffed with vegetables, all home-made as well, followed by the cakes Danica made, because we rarely did any baking, a tender layer cake with layers of cream, crisp vanilla crescents and crunchy walnut and jam bars, and even a wonder cake, the wonder being that it was delicious, that it melted in your mouth, with just a few walnuts and a bit of chocolate, and it hardly cost a thing – was a chance to laze around for a few days before the advent of the dark future that was about to knock at the door.

Adam stopped pushing his Sanitation wheelie because his father threatened to kick him out if he continued to park it in front of the house and embarrass him before the neighbours. He found him a job at a petrol station; since that's all you're good for, go and fill up petrol tanks, he decided. He was to start work on Monday. Until then he'll stay with us, he says, if we'll have him, he says, and having risen from the dead he immediately asks for a brandy to clear his head.

Not brandy, coffee, and then a beer to sober up, I announce, but I'm glad he's here, it's more fun. My father liked him, too, he doesn't like my one and only, but he does like *him*, he told my mother, who also likes him, because he's a poor thing, like her late husband, and because she sees that he is in love with her daughter and is unhappy. He stares at me all day, peering over his thick-lensed glasses, which make his eyes invisible somehow, but without which he is as blind as a bat, he sniffles and wipes his constantly wet moustache, and when my beloved leaves the room for a moment, he unassumingly puts his hand on my knee, and I remove it or he removes it himself when he hears the door open.

But he's not here to attack my knee, he is here to talk. Because we are people who discuss, who read books, who ask questions of life that have no answers but we hope to find them, we hope that life will give voice to itself, that it will speak, that it will explain. And we will be prepared when these answers come. So we sit and wait, piles of answers coming from books, answers collected over the centuries, more than we can absorb, some similar, some different, of one sort or another, it is hard to choose the right one, because as soon as you choose one, another appears, which is different but also right, but how can two answers that rule each other out be right, we bang our heads against the question; fortunately these heads aren't made of stone so they don't crack. The discussions go on and on, you're thrilled when you think you've finally got somewhere, like a mountain-climber reaching the top of the world, and then just when you think: look at me, I've made it, you're back down in the abyss again, like a mountain-climber who has fallen without conquering anything. At the end of it all, we're drunk on a life that has hidden its meaning, but so what, we don't care, we'll find, or at least get close to its meaning, and that in itself is something to celebrate, we have time.

Filip and Petra come by to congratulate us, to philosophise a little over a meal and a glass of wine, to sleep a little, and then repeat the whole thing all over again, but then my beloved gets a toothache, or a headache, or both, it hurts, it hurts, it hurts, the words echo through the house that afternoon, so at first it's aspirins, a cold compress, a hand cupping his left cheek where it hurts, a grimace and clenched teeth, my mother boils some sage for him to gargle with, but nothing helps and by evening he can't take it anymore and says, I'm going to the clinic to have it pulled out.

We were supposed to go to his parents' that evening, we had just spoken on the phone, and Adam was supposed to go home, but because of the toothache he stays. He stays as if he can be of help, though I don't see how; he sits with his clasped hands resting on the table, acting as if we'd be lost without him. Finally, he offers to go with my beloved to the A&E, because it's cold outside, and I am sensitive to the cold, so my beloved agrees and the two of them leave, my mother and I will wait at home, otherwise I'd just be in the way.

They're not gentle at the A&E but they do have injections, it's done in a jiffy, you feel a prick, you wait a minute, then the pliers, and two teeth, molars, come out of your mouth, and go into a white, blue-rimmed tin bowl, that's how I imagine it as I listen to him tell his story, because he's already back, with moist eyes (did he cry? I wonder) and a crumpled, blood-stained hanky over his mouth, and when he removes it I can see dry blood crusted in the corner of his mouth, he is still wincing, but the terrible pain has gone and been replaced by a lesser one. Adam looks worried behind his thick lenses, his long nose twitching, as if, like me, he finds something odd about those pulled teeth, that they pulled two teeth not one, I'm angry, I can't believe that they yanked out two of his teeth, they couldn't have both been rotten, the rotten one reflected on the healthy one, they should have realised that, I say to myself.

Did they X-ray them, I ask, no, of course not, it was just take the pliers, jam them into the mouth and pull, they were your teeth not theirs. I should have gone with you and stopped it, I say, looking reproachfully at Adam as if that's what he should have done. He realises what I mean and shrugs, I couldn't do anything, his shoulders tell me, and my beloved says he doesn't care about the teeth, the main thing is that the pain has gone.

And so we return to our old routine of food, drink, talk; he doesn't eat on the side that's sore, but he does drink; we stay up until three in the morning and wake up at ten, it's Sunday and snow has blanketed the city. A thick layer of powdery snow fell during the night, everything is still and in a strange way the snow protects you, it's cosier and you feel as if you are in that glass globe with the fir tree that my beloved brought into the house, which snows when you turn the globe upside down, it's like being in a magical wonderland. If only he didn't have to spend this last day of the holidays working on some programme at the radio, replacing Leon who is snowbound up in the Slovenian mountains. Of course he's going to step in for him, he owes him, sooner or later debts have to be paid, and he has to secure his position at the radio.

Adam is still with us, we still have enough drinks and food and good humour, and stories and my knees, he'll go straight to work from here. As for his father (who is waiting for him), he can think what he wants, he says, let him stew, he says, he doesn't know where he is and he isn't about to tell him, because he can't listen to him anymore. His constant sermons about keeping his head down, being patient, hard-working, persistent, because that's what makes for success, which is why he had brought him to the city, for him to get a degree and not be a tailor like him. Although he himself could have been an opera singer had the circumstances been different, had he had some support, he constantly grumbles, says Adam.

Adam sleeps in our old little room next to the kitchen; at my mother's insistence we've moved to the biggest room on the other side of the flat, where my father died, and she's moved to the smaller room, which used to be mine. Just as well that Adam is sleeping there and not, say, on the big sofa in the hall, I muse, though I don't say anything – because he snores so loudly it shakes the house, and when he gets up he is so disgusting you can't bear to look at him, he slobbers, farts, picks his nose, and when he removes his glasses to clean them, his eyes rolls as if he has escaped from a madhouse.

My beloved left the house at seven in the evening and by eight Adam and I are already discussing Gogol and Dostoevsky, how Dostoevsky said that all Russian writers came out of Gogol's *The Overcoat*, all those geniuses who hadn't existed before, and how wonderful that is, then the phone rings, a call from the radio saying that he's fallen ill, his face is green, he's throwing up, he isn't not strong enough to get up, we have to come and get him, urgently. Adam and I rush off in a taxi to the radio station, wondering if it isn't something to do with the teeth he's had pulled, my heart is in my mouth, it'll all be fine, Adam says soothingly, putting his hand on my back, bringing his worried face a bit too close to mine, so that I can smell his breath, which is annoying. And then a scene I can't even imagine, my beloved slumped in an armchair by the front desk, on a small table in front of him a plastic cup of coffee from the coffee machine, he is green but also as white as a sheet, as white as dead flesh, beads of sweat on his brow, his head stiff, his face contorted like when you're nauseous, he doesn't say anything, he is confused, as if he doesn't know where he is, he mumbles inarticulately, but lets us take him to the taxi, then it's home and to bed, where he throws up. And develops a temperature, a high one, thirty-nine C., so he's in bed for two days, sometimes conscious, when he even cracks jokes, and sometimes semi-conscious, when he sleeps the sleep of the dead, every so often vomiting bile if he has anything to drink, water or tea, because he is off his food, so I make sure he has a basin by his bed and I empty it. He also tells me not to turn on the light, it bothers him. But he won't let me call the doctor, he says it's the flu, the aspirin has brought his temperature down to thirty-seven point five, which is next to nothing.

It's not the flu, not the flu, I tell myself the third day that he's sick, leafing through the worn, brown, post-war *Medical Lexicon* that my mother had probably bought for my father, and which we consult whenever we're in pain and want to see what it is. On Monday, Adam, of course, goes to work the pump at his petrol station. But he drops by after work, reeking. Danica and Frane come to see their son and bring him a cheese pie, only to learn that their son can't hold any food down, everything makes him vomit, so, after dispensing a load of useful advice, they leave worried, with Danica crying, but she leaves, nevertheless. She doesn't offer to stay by her son's side, or empty the basin with his vomit. I look up his symptoms in the book, a book that will never be out of date because it is about us, and we never change, we are made out of flesh, blood, bones and who knows what else, and we're constantly in danger of everything breaking down, in part or all of it, because our armour is fragile.

A fever, vomiting, stiff neck, headache, confusion, what can it be, what can it be if it isn't the flu – meningitis, I discover under M in the post-war *Medical Lexicon,* published for the people to help them help themselves; I run over to Dr. Popijanč's office in the next street, we all like him because he is one of those good-natured drunks who'll give you whatever you need, he'll write you an excuse note for school or work, and he's always kind. The other reason we like him is that he looks like a toy, like a spinning top, with a wide, wide middle like a hula hoop, but narrow at the top and the bottom, his little legs underneath barely able to support his body, and a bald head on top that he covers with a strand of hair. We like him, even though he told our pregnant neighbour who planted the apricot tree in the yard that she was fine when in fact she had the measles and gave birth to a deaf boy. And even though I know that, I still run over to him with my own diagnosis of what's wrong with my darling, meningitis, I say, and he doesn't think that I'm brazenly interfering in his work, this twenty-two-year-old who hasn't got a clue about medicine, who thinks she knows what she's talking about despite having no knowledge, in life everything is secret, he says, and then, as if my diagnosis is correct, he tells me to call for an ambulance to take my husband to the hospital. Which I do as soon as I get home, where I find my darling and my mother, and Filip with his moustache (but no beard), always so full of sympathy, and I go with my husband to the hospital.

XIV.

LATER HE'D say that he was in the recording studio, sitting opposite the sound engineer, waiting for their guest who was late – some expert on recreation, which was the subject of their talk – the minutes ticked by but the guest didn't appear and didn't call, and then the sound engineer played a commercial, because you couldn't have dead air on the radio, and the commercial was about a juice, which went with recreation, exercise, healthy food full of vitamins, yippee, and at that moment he felt his eyelids blinking and his fingers tremble, so he stood up and walked out of the studio. He went to the coffee machine near the front desk, and collapsed onto the armchair to have a cigarette and coffee, hoping to calm himself down.

But when he took his first sip of coffee, which was like dishwater as usual, he felt a blow at the back of his neck, a heavy blow, as if wanting to knock his head off, and his head exploded into thousands of voices, as if a huge carnival parade was coming his way. And then he saw the parade, noisy and colourful, with people dancing, playing music, singing, shouting, performing acrobatic tricks with the ease of a monkey, hurtling towards him, coming but not arriving, and at the end of the parade he saw a woman, her cheeks pale, splattered with rain, and he called out to her. But the pale woman with rain-splattered cheeks didn't hear him, and then he realised that the woman had no eyes, her eye sockets were empty, like Kostja's African masks. And then the woman with no eyes dissolved before his own eyes and a black man stepped out of the carnival parade playing a tom-tom, dancing to the rhythm of the beat, twisting and turning, his naked body painted in a palette of colours, like Kostja's African masks, and the orangey light turned crimson, then purple, and the naked man with the painted body and drum crouched in the corner by the coffee machine, and lay in wait for him.

Then the man laughed, and he could see all his teeth, he had never seen such white teeth, and then suddenly the man turned into a toothless mouth, just a huge hole sucking him in and he fell through it like Alice in Wonderland, hopelessly trying to hold on to the tunnel walls, which were as smooth as glass. Then the stench of rot somewhere reached the hole, heavy and damp, as if it had come from the jungle, and finally he fell out of the hole straight onto the leather skin of the drum, there waiting for him.

The black man grinned and raised his drumstick to smash in his skull, but then the door creaked, the man disappeared and he saw the olive-green wall splattered with blood and scratches. Then a rubber-gloved hand appeared, a syringe between its fingers, and a voice above the hand mentioned a spinal tap. Only then did he realise that he was lying on a high leather bed, waiting for the stranger to stab the needle into his spine.

***

What's he to you, your brother? the doctor on duty asked me after the spinal tap was done, and my darling was carried off on a stretcher into the corridor, until they found a room for him. No, not my brother, my husband, I said, and he was surprised, saying, I thought he was your brother, you look so young.

Young, I felt a hundred years old, and there he was joking that I was young, I'd left my youth behind when I walked into the hospital, not even then actually, it had disappeared, with all its stories, and books and drinking and flirting, with its: what do we do tomorrow? What's playing at the movies? What'll we have to eat? Which lectures shall we go to, which shall we cut? When will we collect the teachers' signatures for the semester, we don't want to be late with that and have problems afterwards, shall we go with Filip and Petra to the talk on Camus and Sartre and their political falling out … Nothing, because we were full of ourselves, of our own endless importance in the world, which needed no proof, that's simply how we were, citizens not of our province but of the world, all of us talented, all of us about to be famous, because that's what talent strove for – to be noticed and acknowledged – and that's what it fed on when it was not yet noticed or acknowledged, as if it were both. An interesting notion, I thought, and wonderful while it lasted, because sitting in our pub was like sitting at the Café de Flore in Paris, on Proust's Boulevard Saint-Germain, where we'd never been, but we'd read about it, which was almost the same thing, it was like having Camus and Sartre sitting with us, sitting in our thoughts and our words, so what more did we want? Sitting with them, of course, was Simone de Beauvoir, the woman Sartre loved, their relationship an example for our future life, even for me, as somebody who married, though I didn't know why, that was something I'd have to find out, but I knew that we would live like Sartre and de Beauvoir, in a partnership of the minds, not the kind with children, that no.

That was my life until that moment, and then all I had left of it were ashes, as if it had burned up in an explosion in my darling's head, and I was left to look at him lying on the stretcher on the floor, upset that he is lying on that floor at all – like all hospital floors it's horrible, too many human legs walking by, too much despair saturating everything and no way to get rid of it, no rags or water or chemicals – lying there looking miserable and scared, and I can't help him. There is nothing I can do, nothing, there is nothing worse than this feeling of helplessness you have in the hospital, and seeing the other person looking at you, expecting you to find an answer, to have an understanding that you haven't got, to cooperate with his fate, expecting you to pass on some of the strength of your health, health that he doesn't have but you do, as if you deserve it, which perhaps you do, but you don't know the prescription for deserving it so that you can pass it on, you simply have something that the patient doesn't and it's horrible to have something unknowingly like that because you can't share it. I already experienced that feeling with my father, but not as badly because I was his child, and therefore, by definition, weaker, somebody you're not really going to depend on. But I still remember his eyes those last days before he died, they were as big as wheels, as they say in fairy tales, and they kept looking, looking, looking in an unfocussed, aimless way, not the way people look otherwise, it was as if they were looking inwards, looking for what was trying to destroy them, but they couldn't see that far, all they saw was the void, and then suddenly, when they saw me, there was a spark of hope that there might still be a chance, that life was a solid thing and would not collapse, that it hadn't all been a hoax.

And now again a pair of eyes, looking for the last time, but these are the eyes of my darling, which are my eyes as well, my life will die with his eyes, I thought at the time, and my whole being is fighting it, don't, don't, I won't let you, all of my support is in that non-acceptance, because any words of consolation ring hollow, and who believes in prayer? In my world, nobody believes, not even my mother. I've never heard her pray, even in secret.

And then two drunks, as he later told me, entered this horrible scene, I assumed they were drunk because of their reddish-purple cheeks, bulbous noses, puffy faces and sluggish movements, as if they were too heavy to carry even themselves, notorious drunks, something my father never managed to become because he fell ill before he could do so. But I immediately dismissed the idea because I couldn't believe they'd send two drunks to carry my darling from the corridor to the room, I couldn't believe something like that was possible. But that's what they were, drunks undergoing treatment and part of their therapy, along with other manual labour, was to carry patients on stretchers, so it was useful at both ends. They came and, with a worried expression on their faces, looked at my husband, who was just under six foot two inches tall, and big-boned, that's to say, hefty, and they knew they'd collapse under his weight.

What about leaving him here, one of them said, and then, after taking a closer look at him, added, he's not going to last long anyway, I've seen it before, he said straight into my darling's terrified eyes, as if he were an object that couldn't hear them and as if I were the same; I agree with you, but the doctor won't, the other one said, what can we do, said the first man, it comes sooner or later to everyone, and before I could jump up and throttle them, they leaned down, one in front and the other at the back of the stretcher, lifted it and staggered off towards the service lift.

I went with them, but I'd already been sidelined, the hospital sidelined you, it was useless. They wouldn't tell you anything or you wouldn't understand anything, or you'd understand only half of it and even if you understood everything it'd be wrong, you still didn't know anything and you had no authority, you were just a passing visitor with limited time here.

Then you go outside, where you have no life anymore, only the remaining stage set of your life, to the apartment where you have nothing to do except ponder what happened, talk endlessly about what happened, empty the ashtrays and pace the apartment like a caged tiger, unable to settle down with a book, or the TV, or in yourself, nothing to do except run to the hospital and come back, through the slush of the snow, your feet constantly wet because your boots aren't waterproof. Nothing to do except freeze when the phone rings, look at the receiver as if it's a funeral bell like the one that sometimes rings at the Church of St. Blaise, near our flat, and heave a sigh of relief when you hear it's Kostja, or Adam, or Filip, or Petra, or my cousin Flora, or Irena, but not anybody from the hospital, and you sit down on a chair, put your hands between your legs and rock back and forth, staring into the void like a candidate for the lunatic asylum.

Two days later, I'm back in the hospital corridor, sitting on a white bench that's harder than anything I've ever sat on, with Danica quietly crying next to me, as if she has an inexhaustible source of tears, so that I can't even comfort her anymore, I just keep staring dully at the olive-green linoleum floor, the hospital is poor, like all our hospitals, we are all poor, and at the pathetic rubber plant by the window which is desperately trying to absorb the last of the winter light, slowly dying. We've been here two hours, Danica and I, here in this corridor in front of Intensive Care, where my husband, her son, is lying, we're waiting to finally learn what's wrong with him, as if that could comfort us, the only thing that will comfort us is to hear that there is nothing wrong with him, but we console ourselves with the thought that it would be progress to hear the exact diagnosis because then he can start treatment, that's assuming that whatever he has is treatable; I'm numbed by the thought but can't get rid of it … I suppose I already know.

Finally the doctor appear, he looks imposing, they all do, even when they are small and ugly, because here they are king, and this one is tall and relatively good-looking, but even if he weren't, because he is a bit too tall and long like a pencil, and his mouth is too small, because he has shrewd, round, coal-black eyes and looks kind, as if he wants to put you to bed with a fairy tale, which, when combined with everything else, is attractive, like a riddle you want to resolve, but you have to work at it, so the two of us immediately jump up from the bench, like students in front of their teacher, and wait for his verdict.

I already know it isn't meningitis that he has, knocking him for a loop and sending him straight from the dental chair to his bed, they've told us that already, but I'm close, this close with the diagnosis I gleaned from the *Medical Lexicon,* written for the people so that everybody can understand it, there is blood in his cerebrospinal fluid, a haemorrhage, bleeding into the brain from an angioma, a benign tumour consisting of blood vessels that could appear as a harmless mole, but its head is a bomb or a dormant volcano just waiting to explode and blow everything to pieces.

You probably already knew about the tumour, the doctor says to Danica, her face puffy from crying, and she blinks like a glass-eyed Italian rubber doll, which she resembles, and he says, it's an old injury, he says, probably from when he was born, he says, it's already had consequences, he says, and looks at her questioningly. When he looks at her like that he purses his mouth and it seems even smaller. She's nodding her head, but says nothing, she's nodding at something inside her, and he knows that he won't get anything out of her, he's known that from the start, I realise. I see him smile ironically, pat her on the shoulder to show that heaven forgives us for being weak, weak and helpless, and then he turns around and walks away on his long legs, each step a yard long, his white coat, with the slit in the back, fluttering behind him like a flag.

XV.

I WATCH those legs and that flag at his back for a second and then run after him, he didn't say anything about the prognosis, what next, what can we hope for, so I run and catch up with him, stopping him at the office door that has his name plate on it.

I pepper him with questions, one after another, in no order, he's the one in charge of keeping order here so let him sort them out.

His round black eyes look down at me pityingly – at least in my imagination, because we all know that doctors can't indulge in pity, otherwise it would mushroom into a jungle and devour them – and then he tells me to prepare myself because a tumour can bleed from other vessels, or from the main vessel, and kill him instantaneously. He is lucky that this hasn't happened, but it doesn't mean that it won't. They'll treat him, but the only treatment for this is an operation, and it's too soon for that. Everything has to calm down first. And he can't predict what else might happen around the area of bleeding or how much bigger the tumour might grow, but grow it most certainly will. And nobody knows what the consequences of either will be.

Then he pats me on the shoulder, just as he did Danica, to show heaven's compassion, because we are so weak, so weak and helpless, and says that all we can do now is wait, be patient and wait, he says, as if talking to a child, and then he disappears into his office.

I'm not interested in the consequences, they'll still be around later, I think naively, dragging myself down the corridor back to the bench and Danica, because I'm not in a hurry now. Just let him survive. Don't let him die. Let him come home, I say to myself.

Danica and I can't leave the hospital, we have to wait for Frane who has gone to inquire about a job at the Institute for the Blind, where he's found somebody he knows; his son is sick and they'll need money, four hours a day, which is the maximum somebody with a disability pension is allowed to work.

My head is like a cage full of exotic birds trying to outsquawk each other, my darling could die while I'm on my way home, while I'm eating a sandwich; he is here and then almost overnight he isn't, you go to bed at home and wake up in rubble, nothing to help you transition between the two, just following the law of the hatchet, it isn't an earthquake and it isn't a war, how can that be ...

And nagging at me are those two extracted teeth, as if they started this whole devastating process, although I know they didn't, they were just victims, portents of what is yet to come, and as such were killed, as in righteous times, extracted while still healthy, and yet, I think, none of this would have happened if they hadn't been pulled out, it could all have been prevented if only we had known, if we had known, but we didn't know so we helped the disaster to happen, to spread, I muse illogically ... But what was logical about him having a toothache, when he was going to bleed in his head, absolutely nothing as far as I'm concerned, the logic of life is only in our imagination, in our desire for power, it isn't reality, it's completely illogical, I think in despair.

I say this to Danica while we're hanging around in the hospital corridors, waiting for Frane, in those desolate spaces where I grew up, my mother and I bringing food to my sick father, in perpetual search of a tree under the window that I can look at to save myself from the desolation, from the fatigue and boredom, that package of horror, until we finally come to what the doctor said – that they had known, they had known about this volcano in their son's head, because it happened during his birth.

They did and they didn't know, I realise from her confused story about her difficult labour that had lasted for two days, because the baby was too big and got stuck on its way out. They had to pull him out by the head with forceps, to clamp and pull. Nobody knows anymore where the mistake was made, but he came out with the right side of his head damaged, with a swelling that looked like a horn and took months to recede. She was told that she could die if she had any more children.

And that's all, I say to myself, but something is missing, what, for instance, if they had taken him for a check-up once the swelling had gone down, X-rayed his head, checked that everything inside was OK, that there was no damage. But she doesn't remember anything, they were subtenants and having a hard time, barely making ends meet, she mutters, afraid that Frane would be arrested, it happened every day.

I know, I say, one morning they collected my father off the street and my mother spent days looking for him until she found him in prison, blind – he'd temporarily gone blind with fear.

We moved three times, she continues as if she hasn't heard me, until she was given a flat by the Institute for Urbanism where she got a job, and with all that moving around they lost everything they had, all their furniture, but later they were given some and they bought some themselves. The only thing they saved was Frane's lamp from Dubrovnik, which is now in our flat. A nice, tall floor lamp, with three lights under a yellow, gold-trimmed lampshade, and a round table in the middle to put your things, books, an ashtray, hanky, ring, if you have one, before you go to bed. It came to our flat later, after my father died, because there was no room for it in the little room by the kitchen. In their house it was shoved into a corner behind the television set, never used, dead, which is why it was given to us.

Then she starts talking about her mother, who died prematurely, poor thing, and she starts to cry, so suddenly that I have no more questions for her, she blurs everything, and when I break through that blur and find her again, her son is already in school, he was good at drawing, at singing, at writing, he was a terrific footballer, they called him Amarillo, Rile for short, after the football player he resembled, and he was a top student straight through until puberty, and though his grades dropped they still told her he was the brightest student in the school, because they had done various tests. I've already heard it all before, but it's as if I haven't, I like hearing her praise her son; so, when she finishes, I say, you never noticed any sign of illness, anything like that, and again she doesn't say no, I didn't, she just waffles and you have nothing to nail her down with, she isn't lying but she isn't telling the truth, and that makes it all more than clear. That she knows but doesn't want to tell me, not even now when everything has come, she keeps hiding it, as if to admit it would change something for me, as if I would say to myself: hey, stop, the man's seriously ill, there's something wrong, get out of here, run for it, the way animals do, the way they teach their young, but me, I was taught the opposite, that it's at such times that I should step up, be compassionate and loyal, like my mother, who taught me to be that way, to love more because this is where it's needed more, because this is where it's missing. They prepared me for sacrifice, I later realised, and I had to pay for that delusion by living as a victim, in the here and now, not in the future, which is a huge difference, because a future victim is notional, and a notion is nothing. What is something is when you live like a victim, which I haven't yet tried. Even sitting with Danica opposite the door to Intensive Care, waiting for Frane, I still don't realise what's waiting for me, what I am intended for, I am just slightly hurt that they kept something from me, because they didn't believe in me. And that they still don't believe in me.

I don't say that to Danica, who is sitting with tears pouring down her face, holding a crumpled hanky, her black hair a mess, and I would never say it to her, because she is a poor woman, as my mother would say, because I felt sorry for her the very first time I saw her, and because I think she is a good person. And also because I still love her son, so I share with her the terrible thing that has befallen us, whether expected or not it is now a fact and we have to accept it. Anyway, I am her son's wife, it has only been two months, but still, I am his wife, and he is now my responsibility, mine first and only then hers, even though she is his mother. That is confirmed that day in the corridor, in front of Intensive Care, despite the fact that Frane had gone to look for work, because being sick costs money, and even though he is sick himself, he will sacrifice himself for his sick son. Not by taking care of him, but by helping us with money, if and when it's needed. It goes without saying that we were living off of my mother's income and I will be getting my father's pension. And when he recovers, my husband will return to his job at the radio, because he is sure to recover. The son of Frane's older brother, who also lives in Zagreb, an anaesthesiologist who is currently abroad on a scholarship, but is soon due back, has been informed of the illness and will be of help.

A few days later, Leon appears and suggests that I write for the radio under Rile's name (that's what he calls him, though I never do), so that he can keep his job and not lose it to somebody else, and I happily agree.

XVI.

MY HEAD. I'm off my head ...

I'm running through life in a deranged frenzy, like a headless chicken.

I've got too much on my mind, I say, if anybody phones – my relative Flora, or Adam, or Kostja, or Filip, or Petra or Irena, who recently married her engineer boyfriend – and asks me how I'm doing, suggesting we get together and talk, I say I can't, I can't, I can't, and after saying it I sit there with my head in my hands, rubbing my sleepy eyes.

I don't sleep well; I toss and turn on the sofa that we moved over from the little room. Because we threw out my father's sofa, and bought a nice small dark green sofa for the little room, which even when you open it up into a bed leaves enough room for you to move around, and that's where Adam sleeps when he stays over, because to get to his house, the one that's being built on the north side, he has to take a tram, then a bus and then walk, and the last bus is at eleven in the evening, and he's always late for it.

The worst thing is when I wake up too early, say at five in the morning, and I went to bed at midnight; it's not a time for sleeping and it's not a time for getting up, so I wait for day to break in the winter but it takes forever and when it does break the day is enough to make you weep, it's so grey it's as if there's a huge dull lid over the city, not the sky, because what sort of colour is grey, or the sun, or thick clouds shaped like a dragon or crocodile to cheer you up so you have something fun to look at above, not wondrous snow that blends everything together into one, into whiteness, with always something quiet and formal about it, as if you were in the theatre. And then you spend the whole day traipsing from one job to the next, as if you were surrounded by Harpies, not three but countless numbers of them, competing in a championship.

I don't even fold up the sofa bed, I don't put the bed linen away, I leave everything just the way it was when I got up, rumpled from tossing and turning and from the sweat pouring out of me like water, sweat from worrying and from images such as the empty bed in the hospital room where you're standing devastated, like his former girlfriend Dunja, when she came to see her father and brought bowls of food. I have nesting nickel bowls like that, on a stand with a handle so that you can carry it. There are four bowls, one for the soup, one for the meat, one for a side dish and one for the dessert, I fill them and bring them to the hospital every day, every time with a different meal, until I start all over again, because I haven't got the energy to be imaginative. At least he's not eating slop, as he calls the hospital food, their soup is like dishwater, he says, it tastes of dirt, and the meat is so tough you could sole your shoes with it, he jokes, he doesn't even mention the revolting side dishes. I bring him beef or chicken soup with home-made noodles or dumplings, sometimes with liver dumplings, and the meat is veal or chicken, roasted or breaded, or meat patties, or boiled beef in a sauce, or a stew or goulash, which he liked to dunk his bread in while it was still cooking on the stove, an image that makes Danica cry, and I'm close to tears myself, as if nothing is more moving than the image of somebody being fed and nothing is worse than to think of somebody dying of hunger. The side dish is potatoes, either sautéed or mashed or as a salad, or rice, or pasta, with or without vegetables, peas, carrots, chopped spinach with butter and milk, all of which my mother usually makes, I do the food shopping, the only thing on the hospital menu that he takes is the salad, because he doesn't care. Twice a week Danica provides the dessert, she bakes whatever cake he wants, a layer cake or wonder cake or *Dobos torte,* there's enough for the next day as well, and for the remaining days I make him floating islands with gelatine, or chocolate-sprinkled rice pudding, or my mother makes an apple pie with cinnamon, walnuts and raisins in one half of the baking pan, and a cheese pie with cream and eggs and raisins again, in the other. All these desserts look delicious and tempting, their aroma fills the room. When there are cakes for dessert, we share them with others. For breakfast, I bring ham and cheese, some fruit, oranges, bananas, when necessary, and since it's winter, thank goodness, I can keep everything outside on the window ledge so that it doesn't spoil, and I also bring him cigarettes because he hasn't stopped smoking. They let him smoke, but only in the corridor, and he can walk, though not too much, because the most important thing is for him to rest. He's got a transistor, so has everybody else, at least those who can hear because some of them are barely conscious, calling out to who knows whom – there are six of them in the room, which is considered a comfortable number because in some rooms there are ten or more – but the competing sounds from the different transistors irritate him so he keeps his switched off. Except when his own articles are broadcast, the ones I started writing under his name, all of them aired in the morning. I write about important dates in the arts and sciences, in history and politics, about events and personalities, when something happened, when they were born or died, what they wrote or painted and when, what they invented or whom they defeated, or were defeated by, whatever you can find by leafing through the encyclopaedia and going to the library, digging around like crazy. I also write for a column called "The History of Everyday Things", and that's even more complicated, you have to work hard to dig up who invented napkins, or matches, or lighters, or umbrellas, or toilets, or nail files, because everything has been invented by somebody, nothing useful simply dropped out of the sky. And I write – again under his name – humorous pieces about modern-day life in the city, stories from the tram, the street, the marketplace, the café, from our impoverished universe, which depicts itself as the best in the world and is not to be touched – because politics, on which that universe rests, is untouchable, keep your hands to yourself if you don't want to lose them, I've been taught since the day I was born – I think up these pieces when I'm exhausted, my throat tight with fear over what will happen to him tomorrow; and I'm supposed to make my listeners laugh.

We had left the September exams for February, because we were only just married and because my father was dying, for real this time, we could feel it, and we figured that we could take the exams in February, but in February life went topsy-turvy, in February whatever was important became unimportant, making you wonder about the real importance of these important things, because surely what's important can't become unimportant until it is resolved, and so that's what happened, the exams became unimportant, we didn't take them and that left both of us without health insurance. And now he is in the hospital.

Who is going to pay for the hospital, or for a possible operation, which is still up in the air because his tumour is going to grow, it isn't going to stay as it is, because those damaged blood vessels have created a bomb, who will pay for it, who, I wonder in despair, running to the head of the university's literature department, who's a holy terror because that's how he behaves, because he doesn't really have any power so he likes scaring people. I have to ask this same man, who loves putting the fear of God in you, to set a precedent by allowing my husband to enrol in the next semester without having taken his exams, so that he can keep his health insurance, and take his exams later, if he survives. I have to say all this because it's a serious matter, I don't want him to think that I'm trying to fool him, and I'll probably have to hear him say that he could have taken these exams earlier, in September, so why didn't he, and I will then have to let him rap me on the knuckles and stoically take it. I'm not asking for myself, I don't like asking for anything, and if I have to ask I forget how to talk, I have to drag the words out of my mouth, and it's not attractive. And so I walk and walk, never reaching the office of the department head, it's as if I've strayed into a labyrinth several times over, because either he didn't come to work that day or I'm too exhausted and give up.

Now, a different picture emerges from the menace of all these dangers, a different picture of the building and its corridors, as if I've never been here, every corridor seems a mile long and there are so many of them, and so many doors, but I can't find the department head's office because I don't want to find it, and I can't remember where it was yesterday when I did find it but he wasn't there. I've been here three times already and something odd is happening, I seem to have gone deaf for a moment, like when you turn off the volume on your TV and are left with just what's on the screen, somebody talking but no sound, just a moving mouth, like somebody who's escaped a lunatic asylum, like a caricature of itself – it's like the faces I see in the corridors, students on their own or in groups, whose eyes follow me as if I were an alien, an intruder, a magnified character from a cartoon who's pushed its way into reality. Even with familiar faces it's as if I have never seen them before, God forbid they should ask me anything. I make my way, moving on, and then there's the door with his unmistakeable name plate on it, I can't miss it, but it won't open by itself so I knock, I hear a voice inside say come in, and I walk in.

The department head, he looks like a badger, is good-naturedly chubby but inside he's a brute, indifferent to feminine charms though I could do with some right now, they would lend a different tone to the scene, one in my favour, but this way he just looks suspicious, there's no sympathy, no smile, a face that refuses a priori, that says no before you ask, a wall, not a face. I'm trying to figure out how to begin talking to this wall, how to start my story, but there is no start to it, I realise now that I'm searching for it, I'm at a loss, I pluck words awkwardly out of the middle of the story, which his logical mind immediately deems to be unimportant, maybe even false, he doesn't see me, I'm of no interest to him, not me and not the person I'm telling him about, he doesn't remember ever having seen us, he has no questions, asks for no explanation, he just says stiffly that there's nothing he can do, that my request is against the rules, so leave, there's no goodbye.

I'm outside of the door, I don't know how I came out, it's as if it took me years to get out, I stand there as if I've been turned into a pillar of salt, I have nowhere else to go, no one to go to, and at that moment I think it's all over, I can only withdraw into myself. And it's there, in my inner self, that I discover the fury of impotence and in my fury I want the department head to go through what I'm going through, to face an illness, let me be precise, an illness affecting the brain, I want a replica of what's happened to me, of somebody close falling ill, and I whisper these words hoping they will embolden the thought, give it body, who knows who's listening beyond this reality, there where fairies and demons live, who knows who's waiting for you to ask them for help with such a terrible task as mine. There is just as much good and bad on that side as on ours, we're told in fairy tales, which are true if you believe in them, as I do now. And wouldn't you know it, a few years later the damned man's son gets a brain tumour, just as I had wanted.

Impossible, I thought when they told me, it's just a coincidence, I'm not responsible for it, though I know I am, and I'm not sorry, I'm not, even though an innocent person has suffered, at least at first glance, because innocence in general is debatable. And I want him to know that this was my doing, actually it was his, because he retaliated first, but I won't tell him, not even when the opportunity arises – as it did years later when I invited him to the radio for an interview – because every side of that story is closed and there's no way in. I wouldn't have asked him for the interview if his son hadn't recovered, I despise cynicism, even the surreptitious kind that mine would have been if his son had been dead when I phoned, but his son's recovery liberated me from that, he and I could confront each other not as individuals but rather in our roles aimed at raising his public image, along with the demons I invoked. About them he knows nothing.

We have a nice talk before the interview, while we're waiting, he is a different man now because I am not his subordinate anymore, he even laughs, and when he does his teeth gleam, but he's still a badger, just a little chubbier, and his closely cropped hair is greying, he remembers me from my final exams, that I was brilliant, he flunked students as if they were pawns he was knocking off a chessboard, but he didn't flunk me. He doesn't know anything important, he knows everything unimportant, which he would depict as important and convince others of the importance of this unimportance, because he could scare them, but now he's famous and everybody wants to hear what he has to say, they have no idea that they won't learn anything, not anything important, or that he will shower them with the evil that he inflicted on me, on his son, and through him on himself, because he doesn't know otherwise. Because he's comfortable with falsehoods.

But now, I'm still standing in front of his door like a pillar of salt; I've invoked demons from the reality of the other side, but I have done nothing in the reality of this side, which is why I came. So what now, what now; I decide to shake off the salt and look for another door, I feel stronger somehow after performing that ritual of invoking demons, the corridors don't look miles long anymore, they don't interweave, I don't get lost in them, and the students are once again people with voices, not silent apparitions, so I move on and immediately find the other door, on the other side of which is a woman, his deputy.

I remember her for once saying that we should read at home, and come to classes when we have nothing better to do, and it still makes me smile to think what a powerful sentence that is, how much she knows and how much she despises cheating – there, in her office, its furniture the colour of fresh wood, enlivened by the different colours of the books that are everywhere, she immediately emerges from that sentence as somebody who sees, who understands, who is empathetic. She knows who I am, who he is, she remembers our names and the essays we wrote for her, mine about Thomas Mann, his about Jack London, she can't get over her surprise at his choice of writer, she has her doubts about the impressionism of that essay, but she's interested in everything, what happened, when, the diagnosis, his present condition, future plans, she'll resolve the health insurance issue right away at the Registrar's Office, it'll be done in a jiffy, she says, no problem, she says, and my eyes well up with tears.

I'm not a crier, especially not when there are witnesses, I'm embarrassed to cry even when I'm alone; look at her, I sometimes reproach myself when I flounder, especially if I start to cry, as if I'm talking about somebody else, but I suppose that visit to the badger was the straw that broke the camel's back, and this camel already had a lot on her back, had carried too much on her back for days it just took that last straw to break it.

No, no, she says and the two of us are already smiling, she with her round face, round and long, and her red-framed thick lenses, and I with my round face, without glasses, she a dark brunette and I a blond, she with her hair in a bun, and a long leaf-shaped hair clip, a red precious stone at the tip of the stem, and I with a bowl haircut, the ends curling in, with both of us plump, she a bit too much, especially her bottom half, in the legs, though her waist is narrow, with me unhappy, her happy, a wonderful husband, gorgeous and successful they say, I saw him once from a distance – tall, blond, straight-backed and strong, as if he'd just stepped out of a Greek myth, somebody you can lean on, or at least you think you can.

She says she'll immediately ask her father, a doctor, chief physician, professor, there's nobody he doesn't know, to inquire about my husband's condition and what needs to be done, how to help him, where to go, to whom, which is the most important thing, and he will intervene.

That afternoon I run to the hospital with his food and the news, but he already knows, she's already intervened, they already know that he has the protection of such and such a head physician and professor, who is a name in the world of medicine, and his cousin, a doctor, also called, he's returning from abroad and when he gets back he will decide what future steps to take and which treatment to adopt. He's red in the face and his breathing is laboured as he tells me all this, he says that when he heard the diagnosis he thought of committing suicide, it was either that or finishing up in an insane asylum, but now he thinks there may be hope after all, he's relying most of all on his cousin. I've never met that cousin, but I have met the cousin's parents, twice, Frane's brother, a gentleman and tall like Frane, but with a head full of hair, and his wife, self-important, too loud, with a mouth like a frog. The story was that the cousin had divorced his wife, with whom he had a daughter, after taking up with some nurse, as is so common in hospitals, and later married her.

Two weeks later we celebrate his twenty-fourth birthday, my mother and I cook up a storm of good food for him, what my mother calls 'špampandale'; we stuff veal scallops with cheese and ham and then fry it in batter, and we stuff beef scallops with bacon, garlic and parsley, then close them with toothpicks and braise them with onions, it's a delicacy called Spanish Birds, and along with that we make all sorts of salads, a French salad, Waldorf salad, *shopska* salad, tuna salad, and Danica makes the cakes. We invite our friends, Adam, Kostja, Leon, Petra and Filip, and we all take the food to celebrate his birthday with him in the hospital. There we open his presents, books, monographs, coffee for the nurses and liquor for the doctors, whiskey, wine, and there are some black leather slippers, as elegant as anything I've ever seen, from Kostja, and they make his eyes shine. I give him a new dark blue, ribbed velvet dressing gown, its lapels bordered in red, with a red-and-gold crest on the breast pocket, because the one he has is old, it was my father's, and he immediately puts on the new one. We share the food with the others in the room, who are sitting on their beds watching us hungrily, and then we all go back to the flat because I want to treat everyone to some food and drink, after all they came and brought presents, I can't send them away without anything, so I have some food for them, because I don't want to return to the flat alone.

The only one who doesn't join us is Kostja, he feels that you shouldn't celebrate a birthday when the celebrant isn't there, what's more he's in the hospital, maybe even dying, he says, scowling at me, his magic eyes looking at me darkly; so he leaves, resentful, driving himself home in his little Fiat 500.

After that, our relationship was never the same, although we still saw each other, and later I was even a bridesmaid at his wedding.

XVII.

KNICKERS, BRAS, tights, slips, clothes for cold weather and for warm, because it may be the end of April but you never know if you're going to boil or freeze, and I despair because I can't close the suitcase, it's too full. I'm excited, I'm packing, I'm going to Rijeka where my darling is in the hospital and has the best doctor for this kind of tumour in the Balkans, and beyond, according to his cousin, who arranged it all, he was Tito's doctor, he says, and our jaws drop. He will be the one operating on him.

He's been there for a month already, but I couldn't visit him before because there'd been an outbreak of smallpox in Serbia and we were under quarantine. We all had to be vaccinated and I stood in line for five hours waiting to be inoculated. If you were here at least we could have waited and grumbled together, I lamented in a letter, because the post could travel. It was just humans who were contagious.

During the quarantine Danica and I made our own clothes, I would take patterns from *Burda,* draw them on a big sheet of wrapping paper, then cut them out, lie them down on the fabric, to trace the pattern onto the fabric with chalk, cut the fabric along the chalk lines, and then that part was done. Next Danica would pin and then sew the different pieces together by hand, as a first go, then she would sew them on the machine, where again she would adjust the width and length with pins, and then it was back to the sewing machine. If there was a collar or cuffs, Danica would make them separately. The next-to-last bit, the hem, was Frane's job, followed by sewing on the buttons, if there were any, the zipper, if there was one, and finally ironing the finished piece and hanging it on a hanger.

We made a dark blue suit with red buttons and a collar for me, it had a fitted jacket and fitted skirt, short, because I had lost weight, and I was going to wear it on the trip to Rijeka once we got the green light, and another two dresses for a change of clothes if I stayed longer. To go with the suit I bought a dark blue purse with a gold-like metal shoulder strap, and dark blue shoes with a gold buckle, and a beige silk blouse, with a hint of gold in it, which I barely managed to iron, I had to sprinkle water on the whole thing. I don't know why I bought all these things, I suppose so as to have something new for the hospital, to begin a new chapter in life in which he would recover and I would arrive as the advance guard.

The days passed by but there was no word about the operation, and it was making all of us nervous. The operation was given a fifty per cent chance of success, which was not much and it was risky, but it's even riskier to do nothing, said his cousin, who was for the operation but even he didn't know why it was being delayed. All the tests had been done, but he wasn't being operated on and he wasn't being sent home, and then I got it – the operation had to be paid for.

They won't do anything without money, I know it, I said to my mother, to Danica and Frane, to friends, among them Filip who immediately offered to help, he didn't have any money but his father would give him some, his father was a Partisan veteran, a Serb from Bosnia. Frane got a job at the Institute for the Blind, working on nutrition plans, on what's known as a "bordereau", the money was better, they had managed to save some and would also borrow some, and meanwhile I had received the official decision on my right to receive my father's pension, which included money in arrears, so we had enough to put together.

I had decided to rent a room in Rijeka, nothing bigger than the little room in our apartment, one in an old pre-war building somewhere in the centre of town, so that I could step straight out into the hubbub of the city, with its shops, window displays, cafés serving espresso, newsstands with cigarettes and newspapers, human bodies rushing to work or simply out for a stroll. And all that in the sunshine, which was plentiful because Rijeka was by the sea and smelled of salt, of fish, of pine, of the joys of life in the south. As soon as I arrived I would join the library and continue studying because I had to think of my exams. Otherwise, I could forget about keeping my father's pension!

Danica would come as well, not to Rijeka but to the island of Krk, just a hop and a skip away, her sister lived there in her lover's villa, because she had struck lucky; yes she had a hard face and voice, was a garish peroxide blond, busty and stocky, walked like a goose with her head high, swaying her chest right and left, and was fifty years old, but all the same she had a lover and enjoyed her life in his villa, doing nothing from April to November.

And so I took the train, wearing my new suit, carrying a suitcase I had only managed to close by sitting on it until the locks clicked.

I stepped off the train straight into my childhood when my mother took me via Rijeka to Omišalj, on the island of Krk, because I had rickets and she had found a job at the seaside so that I could get some sun and finally start walking. The porters were still there, calling out, Porter! Porter! All of them skinny, their faces furrowed with wrinkles, holding the handles of their wooden carts like the Chinese in rickshaws, because they hauled the carts themselves, with them at the front and the cart at the back, and there were always children sitting on top of the luggage, like at an amusement park. It was always the same and yet new, because it belonged to a bygone time that was hard to fathom, you couldn't believe that you were once a child and now weren't, you could accept it but you couldn't understand it, it was too weird.

And then the room: I immediately found what I wanted, in the centre of town, in an old building, with a broad staircase and steps that were so low you could skip two at a time, they were smoothed by the tread of generations, sinking in places, hemmed by a wrought iron railing studded with iron flowers. A fat old lady opened the door, her hips had gone to hell so she waddled right and left, almost like a pendulum, she was dressed in black, a widow I decided, though I don't remember her face, it's as if I erased it from my mind, just her sallow skin and the hairs on her chin, a woman transformed into a man, old age had seen to that. She opened a dark door and showed me the equally dark room, with a bed, wardrobe and desk, its yellow ornamental mat lit up by the sun coming in through the closed window – peace and quiet, I liked it, I could already see myself sitting there studying Spinoza, Hegel and Kant, whose books I would borrow from the library that I would join.

I left my things there and went to the hospital where I found my darling mobile, in a good mood, I was glad to see that he had even gained a few pounds, then he went to have his lunch and I went to the post office to phone my mother and tell her I had found a place to stay.

***

Cancel it, my mother said, why pay for something when she had found me a place to stay with the daughter of an old friend of hers who had married somebody in Rijeka, and they're already waiting for you; the granddaughter was a nurse in the same hospital where my darling was a patient and she was ready to help. All splendid arguments but my heart sank, I had already imagined myself living in that dark quiet little room with the ray of sunlight slicing through the air and landing on my open book, I had already seen myself happy there.

Why did you make such an arrangement, I snap at my mother, but there's nothing I can do, her arguments are too strong, especially the part about the nurse, I can't miss out on such an opportunity; fine, I say, sulking, back it is to get my things, tell the old lady I'm not taking the room after all, and then off to a houseful of people I don't know, whose kindness is already exhausting me.

And she doesn't live in the city centre, where I want to be, by the sea where I can feel the city but also be on my own, where everything is exciting, no, they live on the outskirts of town, in a new building, without the layers of previous lives that make me feel alive, that keep me company without my being in their company, no, I have to take a bus to get there, look for a difference in the sameness, lose my way, ask, until my hands go numb from carrying the luggage, bag, umbrella, overcoat, and I really want a cigarette. At last, fed up, I arrive and am greeted by their smiling faces, mother, father, the nurse and her pubescent brother, good-looking though pimply, curly blond hair, a few years younger than his sister who is barely nineteen and already working, though she looks like a child. She has curly blond hair, like her brother, they are both tall and well-built like their father, the mother is petite, heavier and dark, I am barely a year or two older than the girl, but compared to her I feel like a grown-up, no, not like her mother but a hundred years older, as if I am from a different dimension.

I am given a room full of light, and lunch, and solace that I don't need, because they can't comfort me, and I am given the nurse, who is a hundred years my junior, to take me to my darling in the hospital and be a nuisance there, along with a poppy seed cake and little pail of strawberries for him, and a life that isn't my own to live, because that's what my mother wants, my mother who is always in need of people and therefore can't understand me.

No studying, it is impossible to study at their place, they want to be with you all the time, you are interesting, you've brought them your city, they've never been there, and it is the capital city, and you're bringing them your interesting student life, at least that's how they imagine it, you're bringing them stories about one thing and another, because I have to keep talking, because that's how I started and that's what they now expect of me. And I can play chess. The boy can't get enough of me, it's as if he's fallen in love with me in his childlike way, everybody is constantly at my heels and so kind that all I can do is sink into this communal life until time rescues me, until I return home.

But I am with my darling, the weather is beautiful and during visiting hours we sit in the park. He admires my suit and shoes, and likes showing me off on the ward, especially my legs, which I've finally revealed. He likes the fact that I've lost weight, but he doesn't want me to lose any more, he prefers me with meat on the bones rather than skinny, clothes are one thing, a girl in bed is another, he says. He becomes excited when he talks, which isn't good for him really, and wants to fondle me on the bench, he wants to put his hand inside my blouse, between my legs, ah, it seems you've recovered, I say with a smile, pushing his hand away, cupping his face with my hand and looking into his eyes.

Even in his letters he was always writing about my body, I remember, always my body, how glowing it was, how he couldn't stop thinking about it, how wonderful and beautiful I was, and I wrote about his eyes, about his profile which for some reason made me sad to look at, about how I wanted to be as small as a fingernail so that I could slip into his pyjama pocket and he could take me out whenever he needed me. I gave him a toy, a black cloth cat, with whiskers and a red bow tied around its neck, and a cute face, to sit on his night table and cheer him up, to remind him that I was his kitten and he was my tom, that's how we signed our letters to each other.

I've been here for a week already, and we're racking our brains about when I should offer the doctor money and how I should do it. Suddenly I feel unsure of myself. I've never offered anybody a bribe before, I haven't a clue how to do it, I might offend the man, he's not a porter or a waiter, and plus he was Tito's doctor, what if he turns me down, I think glumly. I still think it needs to be done, but not by me, maybe Danica, when she comes to visit him, she's timid and docile anyway, she cries at the drop of a hat, and, anyway, she's the mother so she's more likely to be forgiven if we've misjudged him. But my darling wants me to do it, he believes in me more than in his mother, who could screw everything up, he says. Just smile, talk to him, shove the envelope into his hand and say: this is for you, he'll say thank you and then you can leave, he says confidently. We decide to wait until Monday and see if he's on the list of scheduled operations – they announce the operations on a board in the entrance hall – and if he isn't, I'll come with the money.

On Sunday night I can't sleep, all I do is imagine that moment when I take the envelope out of my dark blue bag with its gold-like chain, make sure it's a white, not a blue envelope, he warns me unnecessarily, because I know the difference between the two, blue is for workers, white is for their bosses, and then I say, this is for you, and I smile and push the envelope towards him, oh hell, how am I going to do that, we never bribed anybody when my father was sick, we just invited his doctor to dinner when it looked as if he was recovering.

But on Monday, no mention of the operation, so I have no choice, I'm going to have to knock on the door of the best doctor in the Balkans and beyond, this fifty-year-old man with sharp features and a face furrowed with wrinkles, but who looks calm, confident and kind, yes kind, I notice, and that unsettles me, I'd prefer it if he looked nasty, they are easier to bribe. I haven't slept, but I've made an effort to look good, I've put on make-up, combed my hair, put on my new suit, with the matching bag and shoes, a bit of perfume that I stole from the nurse because I didn't bring any of my own. I sit down, cross my legs, and ask about my husband's condition, casually taking the envelope out of my bag, offering it to him, saying: this is for you; and then, oh hell, he immediately stands up, pushing the envelope away, thank God I didn't drop it, I catch it at the last minute and put it back in my bag.

How could I even think that he would accept money, he says, I blush with embarrassment, I stammer something to the effect that we've been waiting for the operation for so long, and we thought, we thought, I can't finish my sentence, I just fall silent, my face burning. He understands, explaining that he still hasn't decided, he's still in two minds, because when he removes the tumour, the thickness of the knife's blade will also remove a part of the brain, he's precise, and nobody knows exactly what is in this area they call hollow, because it's not dominant, it doesn't contain the centres for survival, but something will be removed, something will be missing. And nobody knows, he says, how he will behave afterwards, he may change beyond recognition. He may not even survive. So it's better for him to stay as he is, while he's alive, he's still young, he's still got a chance, better that, he says, than maybe being sectioned, conscious but not quite himself, that's the worst thing that could happen. But, if we insist, he'll do the operation, the day after tomorrow, he says, after all, everything is ready, all the tests have been done, it's just a matter of deciding.

We immediately phone his cousin, who is adamant – operate, and the next day my darling's name is already on the board in the entrance hall, I shiver when I see it, he's having surgery the day after tomorrow, and that may be the end of it. I call Danica in Krk and tell her to come to the hospital to see her son, perhaps for the last time, I think, although I don't say that, because she knows, to come for us to wait together, to support him, and each other, I say. But that day the weather suddenly turns and a strong northern wind starts blowing, so I wind up wearing my overcoat, which I had started to think I shouldn't have brought, and Danica calls to say she can't come, the only way off the island is by boat and she gets seasick, she'd throw up like crazy, she says. She'll come when the weather calms down, forgive me, I can't come now.

I don't forgive her, I don't forgive her for not coming to see her son for what's maybe the last time, to embrace him for the last time, I'd swim the ocean if my son were in the hospital, never mind dismissing a bit of vomiting. What kind of a mother is she, I ask myself horrified, a stepmother not a mother, where were my wits when I felt sorry for her, it's him not her I should feel sorry for, him for having such a mother. But he has me for a mother now that his own mother has let him down, me to support him in life, and no, I don't forgive her, I don't ... because I don't understand.

Morning dawns dark and grey and still windy, the wind whips through the chimney, the shutters, the treetops, the clothes; the northern wind in tandem with clouds, the worst possible combination, the northern wind is supposed to chase the clouds away, and the southern wind to bring them in, not the other way round, they tell me. The wind, with a splattering of rain, has literally blown me off to the hospital, to his room, where he is waiting, ready. He doesn't even mention his mother, which I find a little odd, but I don't say anything. Minutes go by, then an hour, both of us have empty stomachs, mine is knotted, and so is his, and anyway, you don't eat before an operation. We wait and wait, I smoke, which makes me nauseous, he doesn't even smoke, he doesn't think he's allowed to, he just bites his nails. And we're surprised that nobody has come to shave his head and do all the other horrible things that need doing before an operation, such as being given an enema, which he's already been warned about. Finally I say: I'm going to check the board to see if anything has changed; and it has changed, it has changed, I can't believe my eyes, his name has been removed again, and this time it's for good.

Because the doctor has changed his mind. I guess the best doctor in the Balkans and beyond knows what to do better than the anaesthesiologist cousin, he and I decide, he happy that he can finally go home after four months of hanging around in the hospital. True, he's not healthy, but he's no different from the way he was, he feels fine, he's eager to get back to his life as soon as possible, tomorrow, in his mind he's already there.

You know that kind man in whose house I'm living, who's allergic to garlic just like your father, I tell him, as if this means something, as if it is an important connection because I'm looking for an excuse for what I'm about to do, I'm going to borrow a pair of trousers from him, a shirt and a cardigan, you're the same height and size, so that you have something to wear when you go home. He was taken by ambulance to Rijeka in only his dressing gown and pyjamas, he brought some underwear with him but nobody thought about the rest, it had all been so sudden, and afterwards it was too late. While you're saying your goodbyes to the hospital, the other patients and staff, and waiting for your discharge papers, I say, I'll go out and buy you a pair of shoes, size forty-five, I check, planning for tomorrow morning's train trip home. We'll spend the night on the sofa where I sleep, it's a tight squeeze but big enough for the two of us, I say, he likes the idea of squeezing on the sofa and he's got nothing against wearing somebody else's clothes, he's just happy to be going home. I'd even go in my pyjamas and slippers, he says, when we're all together in our hosts' house, having a good laugh.

No need to mail the clothes back, says the wife after we've dressed him, she'll send the kids to stay during the school holidays so that they can finally see Zagreb, they can bring the clothes back when they come home, she says; the girl will take a few days off so that she can go with her brother, they've already arranged everything and are looking forward to it.

I'm slightly taken aback by the speed of this trade-off, this express repayment of debts, and I say to myself it'll never happen, they'll forget about it … But no … They came the first day of the boy's school holiday and stayed for a week. I didn't know what else to do with them except take them around Zagreb until our feet almost dropped off, and feed them until they burst, cold cuts, meat, side dishes, and since we weren't into baking I bought ready-made cakes, except that twice my mother made strudel, once with apples and the second time with cheese, and I lugged tons of candies and chocolates home, stuffed them as if I wanted to kill them with sugar, and finally, not noticing that I was stuffing myself as well, I gained back all the pounds I had lost while he was in the hospital; I wanted to kick myself.

XVIII.

Something's missing, something's missing. Let's get a cat.

I realised that something was missing when we were at the seaside, we had paid for the trip with part of the unpaid bribe, my money and what his parents had contributed, we just returned what we owed Filip. Go ahead, kids, get some rest, Danica and Frane said, and my mother said so, too, so we went. I was in seventh heaven, as they say, because at home he was depressed, almost apathetic; he could sit for hours staring into space. And if I asked him what was the matter, he'd say nothing, what did he mean nothing when I could see it was something, I just couldn't figure out what that something was, it was there but invisible.

The sea will restore him, I think, but it doesn't, it doesn't, he lives with me but is lifeless, like a doll you have to wind up, I make him move, he eats, he walks, he swims, he doesn't sunbathe because it's bad for the angioma, and anyway he has a fair complexion, he doesn't like the sun, but he drinks, the red wine has been on the table since lunch, he sits, smokes and sips his wine, gazing out at the sea from the shade, and I'm next to him reading, because what else is there when all the joy has gone. There's a huge gulf between us and nothing to fill it, it swallows everything up and remains what it was, an absence of something, I wonder if I didn't produce that absence because his illness scared me, because now there is a cautiousness that didn't use to exist, that bomb inside him hasn't been removed, it's still there like a threat.

When we were at home I could barely wait for this trip and now we can barely wait to go home, to stop this torture of emptiness closing in on us. When we get home, we have to get down to the books for our exams, but that's another story, that's a clear objective with all the tasks that go with it, it's a different way of being together. Maybe he'll start to write those radio pieces that he signs, it would be only fair if he wrote them and earned some money. I'd worked my tail off to write those articles and cover the three weeks we were going to be away at the seaside, it had been hard, and he had to be catered for as well. But he never said: let me help you, let's share it, no he watched TV, read the newspaper, went out to buy cigarettes, to visit his parents, he met up with Leon, and all that time I was writing his articles for him. Sometimes he would come home after midnight and be surprised that it upset me, but you were working, he'd say, raising my blood pressure, especially when he'd add: I thought you'd already be asleep. As if he'd been waiting for me to fall asleep! Because he knows that I don't stay up late, that I'm a morning person, I get up with the sun. But I'm still not angry, memories of the hospital are still fresh in my mind, I'm still afraid of something happening to him, I'm still glad that he's alive and breathing and moving, that everything still exists.

Home at last!

I've been planning to renovate the kitchen for some time, to move it into the pantry and turn the kitchen into a dining room on the southern side of the flat, where there's more light, because the hall is steeped in semi-darkness no matter what time of day, unless we turn on the light, and the only natural light there is comes from the rooms, if the doors are open.

There is still enough money left for the renovation from the money we'd collected for the bribe, it would have been frittered away anyway, he just keeps asking for more, but never asks where it comes from or how long it will last, so let him get involved a little, I say to myself, thinking about the renovation, let him do some work, he can't just laze around all day. He's not allowed to carry anything, nothing heavy, not even the luggage, so I'm the porter and he trudges along beside me, that's an upsetting image – a porter for the rest of my life! – it's like being diminished, I hadn't counted on that, I had counted on the opposite, but then I chase the thought away ... It's not his fault, I tell myself, I mustn't be like that, what can't be, can't be, but there are things that can be, for instance, we can plan the renovation and go around the shops together. And he can help out with small jobs, or at least supervise the work. Danica and Frane send us a man to give him a helping hand, he's old and cheap, he's known him since childhood, and if nothing else he'll have somebody to sit beside him and drink with. But I have to do the run of the shops with my mother, he's too tired for that.

Leave him alone, the poor man is unwell, my mother would say whenever I had a go at him to get off his ass, to do something, but she would say I'll do it, I'll do it, she was retired and had the time and the energy, she and I were enough. Not for me we're not, I thought, had you been enough for me I would never have married, but how can I say that to her when we're living in her flat, though it's true that when my father died I took over as boss, because she never knew how to be a boss, and somebody had to do it, but it is still us who have invaded her life, not she ours. I'm not obsessed with the thought, I have resolved to live with her, I'm not going to leave her, but it does cross my mind now and then that everything would be different if we lived on our own, that he wouldn't be able to get out of things on the grounds that my mother is helping, or use the fact that we're not alone as an excuse to disappear from the house, an increasingly frequent occurrence.

He needs something to tie him to the house, I think to myself, children are out of the question, we're both students and he's sick, and anyway, we haven't planned for them, no we'll get a cat! The black cloth cat with the red bow around its neck, and its cute whiskers, is sitting on the shelf but now I want a real, live cat to prowl around the house and to play with. I'd rather have a dog, I've already had one, I prefer dogs, they are more loyal and sweeter, but they're also more work, you have to walk a dog, whereas a cat practically takes care of itself, just give it a litter box and food and that's it. He agrees to the idea, but not just any kind of cat, not, say, an alley cat from the courtyard, where there are lots, when it's sunny they stretch out on the roof of the shed, it was once a barn built by the previous owner for his dairy cows, a crazy story, he died in a madhouse a long time ago but the shed with the nice flat roof remained, it's like a terrace without a railing for the neighbourhood cats that don't belong to anybody, as far as I know, though everybody feeds them. They mate all year round and at night they yowl like babies, crying and wheezing, you'd think it was a massacre.

We don't want that kind of cat, or its kittens, even though they come free, we'll buy a cat, not an ordinary one though, a Siamese cat, he says, but they look nasty and mean, I say, however, he won't let it go, it's either a Siamese cat or nothing; well, alright then. So we look in *Večernji list* under "pets", cats, cats, not ordinary cats, aha, there they are, Siamese cats, with the phone number, address, Martić Street, not exactly around the corner but not too far away either, we can walk there. It's an Indian summer, and I'm skipping by his side, because it's warm, it's a riot of colours, not grey, because I'm young and because we're going to get a pet, a cute kitty will come into the house, for us to look at and cuddle, to add something to our lives, to bring us together.

On the way, there'll be lots of shops and window displays for us to see, because we'll be walking down Ilica, the longest street in Zagreb, a street of shops and display windows, of clothes, shoes, hats, appliances, newsstands, cinemas, bistros, pastry shops, lottery ticket vendors, all full of people, of shoppers, strollers, no matter what the hour, everything full of colour, the trams running in two directions towards the outskirts of town, one eastwards and the other westwards, the route armies take on their way in and out. The north is reserved for the elite, for doctors, lawyers, politicians, and in the south new housing projects are mushrooming for the new poor, for blow-ins as we natives of the city centre call them, we who got here first and think that makes us privileged.

At the radio station, an old building that has seen everything, all sorts of comings and goings, and still managed to survive in one piece, we run into Leon with his goatee and hawkish eyes, stocky, short, slightly hunched, wearing a dark blue suit and dark red tie, we're journalists, we've got to maintain a certain standard, his clothes say, hey, you two, he says, where've you been, where are you going, let's go for a drink. And he immediately reminds me that I owe him two articles, he reminds me, not him, his Rile, who is here right beside me, and who is still signing them, his name travels through the ether into the listeners' ears, he's already famous, you'll get them, I say, you'll get them, when I'm late with something I always keep my word. But my darling says nothing.

We'd love to go for a drink but we have to pick up the cat, we say explaining the inexplicable, the cat, he says in surprise, he can't believe that with so many stray cats around somebody was actually going to buy one. And what do we want a cat for anyway, what will we think of next, he says; Rile probably can't chase pussies anymore because you've nabbed him, he says laughing, and suddenly I remember what he said at the beginning of our relationship, that "if that guy ever saw Italy, I'm the pope". It had upset me because I didn't want to believe it, so I accused him of lying, of wanting to break us up, who knows why, maybe he was jealous because he felt he had lost a friend. But now I suddenly think that he had been telling the truth, Leon, not my darling, or his parents and cousin from Rome, all conniving in this lie; impossible, I'm going crazy, I fight the suspicion that has buried itself in my heart but I can't get rid of it. My darling is here to dispel any doubts I may have; embracing me, he tells Leon that he's leaving all those pussycats for him now, enjoy, he says, see you around, he adds, and everybody laughs but there's a frown above Leon's hawk eyes and he shakes a finger at him as if to say: be careful; we leave with our arms around each other.

And now we're in the flat of the people who own the Siamese cats, an elegant and spacious flat like the others in Martić Street, built before the war, not during the war like mine, or after the war like his, and we're in the living room with the owners and the cats, its big French windows and balcony overlooking the street, the southern sun bathing us in its light. Mama cat and her kittens peer out of the basket, curious, raising their heads with their little brown noses and brown pointed ears, their fur the colour of café au lait, their eyes as blue as blue can be, so sweet you want to eat them up. The owners are sitting next to each other on a sofa the same colour as the cats, and invite us to sit in the armchairs. They tell us how active the cats are, how energetic and cute, what fun they are, and we stare at the scratch marks and tears on the sofa, which looks as if it had been taken off the street, and at the ragged curtains. As if they want to show us what they can do, all three kittens jump out of their basket, tear around the room and sharpen their claws on the sofa, and then one of them leaps onto the curtain, hanging and swinging on it like a kitten out of a cartoon, they really are lively, my darling laughs sardonically, lighting up a cigarette, because he's spotted an ashtray on the table.

How much for your kittens, I ask, since I'm in charge of the finances; our hostess stares at the carpet, which is oddly undamaged, and then her husband speaks up, saying, well there's the birthing, the vaccinations, the food, he waffles, not mentioning the damage to the flat though he's included it in the price, I realise, when he finally comes out with it; that's too much, I say, because I'm not one to equivocate, and with those words the two of us are on our feet, we've got no dilemma, thank you, it was nice, thank you, goodbye.

On our way home we decide to get a dog, a cocker spaniel, a bitch, I say, because it's my turn to choose now, and I'm thinking of Lady in Disney's *Lady and the Tramp*, those sweet eyes, those floppy ears, and of taking revenge for the Siamese cats, I say, and we laugh our heads off thinking of the Siamese kittens, especially the one that dug its claws into the curtain, so it's back to looking at the "pets" column in the newspaper, and before you know it there's a dog in the house. Out of habit, we continue checking the ads and a few days later there's the name of the owner of the overpriced Siamese cats imploring Mr. so and so, his only buyer, in big bold letters, to come and pick up his kitten.

I chose the breed and he chose the name. Tanga, he said, let's call it Tanga, which is the name of a seductress in a Peter Cheyney detective story – he probably masturbated just reading about her, I realised, when I got over my romanticism.

XIX.

It's November, the worst month of the year, neither autumn nor winter, a time of shadows, it's early afternoon, but we've already turned on the lights, and my mother, the dog and I are sitting in the dining room, she's darning the heel of my husband's sock on a wooden mushroom because she refuses to throw things away, she mends them, the dog is curled up on the chair, dozing, and I'm leafing through the newspaper, which is empty; suddenly there's a blood-curdling scream from the other room. The dog leaps out of the chair terrified, my mother and I stand up, the darning mushroom rolls under the table, what is it, what is it, we shout, the three of us running into the hallway, and then into our room where we find my husband on the floor – he'd fallen off the sofa he was sleeping on – his back twisted, shaking as if he'd had an electric shock, his face distorted and blue, his mouth spewing blood-speckled foam. An epileptic seizure, I immediately realise, I'd read about it in Dostoevsky, and there was a boy in my secondary school class who was epileptic and had a few seizures during our lessons, he was dark and his last name was Habulinec.

We're standing there feeling helpless, me with an image of Habulinec in my mind, when my mother, who is more level-headed, quickly grabs a pillow to place under his head. But how, when she's afraid to approach him, so am I, I'm shivering as if it's cold, the dog sneaks under the four-legged table, watching quietly, resting its head on its paws; we keep waiting, waiting for this horror to end, we wait forever, until he finally looks peaceful, though he is still unconscious, but at least now we can put the pillow under his head, and he opens his eyes, which look faded. What happened, he asks, because he doesn't remember a thing, not that he screamed, not that he fell, not that he shook. He sits up, running his tongue over his lips in astonishment, he can taste the blood in his mouth, he says, I bit my tongue, he says, wiping the spittle away with his finger and then cleaning his finger on the track suit he had been sleeping in. I help him get to his feet, he stands there not knowing why he got up, do you have to go to the toilet, I ask, no, he says, he's tired, he says, and I help him lie down on the sofa again.

The doctor in Zagreb, not the one in Rijeka who's too far away to contact, tells me what I need to do the next time he has a seizure, a *grand mal*, he says, the worst kind, he says, which I already know from my *Medical Lexicon*, I keep it on my bedside table close at hand; just put a pillow under his head, he says, or anything soft, a roll of clothes, that sort of thing. Don't touch him while he's having a seizure, he says, that can only make it worse, and when he comes to, keep him calm. Do I have to put something in his mouth, like a hanky, to stop him from biting his tongue, I ask, but he says better not, he could hurt himself on a foreign object or it could block his breathing, no just calm him down. And he gives us barbiturates to prevent or at least minimise the seizures, but they have to be taken regularly, he says.

So that's that, epilepsy from a brain tumour that's still there because they didn't remove it, and now we have to live with it. Illness has been a part of my life for as long as I can remember, first my father's and now his, isn't that strange, I think, feeling guilty because it's unkind to think like that, one should be compassionate and make one's peace with it, not complain, which is anyway pointless. Because you're certainly not going to show illness the door, you're not going to pass the buck, and anyway there's nobody to pass it to, Danica and Frane have long since dodged the issue, behaving like guests. My poor son, Danica moans, crying her eyes out, while Frane just nods inconsolably, shakes his head and brings her coat so that they can return to the peace and quiet of their own home, or at least the peace and quiet of a place where they don't have to look at a sick person all day.

They don't have to wait for the next seizure, to jump every time there's an unexpected sound in the flat, the sudden flushing of the bathroom toilet, the door slammed shut by the wind, shouts in the street when the windows are open, they don't have to tremble if he calls out from his room to the kitchen – not knowing if he needs something or is screaming – and then run over to him, prepared for the worst. Make sure he takes his pills, and if you discover in the middle of the night that he's run out, go straight to the duty pharmacy, wherever it is, on foot if need be, and get a hold of those pills, even if you have to do it without a prescription.

The nights are the worst, we still sleep on the sofa, but not the way we used to, with my head on his chest, or me spooning him, no, now I always turn my back to him, as if that will save me. I stay awake afraid that he will have a seizure in his sleep, that I'll be awoken by him screaming, that the *grand mal* will explode in my face, that I won't survive it. I lie there curled up, staring into the dark, thinking,

thinking, but not really thinking about anything because there's nothing to think about when there's nothing you can do, it's like thinking about how to get out of your body when you discover it's a prison, how to get out alive, not dead, how to leave and still stay inside it, you feel so helpless that you grind your teeth until sleep gets the better of you. But the real torture is when he reaches out for me in bed, because I don't like it but I can't tell him that, I don't want to kill him, I'd rather simply endure it, I just have to keep my legs together so that he doesn't push in too far, because it's too big, it will hurt me.

The nights are a nightmare but everything changes in the daylight, when I get out of bed and slip on the human skin of the day, like in a fairy tale, although there, it's the other way round, a swan by day, a beautiful girl by night, never mind, one way or the other it's two different faces. My daytime face is happy because dawn has finally broken, everything will be alright, it'll all be alright, I tell him, his mother, me, I spread the optimism of believing that he will be fine, we'll stop the epilepsy with the pills, and anyway you don't die from epilepsy, I say, as if in cahoots with the keeper of the keys to life. See, I say to my darling, now you're Dostoevsky, you just have to write *The Brothers Karamazov* and there'll be no stopping you, I joke, not to go crazy, and you'll buy your Lincoln Continental with the money you get when you're published in the U.S., I laugh, not to go crazy. He responds with an ironic grin behind his beard and moustache, nodding only half good-naturedly because he does and doesn't like the joke, it's a joke, yes, but on a serious subject, and he plans to be Dostoevsky and to be published in the U.S., and he swears it's all going to happen, you'll see, he says ... And for a second, that never-to-be famous, rich and successful person is standing on the prow of the *Queen Mary*, sailing into New York, greeting the Statue of Liberty where he'll be welcomed with speeches and flashing cameras.

Because fame and wealth exist only in New York, as his father Frane told him when he was thirteen, on a boat trip to Opatija, standing on the deck, looking out at the sea and the ships and the distances they imagined lay ahead, his father's dream, one he did not fulfil but he had a son to leave it to, a son who could fulfil it for them both.

And that turned out to be my entire inheritance, he says sardonically when he's finished his story about his father, himself, Opatija. New York, the *Queen Mary* that would take him to all this, furious at his father for having deluded him – because other people's dreams never take you anywhere – yet still perfidiously in the grips of that subversive dream.

And then his disappearances became more frequent.

The first time he disappeared was in Pula, when I didn't kick him out because of his fragility, which I thought would be lifelong, and how could I go against that, and now, of course, there's his illness, an excuse for everything. Bad boy has become poor boy, you can't rebuke him, as my mother says, at least not too much, you can't get angry at him, at least not too much, until I go crazy because I can't take it anymore, I'm going to explode.

I usually sit on the sofa in the hall, in front of the TV, it's evening, then night-time, it's just the dog and me, my mother's not around, she's probably already left to work, saying that she has to earn money for my father's headstone, because his grave looks pathetic without it.

I sit, I smoke, I drink, I'm grey with fatigue and worry, my greasy hair lank around my face, even when I wash it, which isn't often, because I don't wash much anymore, I smell in the hope that it'll disgust him and he'll leave me alone. Because he's obsessed with cleanliness, he always scrubs himself down with soap and splashes on the cologne, he keeps 4711 cologne in his toiletry bag, along with some face and hand cream, which I used to think was funny but now I think is sick. I wait to see when he will unlock the front door, at one, two, three in the morning when he comes home, having gone out to buy cigarettes or see Leon, or whatever, ten, twelve, fourteen hours earlier; he unlocks the door as silently as he can, but it's no use because the dog has already heard him and runs over, the little traitor. But he keeps hoping that I'm asleep, although I never go to sleep until he comes home, not anymore, I wait until I drop. Because I never know if something has happened to him, maybe he had a seizure and fell in the street, under a car, under a tram, maybe he's already dead in one of the hospitals, bad news travels fast they say, but I can't help it, I have to see him walk through that door. And when he does, I can't not be angry, not be furious that he does what he does, that he disappears without a word, I can't not have a go at him, ask him where he was, and why, why, repeating it a hundred times, not choosing my words, until he slaps or punches me, because he can't listen to me anymore.

I never hit back, he's sick, I might hurt him, so I just twist away, try to fend him off with my hand, as I used to with my father who also hit me, when he was drunk, not on the head, my mother would cry out, but it was no use because, if I protected my face, his hand would automatically go for my head. And it stopped when I told him that the next time he hit me I would kill him, I was already of age. And then I brought my husband into the house only to have it continue, as if I couldn't live without being hit.

I don't hit back even when he hits me because I haven't written the article for the radio; the money for it goes to him, to his bank account, but it doesn't come into the house because he spends it on himself, on his disappearances, so I never see any of it. I won't do the writing and have you do the spending, I say, which seems logical to me but not to him, because he was counting on me, he shouts. Because I promised him I would write it. I say, no I didn't, I'd warned him that I was done with it, but he shouts that he can't just jump in and take over like that, that I've got the hang of writing these pieces and he hasn't, so until he has I have to write them, or else.

And here I am, with a black-blue-and-yellow eye, behind sunglasses that I still have to remove sometimes, and Filip, who has dropped by, asks me what happened. And I say, you know that high shelf in the kitchen where I keep the scales (an old iron one with weights), well, I was trying to take it down and it fell and gave my face a hard smack, I say. But Filip looks at me doubtfully, that was wasn't caused by scales, he says, and he's serious, he's not laughing at me.

He's come to advise me how to continue my studies so that I can keep my father's pension, I lose it when I graduate, and I don't expect to find a job. Make your second subject, philosophy, your first and that will give you another two years, and by then he'll probably graduate as well, he says, thinking of my husband who, of course, isn't at home even though it's already dark outside.

In the morning, he was going to write his senior thesis for his second elective subject, also philosophy; I'd already finished mine, all I had left now was my thesis for my first elective, comparative literature. But he didn't do anything, he was tired, tired today, tired tomorrow, I can't, I'm not getting anywhere with it, he moaned, and anyway what was I going to do with a degree in philosophy and comparative literature, I could wipe my ass with it, it wasn't going to get me a job, and so he put a stop to all our efforts, the ashes and dust of life. OK, we'll study together, I said, because I can't stand leaving things undone, and I took out the notebooks I had studied from, and the summaries of the books I had read, because that's how I study, by writing, not just reading, I have to rewrite the book if I'm going to remember it. You can learn everything you need to know from these summaries without ever having to read the original if you don't want to, I said, determined not to give up. And he agreed to it, because he thought it would be easier to learn the summaries by heart, with somebody who could explain everything to him, lay it out on a platter, and so we started with philosophy, to finish with that first, because officially it was his first subject.

And now, just before his written exam, he's disappeared, disappeared, can you believe it, after months of studying, I say to Filip, who doesn't know what to say, he just stares at the bruises on my face, keeping his opinions to himself, probably thinking that I'm an idiot to go to all this trouble for nothing, which is what I think, too. All the same, I get dressed and go out to look for him, having first seen Filip off because I don't want him to know what I'm going to do, how pathetic I am, and I cover my bruised face with sunglasses, which nobody sane wears at night.

Like a machine, I walk here, there, street after street, from the restaurant to the café, in, out, sweat pouring out of me, but I keep on walking and walking, then I stop to light a cigarette and look around as if I expect him to appear out of nowhere, out of a shadow that's swallowed him up and is now going to disgorge him because it can't digest him. At "Peščenica", his old restaurant, all his pals are still at the table, all except for Leon, and they shrug, saying that they haven't seen him in a long time; the hunchback, sitting like a frog on the armrest of the chair, swinging his legs with their laced shoes, scrutinises my sunglasses, It's not easy, he says, as if he knows what happened and understands, though we both know whose side he's on, and he asks after his health and says to give him his best when I find him, but I won't do that, there's nothing here for me. I catch a glimpse of myself in the mirror at the front door, unable to recognise this face behind the sunglasses that claims to be mine, the face of the madwoman I've become without realising it.

But then I run out of places to look for him; everything in town is closed, maybe he's gone home, I think, and I'm not there, well, never mind, now it's his turn to worry about where I am, I think, feeling mean. Still, I give it one more shot and rush over to the bus station, to "Gumenjak", that's what they call this drinking hole, "Rubber Boat", and there he is, sitting at a table, hunched over a glass of brandy, his trousered legs crossed, swinging his top leg as usual, a sign that something is eating at him, I suppose. I realise his hand was between his legs, under the tablecloth, when, after noticing me, he places it on the table, as if he had taken it out from somewhere. A fleeting thought instantly disappears in the face of the urgent need to get him home right away. He has to get up early in the morning.

What are you doing, I snarl between clenched teeth, you've got your written exam tomorrow; I don't let him finish his brandy, get up right now, I say, glancing at the two mini-skirted women sitting at the bar, swinging their naked legs, he was probably gawking at them, I think to myself. He immediately stands up, his hands resting on the table for support, and the two women at the bar snigger, their faces lopsided because they're drunk and their skin won't listen to them. He pays at the bar with a crumpled bill that he's pulled out of his pocket, and then follows me out, hunched over, as if he's on a leash, as if he's a slave, not a man.

And now here I am in the morning, my sunglasses still on my nose, sitting on one of the benches in front of the large lecture-room in which students write their exam papers, a prerequisite to having your orals. Beside me is a stack of notes with possible exam topics. I'm waiting for him to come out, allegedly to use the bathroom, to tell me what topic he's been given to write on so that I can pull it out of the folder and give it to him to take inside beneath his jacket.

Socrates and the sophists, he whispers when he comes out, leaning over me, a strand of hair falling onto his perspiring brow; here, I've got it, and I take the papers out of the folder that's on top of the stack because this is the beginning of continuous thought, an easy subject, he's lucky, I think to myself, later it all gets complicated. He turns red as he shoves the papers beneath his jacket, terrified that he'll get caught, even though there's nobody in sight.

He passed the written exam with a B, and got another B on his oral, which we celebrated with friends and a mound of food as the event of the century, and for days afterwards we were eating leftovers, the empty bottles lined up by the front door. But I listened to Filip, prolonged my studies for two more years, and the agony for two more years, blocking out myself, blocking out the obvious – that I was continuing a life where there was no more us, no more, no more, no more, as the song goes, which was hard to understand because supposedly there still was an us, there still was happiness and love and music and dance, so why was there no more us in all this, I wondered, banging my head against the question; there was, but there wasn't, you had no place to return to, no place to go to because you didn't exist; absolute torture.

To thank me for helping her son with his studies, Danica gave me a fur collar taxidermy, a silver fox with a horrible pointy snout, fluffy fur tail and poor little paws, you didn't know what was worse, the glass eyes or the lifeless paws. I shuddered when she took the poor thing out of the cardboard box and placed it in my hands.

Still, I pressed the fur against my face, looked in the mirror, said it was lovely, a marvellous gift and thanked her, which brought tears to her eyes, but when she left I stuffed the revolting thing in the storage compartment of my mother's sofa, under the instalments of *The Witch of Grič,* beside the balls of wool and old clothing, mothballs generously strewn across her petty oasis, although the moths were still in residence, as became obvious in the summer.

XX.

THE DOORBELL rings, who is it, I ask, dragging myself to the door, the dog barking behind me, but I already know who it is, of course, it's Adam, who can be relied on to come the minute my darling disappears, so that we can be alone.

How come you always know when I need you, I say, kissing his cheek; he shuffles in, like a convict dragging a ball and chain, he is clearly dragging something, but it's invisible, because addiction is heavier to drag around than a ball. His whole life has been as heavy as a ball and chain, at least seen from the outside, and how else can you look at it except from the outside, you can't penetrate another person's inner soul no matter how hard you try, you can only guess, and inside that gaping darkness behind these guesses are ghosts that even the person himself won't penetrate, at least not in his lifetime.

And now I need you, too, he says mysteriously, because, of course, I know that he needs me in a way that I don't need him, we both know it, he needs me for a particular reason, something's happened.

I take him into the hall, where I've been sitting because that's where I have the TV, the background sound of the world; my hair hangs in limp strands, like the day, I'm in my house clothes, a washed-out black track suit with worn knees, my face is grey, like the day, and I'm exhausted, because waiting for my vanished husband is killing me.

I look awful, I say, but he doesn't see it, he doesn't see what I think he sees, the scruffiness and the fatigue, no you don't, he says, your eyes just look smaller, like a mouse's, he says, that's because I haven't put make-up on, I smile, but I like it that way, he says.

He's not yet drunk because he's come here from work where he can't drink, but he is tipsy. On his way over he must have downed two brandies or a beer, or both, because he's already a bit stiff and sniffly, the way my father used to be when he drank but wasn't yet drunk.

He recently got a job at a bank, again through one of his father's clients, being the good tailor that he is he makes suits for politicians and directors, and also drinks with them, so he used his connections to find a job for his son, for he didn't know what to do with him anymore.

Adam first started studying law, then dropped it and switched to literature and philosophy, then dropped that, too, although he still doesn't know why. Wicked tongues would answer that it was probably because he wanted to drink, not study, which wouldn't be far from the truth, but there was no answer to why he wanted to drink to the detriment of everything else. Maybe it was drink that kept him in this world, because who knows what keeps us here and why we ever came. Not everybody comes into it to be successful, some come to fail and fulfil their destiny through failure, as if they're paying a debt, and that is their peak achievement, I once thought when I saw him sitting on the terrace of a café, waiting for me because he was early. He had come early on purpose, so that he could sit there on his own, drink and stare into empty space, at least that's how it looked, but people who stare into empty space are themselves empty, and he's not, he's a cup spilling over, a cup full of himself. When he stares into empty space he is staring into his own amazing, astonishing, fascinating self. He delights in himself. And drink keeps him to himself, it protects him from society whose demands steer you away from yourself and into the obligations and duties of work and marriage, into acquiring things, into situations where you have everything and everybody except yourself, that being right and socially desirable. That's where he parted ways with the rest of the world, I realised, he couldn't be of use to society so he harmed himself, because society does not forgive. My father drank within the protective embrace of his family and, like most drunks, he never dragged anybody into his drunkenness, except for his parents, them he couldn't avoid. When he realised that nothing would come of his studies, his father tried to find him a wife, he took him to his rich friends in Podravina to marry him off to one of their daughters who would inherit land and a fully furnished house that was just waiting for a young newlywed couple to move in and begin to fill it with offspring. But he would sit there like a log, showing no interest in any of the marriageable girls, just drinking and waiting for his father to drive him home and put an end to this nonsense. He had affairs, but only casual ones, for a night or two, never an official girlfriend, and after so many years, chasing me had become almost as routine as saying Hello, I would tease him; because he kept swearing he was serious, but I would just smile and lift his hand off my knee.

In order to live the way he wanted, sitting at a table with a glass at hand, wallowing in himself, he needed money, a pile of money, he needed, as the fairy tale goes: "table, deck yourself" (with all and sundry), "ass, spew forth gold pieces from your rear" and "cudgel, out of the sack" (to defend the table and ass from thieves); in other words he needed a miracle, because you can't earn a pile of money, and when you have to earn it you don't have time to spend it, so what you have is nothing, he would say, constantly looking around to see if it would appear somewhere. Not in a bag that somebody lost and he found, as my father hoped, no, in a less imaginative form, say, in the form of an inheritance, like in a nineteenth-century novel, where that was precisely what they were waiting for. The grey streak in his thick blond hair confirmed that such a thing was not inconceivable, because anyone with a grey streak, it was said, would one day have so much money they wouldn't know what to do with it.

Then something shifted in just that direction – his father's sister appeared; she owned a big estate in Podravina and on the property were curative springs, so she marketed the water and, combining medicine with religion, founded a kind of sect to compliment the idea of health, and raked in a stack of money. This woman, who marketed the health of both body and mind, now fell ill herself but she did not resort to her curative waters and religious books and prayers to get better, no, she came to seek help in Zagreb, with its hospitals and doctors and science, she came to her brother.

Adam was ready to jump in, because this unmarried aunt was his only living second-degree relative; he had lost three uncles at the end of the war, they'd been killed as presumed *Ustashas*. They were simply liquidated, Adam told me, one was run over by a car, the other was thrown off a train, and nobody knows what happened to the third because he disappeared after they carted him away from home and he was never found.

Adam was preparing to write a novel about his uncles as soon as he got rich and had some peace and quiet; he needed complete freedom to be able to write. Not something he had sitting in the bank every day, settling loan requests and wondering, while serving customers in his thick-lensed glasses, how he had ever wound up here and how he could get away, without having to face the Podravina brides whom his father kept arranging for him to meet in the belief that an unmarried man was a failure. At the end of his working day, when he was released from that prison, all he could do was drink and bemoan his fate in the form of his father, who had never understood or asked what he wanted, but rather had always high-handedly doled out advice about keeping a low profile, because it could save his life. And his father would sing a song about patience, diligence and perseverance, the three foundations of life that provide the basis for everything else, but the message would go in one ear and out the other, and he would do the exact opposite. As a result, and as his father had warned, he risked winding up on the street, despite the protection of his mother. She was ill now (emphysema) and depended on his father, too ill to help him, as she had when he dropped out of law school to study philosophy, against his father's wishes. That's a waste of time, he said at the time.

This was the situation at hand when his extraordinary aunt appeared, with bowel cancer and a well-run estate of curative waters worth a fortune, and no one to leave it to except her brother, thought Adam's father. Or to me, Adam reckoned, because, as he said, such a fortune was too late for his father whose fate was sealed and life coming to an end, whereas with that kind of money his own life could flourish, take a new turn, away from this swamp of a bank where I'm already turning into a frog, he moaned.

An underground struggle began in the house to win over this sister/aunt of crumbling health, to see who would get into her good graces, the father or the son, the brother or the nephew, who would do more to please and help her, so that she would make out a will in favour of the one or the other, rather than die intestate, because then his dead uncles' children and grandchildren would also appear as heirs, and that meant that the whole fortune would have to be divided up, making it worthless.

Adam's self-sacrifice for his aunt proved to be greater than anybody could have imagined because he agreed to everything, not only did he give his room to his aunt and move into what was basically the pantry, not only did he keep her company and comfort her in her pain, but he also helped her when she had to empty her bowels, he washed her and he washed her bed pan, he changed her clothes, and he took unpaid leave from the bank so he could do all this, which even his father accepted as appropriate. He wasn't disgusted by her old, disintegrating body and its excretions, or by the stench of illness and the unholy sights of the body, which is how I saw it, even though I had long experience with illness, had seen all sorts of things and knew that imagining these horrors was worse than having to face them in someone close to you, when you see what real helplessness is and when everything becomes natural. He also had another reason for hoping that things would work out in his favour, and that was that his aunt was extremely well-read, she read not just religious but also secular books, she knew Dostoevsky and Tolstoy by heart, and for years had done a lot of her own writing and had brought those notebooks with her in a big wooden chest.

You've now got your treasure chest, you finally found it, I joked with Adam, not because Adam believed in these writings, which he never even glanced at, but because they were his guarantee of success. He was counting on having a spiritual kinship with his aunt, on the power of such closeness; he already had a blood connection, demonstrably the strongest, and now he also had this spiritual one, which gave him an advantage over his father. Because his aunt never got along with her brother, ever since they were children he had always thought of her as a little too excitable, and her preoccupations crazy. And he didn't change his mind even when she proved to be an adept businesswoman and made a lot of money.

Unlike me, that crazy woman is a success, he said, slapping himself on the forehead, thinking how Adam had inherited that crazy side of the family, but without a sense for business, he was just unlucky that way.

When his aunt's health showed some improvement, he returned to work, and that was the last I knew until about three weeks ago, when he dropped by. Again my hair was lank, my eyes as small as a mouse's, my clothes shabby and my face grey, but we talked as we're talking now, always about the same thing – why was my husband disappearing and what was he doing when he was gone, because we couldn't understand what he got out of his disappearing act, except making me angry. He's crazy, I guess, was Adam's conclusion.

I told him how I had recently gone out to look for him and spotted him through the glass window of the café Dubrovnik, sitting there on his own, alone, I said, and when he saw me walk in he got up and guiltily ran down the stairs to the bathroom, as if that would save him. But it didn't save him because I went down after him, dragged him out of the toilet onto the square outside, grabbed both his arms and shook him and for the umpteenth time asked why, why, but there was no answer. He just shook his head and sighed as if he had done something terrible, he hadn't wanted to, but had done it anyway, he couldn't help it.

At least if I had caught him with another woman, I would have understood, I said, I would have been able to deal with it, but this is enough to drive you nuts. That's probably why I take it, because I can't understand it, because I'm waiting to understand it so that I can deal with it, I thought to myself.

You're eating yourself up for no reason, he's not worth it, Adam said, and we went over the story all over again, hoping to find something that would lead us out of the labyrinth of my husband's life, into which I'd strayed and now couldn't find my way out. And we remembered the myth of Theseus and Ariadne who gave him a ball of thread to unroll when he entered the labyrinth, so that he could find his way back, because, according to the myth, how you enter is how you shall leave. It sounded simple if you had an Ariadne to give you a ball of string, but if you didn't, then you knew how you'd enter but you'd never get out, was the depressingly logical conclusion we reached, after which we fell silent.

Both of us light up, filling the air with smoke rings that disappear as soon as they form, something that's always amazed me, because though these otherwise invisible shapes look permanent, they're not. Everything is like this smoke, I say, we're like this smoke, I say, we appear only to disappear, we disappear only to appear, the principle is the same, only the forms are different, including us, for a second. So much seriousness over something that isn't really a form, I say, it's constant change, change as such, so much senseless drama, I say. We want to keep something that can't be kept, and even though we know it, we still want it, we still hope for it, we still stick to our idea of permanence, which doesn't exist, I say. He understands, he agrees, he's enjoying himself, he always has something to say that opens up the conversation, and opens me up, maybe he would enjoy himself more if I didn't stop his attempts to kiss me on the mouth instead of the cheek, but he enjoys our talks, which are just ours, because we don't share them with others.

There is a bottle of wine on the table, of course, Pharos, I spare no expense when it comes to wine; I pour it into two slender wine glasses etched with white wreathes, they were my mother's, the only two left. There are also some things to nibble on, a bit of hard cheese that you can always find, this time it's Trappist, one of the better cheeses, and some salami, pickles and bread. I put the cheese and salami on a platter, uncut, so that we can slice them as we eat, the pickles are in a plain yellowish bowl and the slices of bread in a white porcelain dish painted with blue flowers and nested in a basket. It looks nice, that's something, at least.

He goes on to tell me what happened, his aunt died, he says. Died, I ask, surprised, wasn't she getting better? It was what they call an end-of-life rally, he says, a kind of remission, only false, because after that she died in such excruciating pain that it was horrible to watch. And now you're rich, I ask, but not aloud, because it's wrong to mention money when talking about pain. He's quiet, he sniffles, he frowns, as if he can see his aunt, she suffered, he says, shaking his head, in spite of all her saints and prayers and faith; they heaved a sign of relief when she died. Nobody should die like that, you should just go to sleep, he says, falling silent again; something bad is coming, so bad that he can't get it out.

Where is she buried, over there or here, I ask. Here, he says, in the family grave, and it was at the cemetery, he says, at the funeral, that a man appeared, a younger man, with slicked back hair, in a black suit, holding a hat, they thought he was one of her clients, but it turned out he was her husband, she'd married him a year and a half before, secretly, obviously. He took his marriage license out of his pocket to prove it, and then the will, in which she left him everything, the property, the money, everything, as a kind of insurance against the family even thinking of challenging the marriage. In the will, which she wrote before she came to them for treatment, she bequeathed to him, her nephew Mr. So and So, because she also had other nephews, her books and the chest of writings that she'd brought with her, as the most important part of her legacy, instructing him to read through and edit these writings, so that they could be published, Adam says, watching me trying to keep a straight face, but I couldn't hold back my laughter, I was about to burst.

She left you her religious books and papers, I shriek with laughter as he looks at me in astonishment because he doesn't find it funny, he had washed his aunt, cleaned off her shit, read to her by her bedside for days, a bit of *Crime and Punishment,* a bit of the lives of the saints, and all that for nothing, he said between his healthy white clenched teeth, wanting to break because he felt duped.

But how did she know that you'd be interested in all that before she even came here, I ask laughing, I just can't stop, it was too ridiculous ...

She knew because I once spent the summer with her when I was a boy, and even then, I would sit in the shade, reading all day, I discovered my first book, *Ben Hur,* in her house, and that's when I realised that this, this is what I wanted, I wanted the life you find in books, not this life in reality, the life you find in books. That's how she knew, he finishes, still ultra serious, smoking, exhaling as if wanting to let out his soul.

What did your father say, I ask, half-smiling to myself, not to him, because the story with his father seems serious, unlike his own story, which isn't even close.

And then I hear what his father did, the man with the narrow face, pointed moustache and stiff bearing, always in a suit, always looking down on people, we called him the "uptight gentleman", the gentleman tailor duped by life – he went into the room that Adam had turned over to his aunt, where she'd kept her things, including the books and the big chest with her writings. He stuffed the books into a plastic bag as if they were utterly worthless, Adam says, I tried to save one or two but he stopped me dead in my tracks with just one look, he says. He dragged the bag into the courtyard and emptied it, then came back for the chest, pulled it noisily into the courtyard, with us following behind, he says, my mother, brother, his wife and son, because we had just returned from the funeral. I tried to tell him that that was my inheritance and he had no right to it, and that I'd at least like to read some of it, but I might as well have been talking to a wall, he says. The notebooks flew out of the chest onto the books and all over the courtyard, and I ran to collect them but he had already scooped them up, making sure he had all of them, that's how bloody-minded he was, he says of his father. Then he lit a match and set them on fire until it looked like a funeral pyre, and he stood right next to it, stony-faced, watching the rising flames, looking up at the sky, enjoying it.

And the aunt was up there smiling, I think, I never met her but I imagine her, who knows why, to be a thin, shrivelled old lady, with warts on her face, curly hair and a raspy voice, happy to make a fool out of her brother who had never appreciated her and was now getting his comeuppance. He hadn't even managed to save her from dying, which she had hoped he would, and he might have received his inheritance had he succeeded, he, not her nephew who had tried from the beginning, but to no avail.

The neighbours rushed over to the pyre, too, Adam continues, they were afraid that if the flames spread to the orchard they would engulf their houses, somebody even called the police, who arrived when it was all over. The fire was extinguished but everything was destroyed, only the ashes remained, he says; they wrote up their report, told us that we would have to pay a fine, but his father just rubbed his hands, nodding. We'll pay it, with pleasure!

Adam falls silent, looking morose, he doesn't see me anymore, he takes his glasses off and starts cleaning them with the tail of his checked shirt, which he wears loose, all the while rolling his faded blue eyes. He'd probably set out to sail the waters of his dashed hopes, hopes that had been real to him, I think to myself, until he was suddenly thrown overboard, like on a sinking ship, and now he's drowning, trying to swim to shore.

That night I let him keep his hand on my knee longer than usual, just to comfort him for his loss, and he withdrew it himself when he didn't need it there anymore, and I realised why he was born half-blind – he'd been short-sighted since childhood, since childhood his eyes had been barely visible behind the thick prescription glasses, since childhood those glasses had been a burden, he was always afraid that they would break and he wouldn't be able to see anything ... he knew what he would see when it happened and he refused a priori to look at it. With others, their sight deteriorates with experience, but he didn't need any experience, it was as if he was born with experience. I know people who fight such a crappy fate, they step half-blind across Persian carpets, but he didn't and wouldn't, he wasn't here to overcome his miserable fate, he was here to live it, an endless loser.

He left as day was breaking, taking the first bus home, because it was Saturday. I didn't walk him to the bus; I'd stretched out on the sofa while he was still numbly sitting there, and was already half asleep when he said he was leaving, rose to his feet and walked out, the old parquet creaking under his heavy step, and then I heard the door slam shut. Left on the table was an ashtray full of cigarette butts, an empty bottle, glasses with dark blue stains and smelling of wine, and leftovers of cheese and salami that would go bad, I thought, opening and immediately shutting my eyes, pulling the big black-and-white scarf off of the back of the armchair to cover myself and tucking my feet under the dog's warm body.

XXI.

I MAKE a decision to pack some underwear, a change of clothes, a few basic items of make-up in a plastic "Adidas" travel bag on the spur of the moment, at six this morning when the bells of St. Blaise tolled; Hail Mary, said the bells, and Tanga yowled, and my husband walked into the house calming her down, be quiet, it's just me, stroking her soft silky fur, probably glancing nervously at the living-room door to see if I would appear. Because we didn't sleep together anymore, he still slept on the sofa in our room, but I had removed myself to the sofa in the little room, a useless act of protest.

I did not get up and have a go at him, I just listened to him step into the dining room, carefully open the door, and sneak into the kitchen to pour himself a glass of water, he never drinks out of his hand like me, that's the only way I can get my fill of water, just as he never eats food out of the serving bowl, only on a plate, thank you very much, I'm not a pig, not that one can tell from the outside, I think to myself. Then, making a noise as he put his glass in the sink, he tiptoed away, accompanied by the dog that would join him in bed because it had divided loyalties. He'd take off his clothes, socks and shoes, sprawl out on the sofa in his undershirt and shorts and sleep until at least noon, when he would get up to eat and then go back to bed again because he'd had an exhaustingly sleepless night. Except this time I won't be waiting for him in the dining room itching for a fight, with eyes as small as a mouse's and a mouth like a sad clown, looking ugly, which I'm not, no this time I'll simply disappear, I decided. Once he's asleep I'll pack quietly and take the bus to my mother's in Plitvice, I decided; this time he can wait for me when he finally wakes up, he can feed and walk the dog and wonder where I am while he's making sandwiches, because there's nothing for lunch.

But then comes the evening, and the night, and I'm still not there, I imagined the scene in my mind, and he can't even run away because who's he going to run away from if nobody's at home except for the poor dog that needs to be taken care of, so he sits and waits, listening for the sound of the key turning in the Werther lock, for the creak of the door hinge, wondering when, when I will come back, imagining who knows what. Maybe I'm with another man, though that's hard to imagine because he's had me focussed on him as if he chained me to him, and yet, and yet, there's every reason for doubt, maybe something has happened to me, maybe I was run over by a tram or a car, he thinks in despair. The TV is on, and probably the light as well, to dispel the darkness inside him, but I know it won't, the flat becomes eerie when you're waiting for somebody and you don't know where that person is, when things are uncertain, the flat becomes a prison.

Now I'm the one who's free and he's the one in prison, I think to myself vengefully, covering the streets in long strides, going from my street to Primorska on the left, towards Ilica, the high street, because you can also take the road on the right, towards JNA Street, which has no shops but is lined with chestnut trees, I used to go that way to high school and later to uni, it was always a nice walk, it felt like being in the countryside, that street was a gift from heaven, special somehow. In Ilica, on the other side, everything is different, shops, traffic, crowds, the tram stop for Republic Square, the city centre, branching out from there in all directions. Opposite the tram stop is what we call *Britanac* – British Square, with its marketplace, and what with summer coming, it's now a riot of colours with all the fruits and vegetables that have just come into season, the flowers releasing their fragrance into the air, it even wafts over my way as I wait for the number two tram to take me to the bus station on the other side of town.

As I walked out the door I kept hoping I wouldn't run into anybody – I was born here and we all know each other – because I don't want to have to even say hello to anybody, let alone be asked even the simplest question, like how are you, how's your mother, when is she coming back from Plitvice. But that's exactly what happened when Dragica, a neighbour from Primorska Street, whom my mother knew from before the war and had now become her friend, emerged from the marketplace across the road. She was pale and covered with yellow freckles from brow to chin, I'd never seen so many; her permed hair was dyed the same colour. Tottering under the weight of her shopping bag stuffed with vegetables and leeks and lettuce almost spilling out of it, she crossed the tram tracks and walked over to me at the tram stop. She automatically put her shopping bag down and stood next to it, hunched over, as usual.

Before the war she worked in a factory and lived in a small room with no water and no toilet, more often hungry than not, until Matek appeared who brought her a bread roll every morning for breakfast, and later she married him;

he was a good plumber, hard-working, not a drunk like most of them, and they had a son and sent him to school to become an engineer. And everything would have been hunky-dory, as they say, if that son hadn't married a girl, with a slight limp, who worked in the factory, and then had fallen in love with somebody else, somebody whose skin was so clear and glowing that she looked as if she bathed in milk, a pretty girl in a cold sort of way, her blond hair always in a bun and a silk scarf around her neck, because she hailed from more refined pre-war circles. So he divorced his wife and married her, as a result of which his ex fell ill, stomach cancer, which you get when you have trouble digesting, people say, and that sounds about right to me, but Dragica couldn't abandon her poor ex-daughter-in-law who was virtually on her deathbed, and so she took it out on her son. The ex-daughter-in-law treated her cancer by eating macrobiotic and organic food, which was imported from the West, along with its contamination, and it was expensive so her ex-mother-in-law, now working part-time making costumes for the theatre, bought it for her.

I was friends with her niece Dora in high school, until we were caught in the supermarket stealing chocolate that was meant to be a present for Mother's Day. As we were being taken away, Dora whispered that she wanted me to take the blame – we had put the chocolate in my bag, so the evidence was on me – but just then her mother walked in to lodge a complaint about some bowl she had bought ... Talk about coincidence! Now she would see her daughter and daughter's schoolmate being hauled off on charges of theft. I whispered back to Dora that I wouldn't take the blame, figuring that two were less guilty than one, because the blame would be shared, that two would fare better than one, especially because of her mother, and she never forgave me for it and I never forgave her. After that fall-out we still saw each other, though not often, and so the first thing I asked was how was Dora, and she said that Dora was fine, she was about to finish her chemistry studies and was planning to marry her boyfriend. Then she asked me about my mother, how was she, when she was coming back, saying that she missed her, that she and Matek had nobody to play cards with in the afternoon once a week, and she had nobody to have afternoon coffee with once a week, and then I asked how her ex-daughter-in-law was doing and heard that she had recovered, completely, she said, the cancer had gone, not a trace of it left. My goodness, that's a miracle, I said, and I really thought that, even if in an uninterested way, because her cancer was hardly my business. I was saved from further conversation by the number two tram loudly trundling to a stop in front of us. My neighbour Dragica picked up her shopping bag, contorting her face into a smile, it was that kind of a face, and told me to say hello to my mother. I will, I said, staring at her flaky eyelashes, so light and red along the edges of her eyelids, like an albino's.

I managed to grab a seat on the tram, which I always take as a victory, especially when it's crowded, like this morning, because it was a Saturday and the tram was full of peasant women who'd come in from the surrounding countryside and now, having sold their goods at the markets, were going home, pushing their way onto the tram with their empty baskets, oblivious to everyone, travelling through town with their bags on their lap, so that I barely noticed the vacant seat. As soon as I sat down, I plunged into my own world, like Alice into the rabbit hole, a world that had been turned on its head, I plunged into my muddle of a life that had trickled through my fingers, something I refused to accept, as if this mess would clear itself up by itself, as if it were a dream, not reality. Everything was clear, everything was settled, everything was in its place, roughly speaking, anyway, because you can always correct the details, and then suddenly everything was all over the place, like a cake that collapses in the oven. But life isn't a cake that you can choose not to bake and so avoid failure, life makes you do things, you have to try even when you're not sure of the outcome, you always have to hope for the best. I was running away from home not to create more of a mess, but to clear it up, to make my husband understand what was waiting for him, where all this was going, to make him come to his senses, as they say, so we could continue from where we had started, despite his illness, which we'd put aside, just as the doctor advised, the best doctor in this part of the world and beyond: don't think, let go, live the life you have, nobody knows how much time one has on this earth, but for as long as you do, for as long as you live, it's forever.

And then, in the reflection of the tram window, I suddenly saw a cat, a Cheshire cat, like the one in *Alice in Wonderland*, I remembered it from the Disney movie, the cartoon, when I was a child; it was fat, soft, striped like a prison uniform, only in pink and blue, with a waving luxuriant tail, always grinning, moving, disappearing and reappearing, removing its head and putting it back on, and it told me that I was crazy. I'm crazy, too, it said, just so I didn't think it was discounting itself, everybody is crazy, it chuckled, and then disappeared until only its grinning white teeth were left. And then the teeth turned into the moon from which they had emerged.

The Cheshire cat is right, I thought, standing in front of the ugly bus station, so ugly that it was like the beginning of the end of the world, with its dilapidated reality, a grimy ruin, like in films, black, grey, dirty, covered with graffiti, reeking, pigeons wading like drunks through pools of oil, an old lady staring at the red vomit on the ground that resembled a sprawling lobster, she stared as if she couldn't get enough of it – we're all crazy because we're all unreal, no foothold anywhere, I mused. Except in art, except in books, I corrected myself, passing through the supposed reality of the bus station as if in a dream, as if it were a picture to which I didn't belong, I belonged to the imagination not to this wretched self-enclosed reality, I belonged to miracles I could imagine, because I am myself a miracle, I comforted myself. The books know.

I haven't told her I'm coming, she's my mother, I'm always welcome, she's always happy to see me, and she knows everything, I don't have to explain anything to her and she doesn't criticise, she knows that life sets unavoidable traps. I don't even know if there's a place for me to stay, I've never visited her there, I couldn't because I had my husband to take care of, but I know that her room on the ground floor of the hotel is for staff, and that it's just a bit bigger than our little room, but square and dark, she had said, because she never asked for anything.

It probably has two beds, I thought, stepping off the bus into the sharp, unpolluted air of Lika, a planet of forests, light, dark, coniferous, deciduous, trees wherever you looked, and roaming among them wild animals, like bears, for instance. You can run into a bear when you go out to buy cigarettes, my mother said, although she didn't smoke but somebody else who did went out to buy cigarettes and saw a bear on the road, and since my mother, unlike me, was chatty, she asked everybody questions and never forgot a thing. If I had stepped onto the bus with the idea of the end of the world, I now stepped off it into its possible beginning, not even a three-hour drive from end to beginning, from death to birth; in my mind I was jumping up and down with joy, free at last, I sang voicelessly, because that's what I'm like when I find myself in nature, even if it's just for a moment. Because happiness doesn't last, exhilaration quickly cedes to disconnection, you're on the outside not on the inside, you're not a forest, you're not a forest animal and you will never be one, you'll just look at this paradise knowing that you've been expelled from it, but your body remembers.

But now my travel bag was on the ground, between my legs, where I'd put it while inspecting the hotel across the way, the biggest hotel in Plitvice, built horizontally to complement the forest, and I knew my mother wasn't there but they'll know where she is, I decided, picking up my bag by the handle. Suddenly there was a pat on the back of my shoulder, a slap almost, I dropped my bag, and, half angry, whirled around. But my anger disappeared upon seeing the smiling face of a virtually toothless old man, his mouth a dark pit, almost bald, with white strands of hair combed over his barren skull, his dimmed eyes sinking into the web of wrinkles on his face, and a moustache just like the beggar's in my street, young somehow, like his red puffed-pillow-like cheeks … Srećko, the park's agronomist, an engineer of horticulture, in his fifties like my mother, though he looked both a hundred years older and a hundred years younger, a child or an old man, I couldn't make up my mind, I was arguing with myself and consequently, as happens, with the whole world. And my mother's "client", of course.

He was from Herzegovina, considers himself to be a linguistic expert, my mother told me, and his speciality was placing accents on words in written texts, which drove everybody crazy – it was a constant battle.

Some ten years earlier he had lost his job in Plitvice – a bureaucratic stitch-up, my mother said he had told her, and instead of looking for another job, he sued to get his old one back and wound up in a ten-year-long legal suit, forsaking work for that entire period because he expected to win his case. He did nothing for ten years, but during that time, when he was still young and in possession of his teeth and his hair, he managed to obtain what he needed from a network of people whom he regularly visited, day after day, taking a little something from each of them. A place to sleep here, lunch there, somewhere a dinar, elsewhere just a few words, an hour or two to warm himself up with a shot of brandy in the winter or cold lemonade – again with brandy – in the summer, and so he lived to hear the court ruling that he was to be reinstated in his old job, where he remained. That's where he met my mother and became her "client", because she gave him a shoulder to cry on – apart from his unhappy love life, because he wanted to get married, but he wanted a young wife and such women eluded him, there was also his battle to receive monetary compensation for those ten lost years, a battle he was yet to win.

There was something almost ceremonial about the way he brought me to my mother, as if presenting her with a personal gift, here's your daughter, he said, putting down my travel bag, waiting to see her reaction, proudly crossing his arms over his chest. Then, since my mother had already eaten and I insisted that I didn't want any food, that I'd have dinner later, he accompanied us to the staff hotel, carrying my bag as an excuse. On the way, he offered to take me for a walk along the lake and to the waterfalls, he'd show me everything, he said eagerly. We'll see, I said, bristling at the mere possibility, and then finally, before departing, he invited my mother and me to dinner, lamb roasted on a spit, at the Lika House, before you leave, he said to me. His treat, of course.

We won't hold him to his word, my mother said after he left, and we went to her ground-floor room, which was smaller than I'd imagined and had a narrow bed that was barely big enough for her, making me wonder where I was going to sleep. By the evening a folding bed had arrived, which when opened filled the entire room, and was anything but comfortable, I realised when I lay down on it in my mother's nightgown, who would even think of bringing pyjamas when you were running away, but I was dead tired after the events of the day and its decisions, so I fell asleep as soon as my head hit the pillow.

The birds woke me up in the morning; there are birds on the apricot tree in my courtyard as well, but just sparrows and blackbirds calling out to each other and whistling, and doves and pigeons cooing on the rooftops, however here it was something else singing in the early morning, something that went straight to the heart and that I had never heard before, and I instantly recognised the bird that sings in books, a nightingale, I thought, it must be a nightingale, like the emperor's, in the fairy tale. I immediately left my bed and stepped out of the room – my mother, like the other residents of the rooms lining the eerily white corridor, was still asleep – but I stepped out like a sleepwalker, in my nightgown, barefoot, at that magical moment in the morning that belongs to the surrounding forest, when life wakes up and you are filled with this sense of awakening, as at the dawn of humankind, when the first human realised that he was alive, because he hadn't known it before, it came to him suddenly. And it's no different today, the wonder of life remains hidden from us during the day, and turns into fear at night, and it is only like this in the early morning that we understand it, when we are alone and when it's spring and when the forest within us breathes, or the sea within us breathes, when we imbue each other.

But the nightingale fell silent when I stepped outside and the moment passed; I tried to hold on to it, searched for it with my eyes and my nose, but I had disturbed it the second I understood it, and was back in my life, which was longer a wonder, just pain or pleasure, as the case might be and depending on how you saw it, never pure and simple.

For three days I dragged my pain through the pleasure, because everybody wanted to show me the lakes and the waterfalls and all the other magical wonders of nature. A magical wonder is when something doesn't look real but is, I realised as they took me around – like the way Plitvice's waters forged their own paths through the rocks and bushes, through the grey and green, through the air and earth, creating a work of art out of nature, making it look like child's play, untaught, becoming a work of art in itself, based on some primeval memory. It was as if we became a work of art ourselves, rather than creating one, a higher form of existence that we did not sufficiently appreciate, because it eluded us, I thought, walking with my feet in the moss and ferns and my head in the air. Everybody wanted to show me something, take me somewhere, because my mother was popular with both those above and those below, which meant that Srećko never got his turn, then again he didn't insist on it either.

The phone call to my mother came on my third day, around noon, when I had come to her office to take her to lunch; my husband asked if I was there maybe, he was worried because I had disappeared, I hadn't been around for days, he complained. She's not here, I would have told you already if she were, but don't worry, my mother waffled, having been instructed not to tell him anything – the poor man is ill, you shouldn't do that to him, she objected, but she didn't tell him I was with her, she just stammered and was vague and when she put down the receiver I snapped: he read right through you! You shouldn't have tried to comfort him, you should have sounded worried, I said again; my disappearing had become pointless.

As had my staying in my mother's room, on the folding bed, it was unbearably cramped, and it wasn't just the bed, I realised, plus there were no books for me to read, at least before going to sleep. The mornings would fly by, unlike the afternoons, which my mother would sleep through while I, having nothing else to do or see, would, in despair, read the romance stories lying around the female staff's honeycomb-like rooms; it was as if everything had suddenly become smaller – it had all looked so immense when I arrived, I thought to myself, biting my nails in boredom.

I left six days after I arrived, with no solution, with a knot in my stomach that remained lodged there like an axe in a log, watching the rain pelt the dirty windows of the bus, leaving a quivering trickle, and then little rivulets of water streaming into the window's grooves, an entire universe inhabited by who knows what, where even a second is like a thousand years, I thought to myself. But for me, it was simply rain and I worried that it wouldn't stop by the time we reached Zagreb, because I didn't want to get wet and catch a cold, even though it was warm, because then I'd have to take five days' sick leave. And I thought about that ruthless clash of worlds, and how it was the key to *Alice* ... a ruthlessness we laughed at when actually we should be sitting down and weeping, a ruthlessness that was the deepest truth not of dreams but of reality, driving us all mad ...

By the time we reached Zagreb the rain had stopped and the sun was breaking through the steaming city, lending it a touch of enchantment, of light?, of smell?, making me want to hover there and postpone my return and the conversation that was doomed before it started. I was helped by the non-appearance of the number two tram, and, one last time I looked south, at the endless tram track that ran alongside the hedge, bringing the number five tram, which meant I'd have to transfer, shove my way onto two trams lugging my travel bag, no I wasn't going to do that.

Instead, I lit a cigarette, inhaled, then exhaled and the smoke assumed the shape of a cloud, which expanded like a huge mushroom; hey, what's this, I thought when my travel bag suddenly lifted off the ground and floated around my legs; sit on me, I heard a voice say, like in a fairy tale, and I immediately obeyed, never happier. Then we soared up into the sky, me and my travel bag, up into the blue, amidst the woolly clouds left after the rain, and from there I watched the city turn into squares of different colours and sizes, into a patchwork that said everything is possible, that nothing is lost and nothing ruined, things just rearrange themselves.

XXII.

SITTING IN the living room, dressed to go out, is my darling, my love, my everything in life, my forever; when he was in the hospital in Rijeka, I would write him letters with stickers of Peter Pan and Tinkerbell, *I'm Tinkerbell, you're Peter Pan*, and with pictures of a little heart, and I'd also put Lady and the Tramp and Snow White with one of the dwarfs, *Sleepy, for a good night's sleep*, and a lipstick kiss, and a photo of me when I was three, dimpled, smiling like a sunny day, and a pressed violet that I'd picked when I visited Petra, and a lock of blond hair tied with white thread, and a cutout of my eyes from a photo that I pinned to a scrap of paper, and my thumbprint, like for an I.D., all so silly, so impossible to imagine today. And all this embellished with words of love, adoration and devotion, although I did mention some terrible doubts, though they seemingly vanished when he fell ill, when health was all that mattered, everything else was unimportant. But now, doubts are all we have left, I thought, looking at him, still standing at the door, like a wall separating us, an invisible but impenetrable wall, stopping us from reaching each other.

Although I still see the same blue in his eyes, that forget-me-not blue, the same straight nose, the same pink lips, the same facial bones under the stretch of thin, fair skin that blushes so easily, the same high brow inviting baldness, the same always neat beard, the same dark straight hair, everything the same yet nothing the same ... Because if it were, I would go over to him and kiss him on the mouth, on the nose, on the forehead, on the cheeks, everywhere, I would run my fingers through his hair and we would laugh, but I do not go over to him, I stand at the door, petting the dog who's trying to jump on me. And he doesn't walk over to me either, he sits there, watching me from a great distance, as if he had left his body in the dining room and gone off somewhere, it's not him looking at me it's a bloodless, lifeless shell, stiff and pale.

And then I see the mouth of this corpse suddenly start to quiver and the face adopt an expression that says "so, that's it, then", as the blood returns. And, look, he's already nodding his head in recrimination, nodding not to me but at me, at this alien being that has done something bad to him, that tormented him for five days, but that he torments as well, so he has no right to say anything, to attack it. He can only exude silent resentment and plan his retaliation, because one retaliation calls for another, regardless of who started it, maybe it wasn't your fault before you took revenge, but afterwards it is.

The flat looks neglected, on the table the milky white glass ashtray, big as a plate, is overflowing with cigarette butts, the tablecloth is full of breadcrumbs from the stale white bread in the blue porcelain dish nested in the basket, and, apart from the cup in his hand, there are two dirty cups with the dry dregs of coffee, because we drink aromatic Turkish coffee, we drink a litre a day, the coffee-pot was a wedding present from Adam. A piece of greasy paper holds the remains of the salami, there's a plate with the leftover rind of the cheese, a pair of big scissors and a pair of nail scissors, along with a knife, a few sheets of typewritten paper next to some folders; a quick look at the kitchen reveals a sink with dirty dishes that he stacked but didn't wash, and I realise that he didn't do any cooking, he bought everything ready-made, a breakdown of the system, and then I catch sight of the dog's paws, festering with puss.

What's that? I scream, what have you done to the dog! I'm already on my knees, hugging her, examining the wounds between its toes, green, festering, wet, putrid, awful, he says he doesn't know, that they simply appeared, overnight, the day after I disappeared. I say he could have looked for me at my mother's, where else would I go, what do you think, assuming you think at all, I yell, that's how mad I am. He says he did call, your mother said you weren't there, he says, you know she did, he says, you were probably standing right next to her, listening, he snipes, he wants to put the blame on me, as usual. You didn't phone until yesterday, I say, and you didn't mention the dog, you didn't say a word about it being sick, you didn't even take it to the vet, you just watched her waste away, I say, shaking with fury; poor little thing, I say, trying to soothe the dog whose sorrowful eyes blame me, its eyes are the same even when it's happy, it's that kind of breed; it's so sad it's enough to break your heart.

He doesn't answer, he just scowls, shakes his crossed leg, and lights another cigarette, his mouth twisting in disgust as he exhales; the look on his face, which initially wavered between self-pity and accusation, is now utterly cold, there is ice in his eyes, like on a window in winter. He's not looking at us anymore, he's looking straight in front of him, and up somehow, shaking his crossed leg, nodding like a plastic mechanical toy, and says that he has to go to hand in his article at the radio; aha, so he wrote it when I wasn't there, I think to myself, he can do it without me. After that he'll go to his parents, he says, and he may stay there, he says; go right ahead, I say, just go, I have to see to the dog, you don't have to come back.

Fine, he nods, gets up, opens the folder and puts in his papers, moves his cigarettes and lighter to the breast pocket of his light blue poplin shirt, because we wear only the best, and is already opening the dining-room door when he stops and turns around, as if to say something, but he doesn't. I watch all this from the corner of my eye, still kneeling on the floor, hugging the dog, which is disintegrating along with this marriage, I realise, a marriage that never even started, never came to life, it was just a hopeless mess, and it still is, it still is, even though he's gone, because he'll be back, because I still can't let go of him, just as he can't let go of me.

Once again he's left me on my own, without a word, without us talking about it, I think to myself after he left, banging the door behind him so loudly that it made me jump; as pointless as it was, I wanted us to talk, because words always give hope, anything is better than this nothing he's given me, like the way he left the dog to die, watching it fall to pieces, not lifting a finger to help it. That was probably to punish me, I realise, because he knows that I adore the dog; what a monster, what a piece of shit, where was all this hiding that I didn't see it, I keep struggling with all these questions, it's like trying to break free of the ropes that bind you; because I'm not free, I'm a prisoner of this relationship, have been from the very beginning, I guess, a prisoner of sickness, my mother saw it but I didn't, because I was already involved, because I was already infected by it.

And I fell ill, just like my dog, my sunshine, my sweetie-pie, my poor little thing, I think to myself, putting the leash on her and taking her straight to the vet, who's on the other side of town, where I've just come from, I take her on foot because trams don't allow dogs.

Your dog has a serious skin disease, says the vet after examining her, he's an older man with a big nose, in a clean white coat, a pen tucked in his breast pocket, and on the right side of his face a purple birthmark the size of a child's fist; he gives her an injection and rubs a dark blue liquid on the purulent sores between the toes of her front paws, saying it's probably genetic and hard to cure. When you first got her, you may have noticed a little white pimple on her paw, he says, it contained staphylococci that multiplied. You should never buy a puppy like that.

I remember the little pimple, I say, but I didn't know it was a symptom of disease, I just thought it was a kind of mole, harmless. That's what lots of people think, he says, but the person who sold her to you knew what he was selling. And she's pedigreed, I say, as if that's a guarantee against fraud, and anyway, fraud or not, surely he wouldn't kill a puppy because of a pimple, I say aloud, but he simply shrugs and walks over to his desk to write out a prescription for some pills and a liquid, while I take the terrified dog off of the examination table and hold her in my arms. Once upon a time, when she was a puppy, she happily ran into the vet's office for her first injection, but after that I would have to drag her in, she'd brace her paws against the pavement, like a donkey, and wouldn't budge.

It's a serious illness, hard on both the owner and the dog, the vet continues, leaning over his desk, not looking at me, and it requires daily therapy, rubbing down her paws and giving her the pills, the best thing would be to have her put to sleep, he says, trying his luck, but on the wrong person, because I immediately explode. Only if we're put to sleep together, I say, attaching her red leash to her matching red collar, because red looks good on gold fur, don't you worry, my darling, I whisper into her long ear, mama will make it better. Your choice, he says, handing me the prescription and when I see the birthmark on his face twitch as if it were alive, I decide never to come back, we'll find another vet.

The next day, the bastard unlocks the door – he didn't ring the bell, I think to myself when he appears in the dining room, where I'm rubbing down the dog's paw with the dark blue liquid, wiping away any overspill with a cloth. He stands there holding the travel bag he's taken from his parents' place and says he's come for his things. You know where they are, I say without getting up, holding the dog down while she fights me, listening to him move from room to room, thinking that I have to get the key back from him before he leaves, I don't want him bursting into the flat or my life whenever he feels like it. Who knows who might be in the flat, will be my argument when I ask for the key back, my way of provoking him, making him understand his place so that he doesn't get any ideas. But I don't have to remind him about the key because before I can say anything he leaves it on the dining-room table when he's finished packing, and walks out of the flat with a "See you".

"Goodbye", I correct him, and let him leave without saying another word. Then I walk into the room to see what he's taken, just his summer things, I note, summer trousers, tops, sneakers, sandals, underwear and the *Biser* typewriter I bought him, I work on my mother's *Olympia*, which is twice the size and which he also put into his bag, as if wanting to hide it.

And now we're alone, just the two of us, the dog and I, and we roam around the flat; I've never been alone here before and it feels a bit strange. My father's brother and his family, all four of them, once lived with us, for ten whole years the house was full of people, of arguments, of cooking and the smell of browned flour, and then it was just the three of us, my mother, my father and me, with the arguments and the browned flour, and then again three of us, this time my mother, my husband and me, with arguments and stew but no browned flour, because it isn't healthy, my husband would say, parroting his father Frane, a Dalmatian, so instead of browned flour it was sautéed onions and fried lardons, and then it was just the two of us, him and me, with the arguments but no stew, because I didn't make it, that was my mother's cooking, and anyway he didn't like it, especially not leek stew, yuck, he'd say, but now it's just me in the flat, I don't count the dog, without the arguments and without the cooking. The only cooking I do is for the dog, innards, tongue, hearts, in a pressure cooker so it can't boil over, and I don't have to wash the stove and sink. Thinking of my health, I go to the market and bring back fruit, and vegetables to make a salad, and I buy a few tins of tuna and some mayonnaise, it's enough to fill you up, but if I notice a hole in my stomach I just pop over next door for some *ćevapčići* in pitta bread, and eat it in its paper wrapping so that I don't have to dirty a plate.

But I'm not calm. I was calmer when he was giving me a hard time, I think, somewhat surprised, because I expected the opposite, I expected to feel a deep sense of calmness, to enjoy the flat without anybody pressuring me, making demands on me, except for the dog, to have time for myself, for books, for writing my senior thesis in philosophy, on which I'd been procrastinating, finally free, but everything has turned out the opposite, I'm not reading or writing, I spend all day long thinking about what's happened to me and what I'm going to do, as if I'm a burden to myself. I walk the dog three times a day and wait for people to drop by: Adam, Dora, Irena, Filip, Petra ... they all have their own problems and come to share them, because it seems that everybody has problems, that there's nothing else but problems. The only exception is my relative Flora, who's already graduated, found a job and is in a stable relationship, everything is going so smoothly in her life; that's because she's spineless and emotionally hollow, Filip once said after he'd seen her at my place, looking large and pretty and serene, like a celestial queen.

I wait to see whom I'm going out with in the evening, Adam, or Filip, or Dora, who graduated but couldn't find work in her field so she took a job at the Ledo ice cream factory packing ice cream, her boyfriend found it for her, he's about to get his degree in electrical engineering, and then she found out that, while she was packing ice cream and freezing her butt off, he was having it off with some model in their flat.

A model, imagine that, she exclaimed, as if models were something supernatural, to be found in magazines but not in life, in life girls were like her, shorter and chunkier, with imperfections, like hers, her left hand was scarred after she shoved it into hot water when she was a child. She was embarrassed by it and always kept that hand closed. That's why he found me that job, so he could be with her while I was slaving away for the two of us, she moaned and decided to dye her dark hair blond, as if her hair was to blame for her unhappiness, because the model was blond and because, despite his despicable behaviour, she couldn't get over her boyfriend.

Meanwhile, Petra left Filip, that's to say he left her after she'd gone to Italy with somebody else, gone in that somebody's car, which he only learned when she got back, he told me.

Words fell on the table like drunk whores; I remember the day, early on in her studies, when she tried to snare him with a few lines of poetry at the "Old Roofs" tavern, where we used to hang out, and she succeeded because he was a gentle soul and loved poetry, unlike her, she loved poetry but had a heart of stone, he said later, bitter and miserable, because first he had let himself be snared and then he had let himself be deceived, and I felt more for him than for Petra, although she had arguments of her own. After all, she hadn't promised herself to Filip forever, she said when we met after they broke up; she'd had enough, that's all, why should she have to take it, she said, adding that I should take a look at myself and how badly I'd been hurt because I hadn't been able to leave in time, which was undeniable.

You wasted your youth on somebody who wasn't worth it, she said when she heard that he'd left and then later saw him gallivanting around town; once she saw him sitting by himself at the café Dubrovnik (as usual, I thought), but he wasn't thrilled when she sat herself down at his table, he reacted as if she was disturbing him, although later he was more relaxed about it. She also saw him at Republic Square with my friend Irena and another good-looking woman. He smiled and waved, and was very chatty, as if making a play for your friend's friend, in her tight skirt and high, high heels, teetering as if she would fall any minute, Petra said, making fun of her, but I didn't comment.

Sometimes, I go with Dora – who's alone now because she's broken up with her boyfriend, given up the apartment and returned to live with her mother – to an open-air disco, but I don't dance, I just sit and ask myself what I'm doing there. I doll myself up, I want to look attractive, and I do attract, but what's the point when nobody attracts me, I watch people open their mouths and talk, trying to be seductive, because it's all about the opposite sex, hoping to meet somebody, or sniffing each other out, moving their arms and head and body, but there's no expression on their face, it's as if they're on drugs and can barely see. If they're not on drugs, then they're pretending to be elsewhere, I realise, but actually they're on the prowl, trying to make themselves more attractive by feigning a lack of interest, because elusiveness is attractive. I watch all this and wonder how I ever wound up here, amidst all this noise and affectation, after a life geared towards something else, towards books and writing, how I wound up where I don't belong, even in secondary school I wasn't comfortable in disco clubs, I felt like an alien body that had strayed into bedlam.

Rather than go out with Dora, I choose Adam, who has a new plan for leaving the bank, he's going to take a loan big enough for him to live on for a year, and use the money to repay it, he'll rent a flat, a studio, whatever, that's small and cheap, just to get away from his father and his plans, and, of course, from the bank, because his father and the bank are one and the same. He'll write plays, he's already embarked on one, and he's got ideas for another two, if he puts his mind to it he needs only a year to finish them. And then he'll sell them to one of the theatres, and have enough money to continue. What do you think of my plan, he asks me, I've never seen him so excited, he's usually semi-comatose when he talks about the future. Your plan is on shaky legs, I tell him. What if – I want to warn him, we need to say it out loud and face the monster debt that potentially awaits him if he doesn't earn anything, because he'll have to repay the debt even after he's used up the loan – what if, I say, you don't find anybody to buy your plays, because I have no doubt that he'll write them. On the other hand, who cares about buyers when there is something heroic, wonderfully imprudent, unselfish and sublime about the whole enterprise, and when you are famous it will become the stuff of legend; in short, what matters is that he write the plays, not whether he'll find a market for them, and we're both already thinking of these future plays and future fame as if they are happening now, and we're both excited.

Adam comes by more often than he used to now, partly because I'm on my own, and partly to update me on how his plan is going. He's already submitted a loan application and is looking for a flat, and as soon as his application is approved he'll hand in his notice, because he has to be able to work on his plays all day, he says. He still puts his hand on my knee and I remove it with a laugh that sounds hesitant, I know, though I pretend that I don't know, and I still kiss him on the cheek not the mouth and if he moves to kiss me on the mouth I push him away and point to my cheek, here, I say giggling, because I find it funny to touch him. Funny is the right word for the two of us as a potential couple; I see us as incompatible, and he understands that though for him it's serious, but he understands because he's the same as me, because we're like two faces of the same coin that will never meet because we are creatures of darkness.

That becomes evident when one morning – it's already the beginning of autumn – he tiptoes over from the little room where he was sleeping and slips into my bed. I'm awake but still collecting my dreams, putting off having to face the day and its worries, when he pulls the sheet over him and lies down next to me, quietly somehow, like the dog (which jumped off the bed the minute he got in), wearing a white undershirt and no underpants, all stiff and awkward, like me, except I'm the one caught by surprise, and not pleasantly so. It's one thing to have a hand on your knee, and quite another to have a whole body next to yours, a body you pretty much find repulsive, white and fleshy, even if thin, and when he removes his undershirt I see that he's pigeon-breasted, with red spots on heavy legs that are otherwise white as cheese, a body you don't want to be too close to, especially if it's naked. He removes his glasses, gazes at me with his rolling dreamy blue eyes, which are unfamiliar because they are always behind his lenses, so all you can see on the rest of his bearded face is his huge nose.

I register all this in a second, because I don't want to look at him, and while I'm wondering what to do he slides his hand between my legs and squeezes, and I shudder and feel the pain of pleasure rise to my throat. But I don't move, and he takes that to mean that I am OK with it, and the next minute he's on top of me and then, pulling down my panties, he is grinding inside me, it's all over in a minute. I don't feel a thing except for the weight of his body and ridiculous movements, but most ridiculous of all is his face above mine, with its stupid, pathetic grimaces, the kind you make when you're not engaged, with the vein popping out on his broad sweaty brow, and his equally unattractive thick, blond, damp hair, but it's a friendly face that you don't want to hurt, so you push him away, he must see for himself how ridiculous this is, I think with a laugh. He looks at me in surprise, as if he has just woken up, only now realising where he is, and then, of course, he laughs, too, still on top of me, propping himself up on his arms, and then he turns on his side, sits up and slips on his undershirt to hide his nakedness. He puts on his huge glasses with their brown rectangular frame, obtained through his national health insurance, then takes them off, cleans them with the tail of his undershirt, puts them back on, and then leaves to dress in the little room, barefoot, his step as heavy as an elephant's, I think to myself. I jump out of bed, dress to put an end to this story, a horrible story in that it was unnecessary, and hurry to the kitchen to make us a coffee, because coffee opens up space for us to talk, our space, I think to myself, a space that doesn't even need expanding.

After he leaves, I open the windows wide and look out at the huge school playground across the way, where they are having a gymnastics class, like the one I used to go to for years, in my black gym outfit. That was in the good old days, I think to myself, when I was still slim and talented at gymnastics, I was constantly in love, it was one boy today, another tomorrow, I loved being in love, it made the whole day exciting, and I imagined becoming famous, I still didn't know for what, but I'd be famous, that's for sure, I would say, reading the biographies of famous people in the magazine *Discoveries,* which was where my mother worked, so we had issues of the magazine all over the house. By the age of twenty I already knew I would make a name for myself as a writer, don't think I'm going to cook and clean house for you, no, your darling is seriously thinking of devoting herself to writing, I wrote to my love in the hospital in Rijeka, and sent him my first stories for his opinion, because we didn't just love each other we were an association of writers, Sartre and Simone de Beauvoir.

Look at yourself, I tell myself, gazing at the girl in the black gym outfit in the school playground, the girl that I had once been but am no more, you're twenty-five already and haven't done a thing, you haven't graduated, you haven't written anything, you don't even have a husband anymore, he's off gallivanting and you've got a friend moving into your bed, I think to myself, trying to rationalise the situation and see what it looks like from the outside, so that I don't lapse into daydreaming and completely lose it. And as these thoughts run through my mind, I suddenly notice, in front of the house by the railing towards the playground, a good-looking, olive-skinned man with shiny black hair, dark eyes, and the face of an actor, the ultimate in handsomeness, with straight, clear features like a Greek sculpture, no room for anything ugly here, he is slim, not too tall and not too short, everything set in perfect harmony, even his clothes, I notice, they must come from Trieste because we don't have such clear, sharp colours, blue and green and red and yellow, bright but not loud, I muse, watching him step into the parked car that he is probably going to drive to work.

In the afternoon I go to see if he has returned from work and, lo and behold, there he is, crossing the road nonchalantly like a Don Juan who has everybody's eye, walking on the right side of the street, passing the two exits from the Cinémathèque, and then suddenly he disappears, where I wonder ... Probably to the house above the Cinémathèque, I suppose, where you go up the steps and then cross a terrace that is in perpetual semi-darkness and as big as a playground, a building I've never been in, as if it's forbidden, so I find it mysterious. I don't even know the people who live there, they seem to live for themselves, in a world of their own. The only person I know is poor Neda, she has learning disabilities, is short, fat, with huge glasses covering her already wrinkled face, a screechy voice like a crow, and a mouth full of crooked teeth that you can see because her top lip rises up to her nose. But she is sweet and she is kind, she waves to me from far away to make sure that I notice her and then she waits for me to come up to her so that she can ask me something, ask me anything, like, if she notices I'm carrying a shopping bag, what have I bought, or am I going to the movies, and her unattractive face lights up to the roots of her straight red hair, and looks nice. She's Jewish, her family built the house and the cinema before the war, but after the war everything was taken from them by the communists except for the flat they lived in, and they were resentful. It's rumoured that the mother married her first cousin and that's why Neda is as she is, and I notice there's something nasty about these stories. The mother would dart out of the house after her like a wasp, as if Neda had run away from her – and she looks like a wasp, too, dark, thin, spiky, with vicious round eyes – and then drag her back into the house without even a nod in my direction.

That's where the street's Latin dreamboat has disappeared, because it's obviously where he lives, I think, tailing him, becoming increasingly excited the longer I spy on him, the first week it was from the window, but by the second week I had already revealed myself to him in the street, walking the dog in the morning when he was on his way to work, and then again in the afternoon when he was on his way home, until he finally noticed that I was looking at him, that I was there because of him, although I pretended the opposite, because it had been drummed into my head that I must never approach a man, he had to approach me: women don't choose.

Hello neighbour, he finally says one warm Indian summer afternoon when I run out into the street in high heels, and, because I've lost weight again, in a tight-fitting blouse and skirt – beige, I'm taking a little break from wearing black – with the dog running after me, and that handsome face of his smiles at me and I tremble.

He tells me he's already noticed me walking the dog when he comes home from work, he's an economist, he says, from Šibenik, in Dalmatia, he says, he's a subtenant living in the flat of a furrier and his three daughters, whom I must know. I tell him I don't know them, and then the sweet face of a fifteen-year-old girl appears before my eyes, the face of a doll, who could be one of the furrier's three daughters, so I say that I've just remembered, the youngest is a real beauty, I say, and he nods and we both laugh, who knows why. He goes on to say that she is a child and unaware of her looks, that's to say she is fully developed but walks around the house half-naked, as if she were five years old, he finds it embarrassing, but how can he tell her when nobody else tells her, when he is the only person who notices. More laughter, then he looks at the dog and asks what breed she is (an incredible question considering that she is Disney's world-famous Lady), a cocker spaniel, I automatically reply, without elaborating, because it hurts me to see how gorgeous he is up close, and finally he asks if I am free tomorrow, it's Saturday and he doesn't work, we could go out somewhere.

And now here I am, entering my building, my heart in my mouth, as they say, that's how fast it's beating, I'm so excited I have to lean against the wall, put my hand on my chest and take a deep breath while the dog looks at me quizzically, wondering why we're standing here. Then I rush up the stairs and into the flat to look in the mirror and see what he saw when he asked me out, I inspect my face and fix my hair as if he's still looking at me and I have to puff up my hair because it's fallen flat, damn it, and I smile and grin at the person in the mirror who has managed to turn his head.

I spend the whole day thinking about our date, set for eight in the evening in front of my house, getting ready, deciding what to wear, it has to be long, of course, because that's the best look for me, brushing my teeth with bicarbonate of soda, it makes them whiter, removing the hairs from my armpits and legs with depilatory cream, and taking a long shower. I decide I won't have anything to eat, I don't want a bloated stomach, well, maybe just a nibble of a cheese and salami sandwich, but I'll have something to drink, not too much though, I don't want my mouth smelling of alcohol and I want to be in control, although I rarely get drunk. Every so often I give myself a break and sit down at the table with a cigarette, wondering how it will all go. There's still my make-up to put on and my hair to fix, as I check my watch and my excitement grows, these are always the best moments, when you're full of expectations, when everything is still possible and undamaged by the physical, which always spoils everything, because the imagination is always better than reality, because I'm alone when I imagine. Maybe I would have enjoyed being with Adam if I'd closed my eyes, I muse, but I didn't because I seldom close them, not because I know that I have to keep them open, but because I usually want to see everything, even when it would be better if I didn't ... The logical conclusion being that I would be happiest if I were blind, blindness would solve everything. What stupid thoughts! Now I just have to spray on some deodorant, step through a cloud of the perfume I bought when I started going to the disco, take my obligatory cigarettes and lighter, my bag, then take a deep breath and walk out of the flat and into the street, where he's already waiting for me by the car, and off we go.

But where, I wonder, sitting beside him, remembering the perplexed look on his face when he saw my long, dark red skirt with its black stripes and no slit, as if he was expecting something else, bare legs, half-exposed breasts, not this Egyptian mummy, which is how I look with my skirt and blouse, buttoned up to the neck, with elbow-length, cuffed sleeves: I wanted to look interesting.

We're going to "Lagvić" for dinner, he says, hitting me where it hurts because I don't want to go to dinner, who cares about food, I want to get to know him, I want us to scintillate, far above the material world, which for me means wine and delighting in things that aren't food. The first thing I'm not going to do, surely, is masticate in front of him, wipe my mouth and worry about bits of food getting caught between my teeth, not to mention the smell of it, no, that is for the future, if there is one, but the present, at least, has to be clean and fragrant, like now in the car, where our perfumes mingle, because he's wearing some as well. He's in a dark green suit, an ochre-coloured shirt, no tie, the first two shirt buttons casually undone, you can just catch a glimpse of some dark chest hair and smooth, clear, unblemished skin, it's more than exciting, it's the kind of silky skin you want to sink yourself into, die in.

"Lagvić", with its beautiful view of Zagreb, is an expensive restaurant in the north of town, near the village of Šestine, where we used to go as a family to visit our washerwoman, as we called the peasant woman who came into town to wash the laundry, before the arrival of washing machines; actually we came to see my beloved Buco, the shepherd dog we had given to her when our flat became too cramped. When my father first brought him home – somebody had foisted the dog on him when he was drunk – he could fit in the palm of my hand, but then he grew and became this big animal that we used to hitch onto a sled in winter, and he needed a garden, not a small flat, we cried our eyes out.

And now it's getting all mixed up in my mind, my excitement, Buco, his perfect skin and the perfect profile that I keep furtively admiring, the blondish sheen of his maybe brilliantined hair, the unnecessary dinner, my wrong-headed dress choice, at least I'm wearing red high heels on my bare feet, I hope he noticed them, and the old questions of where am

I, who am I, the whirlwind of life, and whirlwinds are dangerous, I sense rather than know, danger lurks everywhere.

At the dinner table I tell him with a tight throat that I won't be having anything to eat, it's out of the question, I'll just drink, I say, and smoke, he can eat, I tell him, and he looks at me surprised, as if he has never heard anything like that – a girl turning down a dinner – surely you don't buy off your dates with a dinner, I think, feeling crushed. I need some wine right away, to recover, to start chatting, to amaze him with words, to captivate him with my wit, because I've wrapped myself up like a cocooned silkworm and there's nothing for him to look at, and he'd obviously been hoping to have something to look at, rather than a not very pretty face, though it's got its charm and there's no accounting for taste, as the Latin saying we learned in high school goes.

And so, while he's slicing the grilled meat on his plate, served with potatoes and onions, not touching any of it though, I go on the offensive, talking about myself, my studies and marriage, a student marriage that broke down, but I do it off-handedly, with humour, because I am a woman of conversation and imagination, well-versed in literature, and philosophers have taught me to think, I don't complicate, I clear paths that one can take with a smile, like me, if only he could see them, if only he understood anything, if only he had something other than schnitzels in his head, I realise, astonished. Because I can't believe that the person behind that perfect face, that perfect skin, that perfect body, the object of my desire, is the same thing as what is on the plate, a piece of dead meat. And since I still can't believe it, I keep drinking, a second bottle of wine is already on the table; well, if you want to pay, then pay, I'd give myself to you for nothing but that's something you don't understand, so, fine, I think to myself, already tipsy. And I'm tipsy, though not stumbling, when I return to the car, disappointed to the core, and I let him drive me to near my house, where he stops in Primorska Street, by the church, turns off the engine and for the first time looks into my eyes, piercing into my very being. Into my nakedness.

I can't see what you're like with all those clothes on, he says ruefully, and without hesitation he lifts up my skirt, it's tight but doable, it's already above my thighs, and squeezes my waist, it was doubly stupid to dress like this, it dawns on me, and now my panties are rolled down and slipped over my shoes, my blouse is unbuttoned, my bra undone and around my neck, and he squeezes my breasts and penetrates me in the front seat of his car which, being the gentleman that he is, he has reclined. Because I belonged to him the minute he grabbed me, I came while he was still undressing me, I came again and again, it was like when I masturbate and imagine some anonymous person touching me, only infinitely better, it was cosmic, it lasted and lasted, I'd never experienced anything like it, I wanted to faint with pleasure, it was utter surrender.

You're nice, he said after I put my clothes back on, annoyed that the sweat had made it slow progress, and finally lit a cigarette, staying in the car a bit longer before leaving and walking home. I didn't want him to drive me to my building, I didn't want anybody to see me, though I wasn't hiding from anybody, except for the phantoms in my head, and they were obviously alive. I sat there sweaty, my hair a mess, and it bothered me, as if my flat hair was depriving me of my power, because power lies in the hair, according to myth, and that's something that should be believed, and I waited for him to ask me out on another date. But nothing. He didn't even ask for my phone number. A smile and a vague "see you around" (while I'm walking the dog, probably, I said to myself miserably) was all I got for a night of ecstasy, which I wanted to repeat, I wanted more of this most gorgeous of men, dumb as could be but he pleasured me, yet it was to be once and never again, as if he realised what I thought of him and was making me pay for it; though I knew that wasn't true, because everybody thinks of themselves as clever, the cleverest even, without exception. He was simply done with me.

Feeling utterly humiliated, for a month I was careful not to leave the house unless I was sure that I wouldn't run into him, and if it did happen, I'd tremble for hours afterwards, tremble with desire, with happiness, with anger, with despair, lying in bed on my tummy, hugging my body, which still remembered his touch.

And then, just before winter, my husband appeared at the door to repay me the money he'd scrounged off me over the summer and autumn, whenever he ran into me in town – which we were now both roaming like stray dogs – and I'd always given him something, beaten down by his pleading, by the obsequious expression on his face when he asked for a loan, by the whispering into my ear, with me unwilling to accept that he had fallen so low.

It's early evening, I am getting ready to go out, my make-up's on, my hair is done, I'm wearing my grey suit, with the skirt above the knee, there's just my raincoat and heels to put on, I'm still in my felt slippers, they're grey as well.

Tanga, unlike me, is all happy to see him, she jumps around, paws him and moans, thrilled by the return of a member of her pack, now reduced to a seemingly disastrous two. I bring him into the hall, it's always gloomy, it needs the artificial light of the wrought iron lamp with its light bulbs directed at the ceiling, the TV is on to cheer up the atmosphere and create a warm feeling, which is missing, to give a sense of company, which is missing, except for the dog, consumed with illness, which always makes it look miserable.

We're both smoking Filter 57, in the green soft-pack, flicking the ashes into the big white ashtray, you've still got that ashtray, he says, as if he'd expected it to disappear in the meantime, like when he walked out of the house twenty years ago and everything changed. I don't offer him a drink, I'm in a hurry, I say, but I don't tell him where I'm going because it's none of his business, not anymore. As usual, he's sitting with his legs crossed, swinging his top leg, nodding his head, red in the face, as if stung by nettles. He's about to say something, but he stammers and I realise that it's the strain of the unsaid that is making him red in the face; once he says what he's got to say, there will be a decision, so he hesitates.

I ask him how he's doing at his parents, what do you think, he answers with a question that is also an answer, and clenches his teeth, making the veins on his neck pop out, then he looks at me wistfully, his eyes, the colour of forget-me-nots, glazed, the expression on his face pleading, his shoulders drooping.

See how miserable I am, his demeanour is saying more powerfully than any words, the meaning of words can always be twisted, but a facial expression is unambiguous, I'm yours, is his message, do what you want with me, he's saying, and he draws up his chair and lays his heavy head of lank straight hair on my lap, signifying total surrender.

Now what, I start panicking, my hands automatically dropping to his heavy, sick head, it could explode right here in my lap, I fret, so I let it stay where it is, I don't push it away, I don't get up, my hands take in the warmth of his head, a feeling from the days when this still meant something to me, along with the times when I was happy and unhappy, unlike now, when I'm just unhappy.

Poor man, my mother whispers in my ear, my mother for whom everybody is always poor except me, even my father was poor although he used to beat me, I resist that voice because, like the head lying in my lap, it wants me to acquiesce, not by resorting to force but by appealing to fragility, because I would fight force, whereas fragility keeps me rooted to the spot like the child who the other day, at the door to a café, grabbed my jacket from behind, hid under it and stayed there like that, so that I didn't dare move.

He'll start studying and he'll graduate, and he'll write for the radio and will stop disappearing from the house, he's come to his senses, he promises, all contrite, and then he stands up, kisses the palm of my hand, strokes my face, as he used to, at the beginning, and his forget-me-not-coloured eyes glaze over again, and all the while, the dog is looking up at us longingly, waiting for us to stroke her back. I remember the day we brought her home, this little golden ball, she was so cute, with her big ears and trusting eyes, it was enough to make your heart burst with joy, and we both cuddled her. And when she was sick, we spent the whole night by her basket, and in the morning, when she stood up and stretched, we cried with relief.

So much effort invested, so many years together, my mother whispers in my ear as I take out a bottle, still in my suit because I'm still determined to go out, it will just be later. When we finish the bottle, having evoked happier times, which moved us both, I finally say, OK, you can come back, but this is the last time, the next time you leave there's no coming back, and I send him home to get his things and bring them back in the morning because I want to sleep on my decision alone.

The dog and I walk him to the tram stop and on the way back I see the car of the man who had rejected me parked in front of my window, and I muse how I had saved myself the pain of humiliation, the man whose memory still makes me tremble, I'm still not over him, but then again I hadn't wanted you either, I say to him in my mind; I've reconciled with my husband, don't approach, don't hope for anything, you have lost me forever. Eat your heart out!

XXIII.

IN MY last year at secondary school, just before the final exams, I changed schools, because my form mistress, who was also my Croatian teacher, had given me a C for the previous year, an injustice beyond belief, because what else did I do except read day and night, books for breakfast, lunch and dinner, books in the toilet, and I became a raging force of nature, unstoppable, so, with the fury of a witch on a broom (as I imagined it from the pictures), I decided to leave my school in the city centre – it was old, venerable and highly regarded, like most things of the past – and when the form mistress ran into me in the corridor one day and asked why I was leaving, I said, without blinking an eye: because of you, and I threw her a sharp look that gouged out her perfidious eyes.

To no effect.

I enrolled in Dora's high school, it was new, on the outskirts of town, neither here nor there, I'd heard, and thank God, I thought, at least I'll get a break from being nagged every day, and though I couldn't join Dora's class because she was taking English and I was taking German, I did meet Irena in my new class.

Irena later recounted how I entered the classroom in a two-toned suit, red and blue against a Burgundy red imprinted with little blue leaves, designed by my mother's cousin, poor Julia, and wearing patent leather heels the colour of sour cherries, as if I was about to step onto the catwalk, and stood in front of the badly erased blackboard, surveyed the rows of heads in front of me, all staring at me, and when I introduced myself everybody's jaw dropped, Irena said. Because it was bold and brave to walk into the classroom like that, where everybody knew each other, and my arrival consolidated them into a group that could accept or reject you, extol or crush you, and it took guts just to stand in front of them, let alone impose yourself like that from the front of the classroom – look at me, remember, you're there and I'm here – it could have made them hate me, but it didn't. Maybe they sensed the truth behind my performance, that I was unsure of myself, that it wasn't me, it was fury that had brought me to that school, the medieval witch on a broom, and it was now receding.

The only person who disapproved was Irena, who would have never dared to do something like that, she would have quietly crept into the classroom, as invisible as a spider, and sat down somewhere in the back, where nobody could see her. Her way of punishing me was to ignore me, not say a word to me, just look daggers at me, who do you think you are, and then turn her back on me, which was as broad as mine, with straight shoulders. But, unlike me, she was thin, scrawny even, with long skinny legs, knobbly knees, big boobs, a long face, thin lips and a slightly crooked, ski-slope nose. And her chin was too small.

She didn't like herself, she thought she was ugly, I learned later, she couldn't see her own knees, though in a way she was attractive, being tall and thin she was modern-looking, she had nice long, thick golden hair and she was popular with the boys, which was the most important thing, because it gave her prestige. Studying came only second, and talents third, especially in sport, followed by art. That's how the system worked, and the system defined our lives, which we both did and didn't know; we knew because we could feel ourselves resisting, as if something was being imposed on us, but we didn't know because we didn't know that it was being imposed on us, because we had agreed to everything in advance.

While waiting together at the tram stop, she gazed around sulkily, but, as before, without saying a word to me; I was standing there looking miserable, when her sister happened to pass by, she was older and at first glance awesome, with eyes like a hawk, and seeing me standing next to her sister she stopped and asked her, who's this, the new girl in school, was the reply, where are your manners, her sister said, you haven't even introduced us. Irena pursed her mouth and pulled a face, which did nothing for her looks, she wanted to kill me for prompting that broadside from her sister, because, as later became evident, she felt like a nobody in front of her. But that was exactly her magnetic attraction for me, I didn't want to give up on her, so, in the second half of September, only two weeks into my new school, when I was making a list of which people to invite to my eighteenth birthday party, I added her name, knowing she'd come because, of course, she didn't want to miss out on it.

And here she was, in a white mohair top, her slim legs sheathed in white trousers, and we were all gobsmacked by her top because we'd never seen anything so beautiful before, so diaphanous, it made her face look unreal, we'd never touched anything so soft, but by ten in the evening, when they left, that top was dirty, sticky, blotched with all sorts of stains, like my two sofas where she'd vomited the cocktails that Edo had mixed for us (he was a lanky, freckled boy from our class). He declared himself an expert at making cocktails when he saw all the different bottles of alcohol I'd placed on the table – along with appetizing sandwiches with salami, cheese, pickles, *ajvar*, mayonnaise and olives on top, and a chocolate walnut cake the neighbour had made – rum, cherry brandy, two liqueurs, one yellow from the egg and the other brown from the chocolate, home-made, using brandy and a store-bought mixture of ingredients, as well as beer and wine. Great, he said, mixing it all together and giving it to us to drink and it was nice and fun until it hit us and we all got wasted, especially Irena. She practically had to be carried out, pale and limp, she looked like a ghost.

They'd already all left by the time my parents came home, and my mother and I worked until eleven o'clock cleaning the sofas with water and vinegar, using a fan to dry them and remove the stink of puke, while my father was drinking in the kitchen, waiting for us to finish, full of understanding for what had happened, a situation all too familiar to him.

Irena didn't come to school the next day, and the day after that she showed up all penitent, apologising to me, almost dropping to her knees, deaf to my assurances that neither I nor my parents were angry at her, because we'd seen it all before, lots of times, we'd already forgotten about it, I said. I asked her about her mohair top, had she managed to wash it clean; no, she said, it's ruined. What a shame! She kept on apologising, day after day, she was constantly by my side, we'd head home from school together, she'd walk me half the way because I lived far away, and we'd talk about our favourite subject, boys, and continued to hang out together.

She married young, a chemical engineer who seemed attractive at first glance, but awful at second, like a goldfish that's turned into a piranha and revealed itself by suddenly flashing its menacing pointed white teeth, an impression I kept to myself because it wasn't for sharing. I was responsible for bringing them together because I gave him my ticket at the cinema, she already had her eye on him, and this was a way for them to meet. They walked into the cinema as strangers and walked out as a couple – sitting next to each other in the dark, elbows and fingers touching, imagining what could be, shortened all the paths to getting together, led to a brief involvement, then marriage and a daughter; I'm glad I gave him my cinema ticket, I'd say sometimes, laughing. And she agreed, though not wholeheartedly, because something was wrong from the very outset, though it wasn't clear what, it was still hidden in the shadows, on the outside everything was shiny and bright, like his teeth, but on the inside the darkness grew and soon she began complaining. And then the darkness spilled out, like an erupting volcano – the little girl had barely learned to say "Daddy" when she discovered that her husband was seeing another woman, Irena found the letters the woman had written to him when she had just given birth.

He didn't even try to hide them, he just left them in the desk drawer, she said, telling me how she had learned from the letters that he had asked the woman if she wanted to be the mother of his daughter and the woman had said yes. He wanted to take even my daughter away from me, she moaned, because she never raged, she acquiesced, unwillingly.

The marriage was over, but she stayed, as poor people do, because she was still a student and they were subtenants, and their respective mothers were housewives, their fathers small-time tradesmen – hers used to manufacture combs made of bone and was now retired – they would have killed her if she had left an engineer husband and landed herself on them. What's more, he claimed that he had never cheated on her, that she was imagining things (he threw the letters away as soon as they were discovered), that he had never even thought of leaving her, and everybody believed him, saying she was crazy. Her sister, actually her half-sister, her mother's illegitimate child, was the most vociferous in defending the husband, son-in-law and brother-in-law as somebody you could only wish for as a partner, somebody no one in their right mind would ever leave.
And then that same husband went to Greece, to Athens, to work in a big American chemical plant that paid well, and she went with him, still mad at him, leaving the child with her mother, until she recovered. She invited me and my husband to Athens, for support, for company, because her husband worked from morning till night, except on weekends, and she would wander around the city on her own, still unsure if she should forgive him, although he'd already given her a fur coat and diamond ring and she drank the most expensive cognac and wine and spent money like royalty.

Of course you're going, my delighted mother said when the invitation came and I was hesitating, not because of him, his illness was dormant, he looked healthy and wasn't having any seizures, the second one had been the last.

We don't have the money for it, I said, the plane ticket is expensive. I'll give you the money, my mother insisted, feeling bad that her daughter had never journeyed abroad, not even to shop in Trieste. My journey was my marriage, I thought to myself, a journey to the end of the night, I would joke, quoting the title of a French novel, I'd certainly had my fill of journeying, what else was there left to see except stage sets, but I let my mother get us the visas and pay for the tickets and take us to the airport and watch me board a plane for the first time, never having been on one herself.

And it was there, in Athens, that my marriage ended, I muse, dipping the bread cubes in drippings, one for me, one for the dog who is sitting and waiting, because we're wide awake and alert when it comes to food, the dripping trickling off the bread cube onto the tablecloth, which absorbs it and turns it into stains, but who cares when there's no room left for the mess to grow or spread, because it's become an absolute. Which must mean the end of disorder since it has nowhere else to spread, and that must mean the beginning of order, I think to myself, waiting to see when this order inside me will spill onto the outside, the way the disorder did. It started in me and it will end in me, I say aloud, placing the greasy bread cube on the tablecloth, as if wanting to provoke it. The dog immediately jumps onto the table and snatches the bread, and I have an image of Irena's little two-year-old little girl, opening the dog's jaw with her two little hands, taking out the piece of candy it had snatched from her when they were playing, and putting it back into her own mouth before we could stop her, and nobody the worse for wear.

She never panicked over silly things, my friend Irena, and she certainly knew how to spend money. The day that we arrived in Athens, where the trees in the street were studded with ripe oranges and, amazingly, nobody picked them, she and her cheat of a husband with the menacingly gleaming teeth drove us to Piraeus, to the long broad sea-front lined with restaurant after restaurant, and no crowds because it was winter, here it was spring, and standing in front of the restaurants were waiters in their white shirts and black trousers, napkins draped over their arms, smiling and trying to entice us to come inside, under the straw roofs, literally tugging us by the sleeve and showing us dead fish on nickel platters, each more magnificent than the last, telling us we can choose; no, says the cheat, tonight we're having fowl, which I had never tried , and we ate ourselves to a standstill.

We spent the days strolling around the picturesque streets and their stalls, where everything was an explosion of colours and sounds, like having confetti constantly rain down on you, where skewered pieces of lamb, sprinkled with oregano, were grilled on charcoal in the open air and served in unleavened pitta bread with onions and tomatoes, known as *souvlaki*, and we drank retsina, a yellowy tart wine smelling of pine, in two-and-a-half decilitre bottles, and we ate mounds of nuts, putting weight on even Irena. We visited two-thousand-year-old sites, the Acropolis, the Parthenon, the Temple of Zeus, the Agora, we spent our days like that because we, obviously, had time, the three of us, because the cheat, obviously, had to make money. And we talked and talked, we discussed Irena's marriage (ours we didn't mention) and other important things in life, they being our only subjects, sober or drunk. The days slipped by, I kept expecting to run into Aristotle or Plato or Socrates in the street, or maybe Heraclitus, the best of the bunch, and was surprised when I didn't, just as I was surprised how ugly Greek men generally were, short, stocky, lumpish and angry-looking, at least those in the street, they looked as if they wanted to beat you up.

To whet our appetite before dinner, when it was the four of us, and for the pure pleasure of it, we'd open a bottle of *Metaxa,* or for, those who liked it (not me), anise-scented *ouzo*, which when diluted with water turned milky white, and then we'd treat ourselves to all sorts of delights prepared by Irena, with meat, fish, cheese, vegetables, sauces of all sorts, and we'd drink the most expensive wines, lining up the bottles in front of the door, to the horror of the neighbours, Irena laughed. Or we would go out for a pizza the size of a small round table, each of us taking a quarter and stuffing ourselves. On weekends, the four of us always went on a road trip somewhere, to the Peloponnese and its groves of newly ripe oranges wherever you looked, hanging on the trees like Christmas baubles, and to Delphi with the Temple of Apollo on Mount Parnassus, nestled among the misty hills, with its two famous inscriptions, "Know thyself" and "Nothing in excess", and you could spend days thinking about them before you realized that you would never know yourself and that you had too little, not an excess, of everything, of love, and happiness, and money, and fame, and even life, which is not forever. For a moment I imagined the oracle Sibyl sitting on her rock, in a trance, issuing ambiguous prophecies, one of which ruined King Croesus, I read, I loved mythology and fairy tales and stories, anything that wasn't real, because "humankind cannot bear very much reality" as T.S. Eliot wrote, for himself and for me.

And it was here, in Delphi, on the ruins of the Temple of Apollo, while Irena was snapping pictures, irritating me no end because I didn't like having my picture taken and I hated it when they would call me away to have my picture taken so that I couldn't enjoy the ruins, that a story took shape in my mind in which my darling – good-looking compared to the average Greek, tall, slim, blue-eyed and with regular features – went off gallivanting during our stay (in the story, not in real life), met a pretty, young Greek girl in a café, fell in love with her, took her to a hotel and deflowered her. He continued to meet her in various hotels, until the affair reached the ears of her three brothers, all dark, short, moustached and angry, who found him and killed him in front of my eyes. In the middle of Athens, in the street, left to lie in a pool of blood. I can still see him there even today, lying on his back on the pavement, his throat slashed, blood everywhere, passers-by stopping to look, his unseeing blue eyes gazing up at the sky.

I couldn't stop thinking about the story, no matter what I was doing, walking, looking, admiring, laughing, talking, drinking, eating, even at night it would be on my mind when I fell asleep, and in town I would look for the fatal girl who had destroyed him. And one day I found her, on the bus, we were going somewhere, probably to a museum with ancient sculptures; she was of average height, her golden-red hair came to just under her ears, she had a fringe, a heart-shaped face and mouth, a splattering of freckles, big purple eyes, like Homer's Hera, and a well-proportioned if pocket-sized body, as lovely as Venus.

That's her, I exclaimed to myself, she's the one who will take him from me and free me of the unbearable burden that he is, which is sure to break me. Only once did I let him penetrate me at night, halfway, I took pity on him, I'd say, and I hardly felt a thing, except that it was boring and I resisted, because now I could compare him with Mr. Handsome from around the corner, who had taken me to such heights, whereas he had become an unbearably heavy body.

One evening, towards the end of our stay, we went for roast lamb and a *shopska* salad to Plaka, the oldest part of Athens, swarming with people like an anthill, a riot of colours, the pungent smell of lamb fat wafting out from the taverns and cafés and the loud hawkers hoping to sell trinkets and phony antique pieces, two of which I bought, two slate blue ancient masks to hang on the wall, one for tragedy and the other for comedy, our life personified.

We've come to break some plates, said Irena when we sat down in the restaurant, which had live music, and to act like we're in *Zorba the Greek,* and to dance the *sirtaki,* she said. Then she stood up, spread out her arms, and started to dance the *sirtaki*, one step to the right, one to the left, one leg raised, then the other, one step forward, one step back, then turn, humming the tune from the movie, which we must have seen four times and knew by heart.

And when we were good and drunk, Irena actually did start breaking the thick white plates that were waiting on the long shelf for just that purpose, although you had to pay for them, in other words, it was money thrown away, which brought a frown to the cheat's face, as he began to bear his pointed, white teeth, saying "Enough", every time a plate was smashed to smithereens on the floor. One more, and another, Irena shouted, I'd never seen her so bold before, this one's for dead husbands, crash, this one for deceased husbands, crash, she kept shouting, smashing the plates until the cheat grabbed her arm, which was about to hurl another plate, and lowered it and the plate onto the table.

Then they got into an argument about culpability, she had never forgiven him and wanted us to judge him, even though he was footing the bill for our food and drink, which made all of it awkward and embarrassing, ruining everything. We returned home in silence, each of us caught up in our own thoughts, disagreeing with the others, and ourselves, and in the morning we all woke up with a headache, at least I did. As soon as I opened my eyes, I took a pill and jumped into the shower, at the wrong time, before our host who was in a hurry to get to work, and that only made me more nervous because I couldn't just run out of the bathroom, I had to dry myself off and he kept shuffling from one foot to the other in front of the bathroom door, murderously baring his teeth, as I saw when I walked out. We were supposed to leave in two days time.

We returned home on Christmas Eve, with a present for Kostja – he'd married, after doing his military service, the only one in our crowd who did, the others were unfit, and he asked my husband to be his best man, which I figured included me as well – a cobalt blue clay tea set and colourful local rug blanket, in which we wrapped the oranges for Irena's daughter. At the airport, the customs officers couldn't have been rougher with the rug, I guess they thought we were carrying drugs or gold or who knows what, they simply lifted it up at one end and let it roll open, so that the oranges spilled out onto the floor, as if scattered by a bomb, and we just helplessly watched.

We barely managed to gather them all up.

XXIV.

My mother came from Plitvice to attend the graduation ceremony, his, of course, Danica insisted, there were tears, mounds of flowers from relatives and friends, mostly gladioli, white and purple, glamorous in cellophane, followed by a family lunch in a restaurant, one of the best in town, said Frane, who had taken charge of that side. Danica came in her new marshmallow white spring suit and dark purple blouse with a bow, and the guest of honour was wearing a new dark blue suit with a Russian collar, a present from Frane, as was the lunch of steak tartare, roast of lamb and bottles of red wine, costing the earth.

He looks so elegant, Danica sighed adoringly in the restaurant, looking back and forth between her son and me with her glassy eyes, seeing us together, squeezing my hand under the table and whispering into my ear that I deserved the credit for this success, she knew that, she would never be able to thank me enough, and I nodded and smiled, having nothing to say except that I was finished with her son, but I wanted to spare her that.

The news was that he might soon have a permanent, salaried job at the radio, where he was freelancing, at first it would be as a trainee journalist, then as an editor, like Leon, said Danica, elated. She overlooked the fact that an editor had to be a member of the Party, which would never happen because his father had suffered at the hands of these people, like his uncle in Dubrovnik, whereas Leon's father had been a partisan commissar, recipient of a veteran's testimonial, a big shot, as my mother would say, who made sure of his son's well-being, both mental and political. Obviously I didn't say that to her either.

A work colleague of hers who had gone up in the world, obtained a doctorate and gone to work in an embassy where she eventually had the power to find her son a job, provided a connection at the radio. Just let him graduate, and we'll get him a job, she told me, Danica kept repeating, she'd never been so happy in her life, except perhaps when she married. If it works, I'll make clothes for her free of charge for the rest of my life, she promised, because the colleague was another of her clients.

Also at the table with us was his cousin, the doctor, without his wife and parents who went straight home after the graduation ceremony because his mother was feeling unwell, it's the heart, he said, not mentioning the non-appearance of the other woman, as if that was self-explanatory. Actually, we had never met his wife, it was as if he was hiding her. He was considered good-looking, although for my taste he was too tall and had an egg-shaped head, shaved almost to the bone, with small eyes and fleshy, chalk-white cheeks, plus, like all doctors, he was self-important, even when with his relatives. He asked my husband if he had had any more seizures, no, he and his mother and I said with one voice; he takes his medicine, I added, because I saw to that, the second seizure was the last, I said. All of us at the table looked at him hopefully, as if this was now leading to a miraculous recovery, and it was in his hands. But he neither confirmed nor denied such a miracle, he simply nodded, saying nothing, leaving the five of us hanging in animated suspension, neither here nor there, suspecting the fruitlessness of all these efforts, suddenly at a dead end with no place to go.

The situation was saved by Frane, that poor skeletal man in his grey, oversized suit, always the same, with his bald head and crooked yellow teeth, who raised a toast to his son's achievement. He was already slightly tipsy, like the first time I ever saw him, and when he smiled his mouth twisted. He stood up and delivered a five-minute speech about the place his son had earned in society by obtaining his degree, and now, he said, all roads were open to him, except for those he closed off himself, he ended didactically, doubling over with a coughing fit of bronchial asthma. Danica jumped up to help him sit down, as if he couldn't do it on his own, but he indicated there was no need, and his son looked down, rolling his eyes, trying to stop himself from laughing.

Everything will be fine now, my mother said the next morning in the dining room, where we were having our coffee, the layer cake that Danica had brought in my mother's honour on the table, along with a bottle of plum brandy from Olga's plum orchard, which she made herself every autumn, and we sold for her to people we knew in town, so she always gave us a couple of litres for free. He'd already left, for the radio, to discuss the programme, he said, which would have rung false had I cared, but I didn't. My mother leaves tomorrow so just be home in time to eat, I said, turning my head away when he tried to kiss me, although with a laugh.

Nothing will be fine, I said to my mother after he left, as soon as he finds a job I'm leaving him; my mother said nothing, shook her head, thought about it, weighed the pros and cons, heaved a sigh and dropping her hands in her lap said, at least wait until you graduate. Let him help you, a salary is a salary, she said, you're going to be without the pension soon, you don't have a degree and you don't have a job, she added, displeased that somebody had exploited her daughter, and without any compensation to boot.

But it was useless, because I wouldn't give in, I don't care about reason or justice, he can go, I said, the sooner the better, I said, I want to be rid of him.

With his degree and job I don't owe him anything anymore, I thought to myself, because I didn't want to talk to her about what was owed, that was my story not hers.

At least wait until he brings home his first pay package, my mother yelled, she simply couldn't take so much injustice, when you give you must receive, when you take you must give back, she didn't say it, because it was inappropriate, but it was implied. God forbid that he should bring home his salary, I said, he might think that I'll stay with him and then we'll never be rid of him.

We were silent, each wrapped up in our own thoughts, but I did pour myself a shot of brandy, knocked it back and poured another, even though I don't drink in the morning.

I had spent all winter helping him to study, because he would never have done it on his own, I mused, I had to funnel the information into his head, simplifying everything and making him learn it by heart, because he wasn't getting it, especially not the theory of literature, he would rehash what he'd read, come up with literary nuggets and anecdotes, but what he needed was to understand the theory of literary style and so much more, he needed to make sense of it and explain it. It was an absolute nightmare. I learned a lot about him that I hadn't known before, or hadn't wanted to see, who knows. I used to think he was bright and funny, but now I realised that he simply memorised lines from films and books, along with all those maxims he had learned by heart from the collection in Frane's red hardcover notebook. His son had bragged about it when we first met, as if it was his own notebook, as if he had been writing in it, not his father who had started it back in Dubrovnik, when he was young. He would insert these ripostes and maxims into the conversation as if they were his, always at the right time and in the right place, he was good at that, and he sounded witty, and I admired the wit and the way he talked, thinking it was original, not a copy. I also wrote his thesis, elaborating on my first-year essay "Music in the Work of Thomas Mann", never in a million years could he have done it himself, I realised with increasing despair as time went by, why on earth hadn't I seen it, I asked myself, but I knew the answer, there was a reason why people said love is blind, as if that was of any help to anybody

What else is love except a kind of blindness, I reflected, you see what you want, what you like, what catches your fancy, what makes you grow, you see what you need but you don't see what you don't need. When you see what you don't need you try not to see it, to attribute it to a random instance, to hide it from yourself, because you compare what you see with the ideal that they've drummed into your head and try to make it fit that ideal. Sometimes it more or less works, unless you completely fail, because basically you always fail, but even an approximation is something, at least it's bearable. The world exists on the basis of approximation. But it's awful when it turns out that what you get is not even close, that it's the exact opposite, that you had imagined somebody else! And, of course, he helped you along, he tried to be what he thought you wanted him to be, not what he was, but he could pretend to be what you wanted until he captured you, until he took away your freedom, in life and, worst of all, within your inner self, because the hardest thing was to save yourself from yourself. By saving him I was saving myself from myself, I realised, from the debt of love, I supposed, a debt you couldn't just discard as if it never existed, it doesn't exist now but it did, it was your life and if it is worthless then so are you and your life; how do you live with that?

That wasn't something I could tell my mother because she wouldn't have understood, she only knew about loyalty and self-sacrifice, nothing in between, about the part of the vow that says to have and to hold for worse, because for better will be easy, she would say, showing she acquiesced unreservedly.

What shall we cook, she broke the silence, as we looked around the dining room, flooded with spring sunshine, take this, take that, what there is and what there isn't, the dog at our heels. When I take her out, I'll pop over to the shop, I said, we've got time, and we stepped out onto the balcony to admire the blossoming apricot tree in the courtyard, it looked unreal, like a painting.

Before long it will lose its blossoms, my mother said, and I could already see a carpet of white and pink petals spreading out on the concrete, turning into red decay, and then into the dirty concrete of winter, rats scuttling across it with their young, their family closeness touching somehow, it made you think.

We made a moussaka with minced beef and potatoes, topped with sour cream whisked with eggs, and for a salad we had pickled peppers, all of which we ate ourselves because he didn't show up for lunch until the evening. He was all apologetic, saying that after his appointment at the radio he'd been invited to a meeting of bigwigs who decide on staff hiring, a dicey story because why would they invite a freelancer, I thought to myself. And afterwards they went out for a drink, he, Leon and one of the bigwigs, and it went on and on, as these things do, he said, a diabolical tinge to his laugh. He would probably be hired for the First Programme, news-gathering, he said, a miserable job, he wasn't looking forward to it at all, but what could he do.

It ain't New York, I thought maliciously, he won't be wearing a Rolex or driving a Lincoln Continental, he'll just be a little reporter barely eking out a living, like all the others. But you'll have a job, I said, and you'll be able to pay the bills (which now I pay, needless to say), and he fell silent.

You'll be able to continue working for Leon when I get my job, he said, as if getting the job was his doing and not the result of my working working under his name for years – and people knew it.

The next scene is from a family film depicting an idyllic picture: he's sprawled out on the sofa in the hall, with a cigarette, an ashtray and a bottle of red wine, there's the roar of the crowd at the stadium where some lunatics are playing football, with him occasionally yelling and swearing so loudly you can hear it all the way in the dining room, where my mother is playing Patience at one end of the table and I'm watching her from the other end, and we don't know what we are or where we are or why we exist, or perhaps we don't exist at all, perhaps we're just dreaming.

XXV.

WINTER IS here, time to think about the heating, that woodpecker we put there keeps pecking away in my head, a *perpetuum mobile,* he never tires, I have to see to the wood, peck, peck, and to the coal, peck, peck, we'll drop the coal down into the basement through the window, and then the wood, seventy cubic feet of beech, after it's been sawed into logs, which later will have to be chopped. We don't have central heating, we have the conventional square brown fireplaces, the kind that were installed after the war, except in the dining room, which has an iron-wrought gas stove and on winter mornings we gather around it while the other rooms are still freezing cold. I chop the wood and bring it and the coal from the cellar, the wood in my arms and the coal in a grey tin bucket, because he's sick and has to be spared such things, like his father in his day. I feed the furnace with kindling and crumpled sheets of newspaper, there's smoke, the fires catches, or doesn't, I take away the ashes and clean under the fire-box, it's such a bloody bore when winter comes.

The flat looks grey and needs painting, peck, peck, and I have to tell him that he can go now, peck, peck, because he recently got a job. A permanent job, with a salary. By six in the morning he's getting ready to go to work, because he has to read the news on air at seven. At six-thirty he's in his suit and tie, his hair washed, beard trimmed, deodorant sprayed, the obligatory 4711 dabbed on the rest of his body, our gentleman journalist sneers at his job as twaddle, but not at the status it brings. The status is a magnet for catching all sorts of things, specifically women, and it's not to be sneezed at, it's not the status of New York but still, it's not to be sneezed at, and he holds his head higher than before, even his step is livelier. The Pink Panther seems to be standing up straighter, I think spitefully when I see him getting ready for work, because I wake up at dawn. He doesn't, but now he's forced to, he's practically blackmailed into it, the cage has finally found and captured him, there's no escape, at least not for now, because I have no doubt that he's thinking about it. Whenever he has the chance, he recounts a scene from an Italian neorealist film, which a group of young men in a red convertible with the top down are coming back in the early morning from partying and a bunch of workers are shuffling around in a factory, its chimney already churning out smoke … *Lavoratore,* shouts one of them in the convertible, standing up on the car seat, and showing them: *fuck you,* making a fist with his right hand and hitting the crook of the arm with his left. Maybe he'll think up a way to get out of the cage, I muse warily, and then I'll be saddled with him again, the only way I can be sure is if he leaves, and even then, not entirely sure. I remember how he once left allegedly forever, just before summer, and then he decided to come back, just before winter, and he sat all day on the bottom step of the staircase, by our front door, kicking it with the droning rhythm of a machine, even when the neighbours passed by, until I finally opened the door and let him in.

It was on the tip of my tongue to say – you're employed now so you can go back to your parents or rent a place of your own, do whatever you want but just leave because I don't want to be with you anymore – I had opened my mouth and was starting with: listen, we have to talk about something, when he interrupted me, saying that the flat needed painting, as if reading my mind.

Incredible that he should think about painting, I couldn't believe it, and that he offered to do it himself, on his days off, I could have expected all sorts of things but not this, because he had never offered to do anything, he had never lifted a finger, he wanted everything served to him on a platter. That was when I discovered something about myself that I hadn't known, I discovered that I could be bribed, because I didn't say to him: thanks, but no thank you, we're finished, no, I hesitated, I computed, I'd been planning to ask Adam or Filip to help me, but why not let him do it, since he was offering. As stage one, I let him take a sheet of newspaper and make a paper hat, which took some doing, and I laughed, and then, with that hat on his head, let him start moving the furniture into the middle of the room and roll up the carpets, creating the mess that I'm still sitting in, can't get away from. Even when he reached the area with the insects, where it was murderous, I couldn't move and create some order, as if I could hardly wait for the demise of order, that external order that concealed the disorder within, to hell with that, too, I decided in a fit of destructive energy, everything has to go to pot in order to be able to start over again, with both order and disorder, because we're doomed to both, I guess.

It was fun at the beginning, fun to turn order into disorder, I remember, constantly forced to serve the needs of order because there was nobody else but you to do it, so it was a nice change to turn against order, to attack and destroy it, there was a kind of surreal justice to it, as evidenced by wars and revolutions that immediately move against the order, as if it were the source of all conflicts; a strange story.

So I bought paint rollers and paint, some white, and a bit of yellow to mix with the white and soften it, give it some warmth, and Filip helped by lending his car, his father's Skoda, to transport it all, and he offered to help with the painting, but I said there was no need. You can help by writing my senior thesis for me, I said, because I had no energy even for my exams, let alone for my thesis, it's you who urged me to prolong my studies so now's your chance to make up for it, I joked but was serious, and he agreed right away. He would write about Nietzsche, he said, almost pleased, Nietzsche had been on his mind for a long time.

And when we'd mixed the paint and laid the sheets of newspaper on the floor of the dining room where we were going to start painting, it's true he did climb onto the ladder armed with the paper hat and the roller, which he dipped into the bucket of paint, made sure it wasn't dripping and then rolled it over the wall a few times before suddenly slapping his forehead and shouting: "Oh!" I thought something had happened to him, terrified, I looked up at him, but, no, he was fine, he'd just remembered something, he bullshitted, climbing down from the ladder, I promised to do a report for the Second Programme, how could I have forgotten, he slapped himself on the forehead again, his paper hat finishing up on the table, and the roller in the bucket as he left to change and rushed off who knows where.

I have to end it, I tell myself, it's become unbearable, I have to be radical about it, like Alexander cutting the Gordian knot because he couldn't untie it so he sliced it in half and then it unloosened all by itself. He did it for all times, for everyone who came after him, including for me, so that I would know it could be done, I say to myself.

I put the leash on Tanga and we go for a walk to the park, Rokov perivoj, it used to be a cemetery but today it's an oasis of peace and quiet above Ilica and the market, beyond the sound and the fury, as Faulkner would say, a quiet path under the trees, it makes you want to weep when you see it inviting you to something that's not there, something that you can only look at and imagine, but never attain.

But even just imagining means something, I console myself as I reach the little chapel of St. Roko, built by the people of Zagreb with their own hands after the plague, in honour of St. Roko, to protect them from disease: plebeians and nobility working side by side, stone by stone, because the plague made no distinction – so that all these centuries later I could sit in its shade and die of love at the age of barely seventeen, my first, platonic, unhappy love. You live what you imagine for that instant that you are imagining it, I console myself, having lost my life, and I let the dog off the leash and gazing at the early autumn greenery that has only just started to turn yellow and red and to decay, a moment with no continuation, but all the same a moment that existed, that fell into place with everything else that existed, the unreal attaching itself to the real which, once it passes, itself seems unreal, and passes in a heartbeat, as if it had never existed, but you know that it did, and so a vicious circle.

After an hour of walking we went down into town, to the food stall at the market where I could see the smoke and smell the meat being grilled, and I bought a large portion of *ćevapčići* in pitta bread for the dog and me, then we rushed home, our mouths watering, so that we could eat it, one for me and one for you, and don't forget the pitta bread, but I threw away the chopped onions along with the greasy paper. You have your water, I'll have my wine, then you go to sleep and I'm going out, I tell the dog as I'm already at the door, heartsick, because I don't like leaving her, I know she'll brood. Dogs don't seem to have a sense of time, to them everything is an eternity and I've vanished never to return.

I've resolved to find him and kill him off in me, this time forever, I'm determined, he can't just leave me in this mess and disappear, the radio programme my foot, lies, all lies and now we're going to uncover them, I say to myself, mentally rubbing my hands as I rush down Ilica to Republic Square and the café Dubrovnik, which, of course, is where I find him. People told me that they would see him there, always by himself, loath to let anyone, Petra, Filip, join him, he just points to a chair, Filip told me because it had happened to him, makes a few witty remarks, laughs and then he's on his feet, nodding, saying – sorry, pal, duty calls – and vanishes.

Duty's calling, I said to him once when he slept until noon after staying up all night who knows where, but he didn't laugh, he just looked at me.

I have nothing to hold on to so my thoughts are all over the place as I approach the café, all encased in glass, the customers as if in a display window, and there he is, he's there, I spot him from the street, he's sitting by himself with a glass of brandy like that time in Pula, when I had seen him perform his escape act for the first time, because what else can I call it, he's as still as a mannequin, smoking, watching, as tense as an animal lurking in the bushes, waiting to pounce.

You get it now? Somebody slaps me on the shoulder, making me jump and it's Leon grinning, I've never seen him so drunk, certainly not in the middle of the day, and he's in a suit, shirt and tie, red on white with dark blue, all spotless and ironed, but it's not him wearing that suit, shirt and tie, it's somebody else, it's Mr. Hyde in Dr. Jekyll, as Stevenson would say, who'd obviously encountered such a monster in a spotless, ironed suit, because it's not a unique phenomenon, and his mouth is wide open so you can see his yellowing teeth, with the prominent canines between his moustache and chin, like a wolf's, and this wolf is about to betray him. So I listen to what my one and only does when he's sitting all tense at the café Dubrovnik, *he wanks*, I hear, *he wanks*, the wolf repeats in between sniggers, and at last I see what he's gawking at, a woman at the next table in a mini, crossing and uncrossing her long tanned legs, as if wanting to excite him.

Once, when I was a girl, somebody rang the bell and when I opened the door I saw a man – tall, dark hair, well-dressed, and I asked him politely who are you looking for, only to notice that his trousers were unzipped and that his member was hanging from his hand like a worm and he was massaging it, raping me with his eyes. I slammed the door in his face, it's a good thing I didn't break his nose in the process, I thought, trembling, listening to him run away down the steps.

This time I didn't. True, for a moment I felt sick, as if somebody had hit me, my throat tight, feeling miserable and humiliated, ashamed that everything had started like a fairy tale but had left me with one of life's cruel lessons, as the only truth, from which there is no salvation, but a minute later I was laughing along with Leon, stepping back from his stench. He continued talking even as we moved away, because there was nothing more for me to see, and anyway I didn't want him to observe me – that Rile is such a bastard, doing the dirty on me with the boss at the radio, when I'm the one who brought him there, he said. He was like that as a kid, he said, he'd break everything in the house, especially mirrors, they had to take a rope and tie it to the dressing table, he said, imagine, a rope, he snickered, and as soon as he grew stronger he'd beat up poor Frane if he wouldn't give him money to go out or if he asked anything of him. And he forced them both to lie, he said, like that story about Italy, he'd never set foot there. And he cheated on you, he said, he'd bring all sorts of sluts to the flat when his parents were away (when he moved in with me and they got rid of him, they'd spend their summers in Slovenia), and if my place was free he'd bring them there, even some of your girlfriends, he said, like Petra and Dora, I bet you didn't know that. Petra, Dora, I listened as if I'd known for a long time, though I hadn't, except as a possibility, because he used to beat me as well, and lie to me and steal from me and I sensed that he was cheating on me, though I had no proof. But now we were going to put an end to all that, I was going to end it with him, and with me, especially with me, I thought to myself as I jumped onto the tram while Leon was still talking.

Home, home and then I'll get ready to go out, to the disco, it's still warm, the dancing is still out in the open air,

I'll doll myself up, clothes, make-up, the whole shebang, as if I'm stepping out of a palace and not this wreck of flat, prepared for painting but neither painted nor cleaned.

Don't wait up for me, I won't be back till morning, I say to poor Tanga, who's sitting, watching me iron my knee-length linen dress on the table, the dress has buttons running all the down the front but the last button is midway down my thigh, and it has a collar, breast pockets and skirt pockets, it's olive green, like army uniforms, and with it I'm wearing dark brown cork heels. And I'll wear nothing underneath, except for a dash of perfume, as a joke I remember says, no bra, no knickers, nothing, I say aloud, doubling over with laughter, which echoes in the dining room like a madwoman's, which is what it is, because I've gone berserk, wild. And nobody can do a thing to me anymore.

I walk down the street pantie-less and bra-less, I've gone out without a bra before but never without knickers, and I revel in the freedom of a body with nothing to constrain it, nothing to pinch it, no revealing outlines, that's something I don't like, and I calm down as if somebody were whispering jokes in my ear, because nobody but me knows that I have nothing on under my skirt, that I've broken the rule. I'm shocked, with only one witness, me, and I feel powerful, I feel as if I'm mocking everybody. If the pavement were made of glass then everybody would see that I have no knickers on, I muse, already feeling very relaxed, I've taken off more than just that, I realise, I've also shed the self-image they slipped on me like an invisible dress that I'm now going to take off, once and for all, and never wear again.

So here I am in the street, with no knickers on, looking for somebody who will want to go to bed with me, for a stranger, it's not that I'm a virgin and don't know what to expect, this is not going to be my first time where I'm expecting the real thing, there was that Šibenik guy, but I was with him for pleasure not love, though at least I was attracted to him, and that justifies everything. But this evening it's work, looking for a stud who will ravish me, not pleasure me, somebody I will offer myself to in order to humiliate my husband, who won't be able to stand it. I know for sure that he won't, my betrayal will kill him. He'd see through it immediately if I pretended that I'd cheated on him, because I'm bad at lying. No, he has to smell another man's body on me, like an animal, he has to understand that he's finally been rejected, and he has to feel that rejection in his bones, down to the last drop of blood in his damaged veins, like a flood that's going to carry him away and he can't fight it. Or like a fire that will engulf him. And, more importantly, me with him, because I have to burn so that I can be reborn and rise up from the ashes like a phoenix, I'm flattering myself, because I don't know if I am a phoenix or if I'll simply disappear. Like the dream he had, the dream about the Wax Queen, I remember, it was a message that I didn't understand.

That's what I'm thinking as I walk in my sandals with the four-inch cork heels, wearing my tight military dress and no knickers, first down my street, then JNA Street, under the blossoming chestnut trees, and I'm smoking, which isn't exactly seemly, as if I'm trying to provoke a reaction. But there's nothing sweeter than smoking in the street, especially when you go out with no knickers on, and you're a woman, because the very fact that the cigarette is in your hand and lit for you and that you're taking a drag – makes it alive, providing a form of support, company, rather than being a mere object, says Sartre in its defence, as a constant subject of attack.

Because I need support for this pathetic, and when I think about it, superfluous sacrifice that I intend to make, in the normal world things like this are resolved differently, you're a bastard, even if you are sick, you're a piece of shit, get out, there's no mercy, but with me there always is, everything is always out in the open, what is and what was, you can always invoke it, I surrender to it, and it's not because I'm weak. That's why he has to make the decision to leave himself, he has to have a reason that he can't ignore, I tell myself as I turn right and past the secondary school I ran away from. You're so harmless now, but you were so horrible then, I say to the building whenever I see it, how things change, I muse, both good and bad, everything becomes senseless, if that makes sense. I'm walking nicely, my back straight, deliberately swaying my bare butt, a cigarette between the index and middle finger of my right hand, raised to shoulder-level, I'm seductive and it works. A hairy, bearded young man in jeans turns to look at me and stops in his tracks, gawking, saying something, I notice him from the corner of my eye, although I'm not interested, I have my goal, the disco where everything will resolve itself once and for all as soon as Osibisa start singing.

It takes courage to go to a disco by yourself, and with no knickers on, I say to myself, building up my courage, because it needs support, too, it takes courage to walk in, sit down, light up, stand up, push your way through the crowd to get a drink and then come back again, pretending that you're not alone, even though you're carrying your own drink, and then to sit down again, cross your legs and wonder if anything's showing underneath. The only thing showing is that I'm alone, which at the same time is an invitation, and meanwhile my glass with the sugared slice of lemon wedged on the rim is turning red from the Americano, a lady's drink, because I need something to protect myself.

I'd barely touched my not too sugary drink, when a candidate summoned from the underworld appears; where've you been, he says, you appeared and then disappeared this time last year, he says, because he remembers precisely, he obviously has certain intentions in my regard. He stands there, cute-looking, a roguish smile on his round face, not sure if it is beardless or shaved, half of him is still a boy; he studies acting. I don't particularly take to him, but that's his plus, not minus, because I don't want to enjoy myself with him, I'm being sacrificed to the heavens to be free of the demons, like in mythology, so I can't and I shouldn't enjoy it. The pyre will enjoy me, the flames to which I give myself will enjoy me, and so will the aroused stripling the gods have sent me so that I can give him my body. After that I won't have to sacrifice myself to my husband, no matter how much my mother whispers into my ear that "the poor man is sick", the way Jesus probably whispered into her ear that her husband, "poor man, is sick", you go ahead and sacrifice yourself for him since you took him for better or worse, even though it was never better, you just pretended it was. Because there's no better in this somnolent world, which doesn't even know what it is, and there's no worse, there's only brutal logic. According to which if you drink a good poison you will die, like Socrates when he was offered poison. And that's unbearable. So we invent fairy tales to save ourselves, except they won't. They'll only put us into a deeper sleep.

We chat a bit longer, he and I, just to be polite, twirling our glasses, the grape brandy in his as clear as the glass, lounging in our armchairs, looking laid-back, that's how everybody else looks so I figure I do, too, a good place for our fears and doubts, for murky secret plans.

Want to dance, he asks, he's already put down his glass, stood up and given me his hand with its clean, hairless, white pudgy fingers and clipped nails, I hesitate, only slow dances, I say, because I don't feel like bopping around, I don't say that I just think it, and I let myself be led onto the dance floor, where the lights swirl in all the colours of the rainbow and the amps are vibrating with the rhythms of Osibisa's *Sunshine Day*, there are slow records and fast, something for everybody, and his hand slowly moves down my back, we're glued to each other. Our faces are pressed together, he holds me tight, not sensing that I feel like that wooden statue of the Virgin Mary who always stands in the invisible corner of the church, her hands folded, her eyes lowered, humble before God and before life, he has no idea whom he'll be taking to the flat (his flat, as he's already said) after we grope each other and have one more drink, just to relax ourselves.

We go on foot, he lives in the city centre, in one of those streets where I always lose my way because they're all the same, like in those new housing complexes, except here the buildings reflect the century they belong to, the second half of the nineteenth century, before the great wars. How did he come by a flat at his age, I wonder, but I don't ask, I'm just glad he has one because even if my place weren't the mess that it is, I wouldn't take him there, I don't want him that near. We enter the flat and he takes me through the gloomy hallway into the bedroom, it's big, with stuccowork on the ceiling, and a bare window overlooking the courtyard. The unmade bed is a square on the floor, with white bedding like our grandmothers'. Embroidered pillow cases and an embroidered duvet cover, I notice for a second, because he's already undressing, always a sorry spectacle before the advent of the act, the same as dressing afterwards, as if a mask is removed and then put on again, ending all that bliss.

He's white, has meat on the bones, his nipples show because his chest is hairless, but his skin is clear, and the boy has an erection, his member standing up, here he does have hair, it's light red, I see everything because I feel nothing. He embraces me as I unbutton my military dress, still in my shoes, he's not really embracing he's grabbing me, my breasts, my ass, he almost bursts when he realises that I'm naked underneath and for a minute he stops. But he doesn't say anything, he has other things on his mind, my dress is already on the floor, I've kicked off my shoes, I'm on my back and he's on top of me, all white, white, white, and big somehow, he groans and sweats, causing me neither pain nor pleasure, this, too, shall end, I think to myself. And so it does, just before dawn, because he kept coming back for more, as if he couldn't get enough.

He says I can use the bathroom to wash myself, but I need the smell of him, I need to take it home with me, I need it on my face and hair, which is matted with sweat and I want to keep it that way, I'll comb it a little with my fingers, just enough not to look dishevelled when I go out into the street. I wrap the sheet around me and reach for my olive-grey dress on the floor, it's all creased as it needs to be, and meanwhile he's smoking a cigarette, the ashtray on the bed linen, sitting and watching me undo all those buttons on my dress.

You don't wear underwear, he says, why don't you wear underwear, he asks. No reason, I say, shrugging, I just don't, I don't know why. Such a pretty woman, he says, looking at me thoughtfully, not finishing his sentence, which doesn't bother me because I'm not interested in what he wanted to say. He's on the wrong track, whatever he says or thinks, because this isn't me, this is me as a weapon, as just a device.

He asks if I want coffee, yes, and, once I'm dressed, I want a cigarette, a little breather before the final battle waiting for me at home. Still naked, he goes to make the coffee, I'm staring at my fingers because I don't want to look at him, and I hear his footsteps, the shower, the clatter of dishes, that's all there is between us, these sounds, the whiteness of his torso on top of me, that's all that will remain.

He returns, a blue terrycloth towel wrapped around his waist, carrying a silver-plated platter with ornate handles, and on it a smoking hot copper coffee pot and two small, white, gold-rimmed porcelain cups. Here, he says, placing the platter in front of me on the table, it's square with one single large leg in the middle, like a metal pedestal. Everything here is old, brown Secessionist furniture with flowers etched on the glass doors of the cabinets and cupboards, on the wall a wind-up pendulum clock, dark oil paintings, still-lifes, portraits, everything here is old except for the square bed, which is his.

His grandmother left him the flat, he says, sitting down, last year when she died. It's a nice flat, I say, I like old-fashioned apartments, he does, too, he says, but it needs renovation, the woodwork, the bathroom, the kitchen. We chat about apartments, studying, where the jobs are, I see through the uncurtained window that dawn is breaking, as if the day is getting up from the earth, so I get up, too, and say I'll be going.

See you, he says, walking me to the door, and I smile and nod, sure, absolutely, and I go down the stairs, watching him watch me, his white torso naked, a towel around his waist. I even wave.

Outside, the air is crisp, I breathe it in, the chill gives me goose bumps, there's nobody in the street, just cars, and the chirping birds in the treetops greeting the morning, the new day they have lived to see with a song. It's two tram stops to my house, counting from Republic Square, which runs parallel to the street I'm on, but I have to cross at least four perpendicular streets to get there so I have to take that into account when I'm calculating how long it will take me to get there. All in all, it's no more than a brisk fifteen-minute fast walk for me, now that I'm no longer invested in my seductive stroll, and assuming I don't get lost, which shouldn't happen, I just have to follow the streets and not stop and think, I tell myself, and be careful. I'm waiting to see the yellow theatre building nestled in the park, because that will be a sign that I'm not lost, that I'm not going in the wrong direction. My sense of direction is so bad that I wouldn't know where I was even if somebody dropped me in the middle of Republic Square, I've been known to say. People answer by saying that most women are like that, they have no sense of space. Interesting, because that means something, except, I wonder, why don't women have a sense of space, or of time, because time is space, so maybe it's because they have a sense of eternity, I muse, because eternity is the opposite of time and space, which are dominated by men. However, it's diamonds, not money, that are forever, Huxley observed, and women immediately recognise the eternity that a glittering diamond promises. I instantly feel better with this eternity inside me where everything has already been resolved, where time and space do not carry the weight they do here, where you have to resolve everything as if it hasn't been resolved already, because that's why you've come.

I keep on thinking and thinking, and then I stop because I've walked past the theatre and JNA Street, and past the Church of St. Blaise, like Jens Sigsgaard's *Paul is Alone in the World*, I dash down the streets because it's Sunday and only just daybreak, even my beggar hasn't taken up his post in front of the church yet, and here I am, already in my street, my throat tight, my lungs and stomach going wild, as if I'm going to an execution site. Which is where I'm going, it's kill or be killed, because that's the kind of execution site it is, where everybody dies, both the condemned and the executor in one fell swoop of the axe; counter to the violent logic that cuts off the head of only one party, I'm off to finish what I started. I push open the heavy, etched glass door and walk into the hallway, climb the fifteen steps and am back in front of my door, unlocking it … And here I am in the entrance hall, music wafting in from the radio in the dining room, the tender, matinal strains of the violin, Mendelssohn, the first movement of the *Concert for Violin and Orchestra in E Minor*, my favourite, as if coming to my aid. So he's awake, I think, he's waiting for me, and I breathe in and breathe out before negotiating the doorknob. He's sitting at the table, smoking, the coffee's made, dressed as if he hasn't changed his clothes, his legs crossed, the top leg swinging, looking at me with both reproach and forgiveness, with hope even when everything is lost, his lips quivering, his face red; it's over.

So, is all that he said before walking out, taller than usual, immensely erect somehow, slamming the door in a last act of protest, my darling, my love, my everything, my nothing. Still in my military dress, unwashed, without panties, I danced around the house, I danced like a winner, hey ho, from the dining room into the other rooms, from the other rooms into the dining room, kicking up dust, kicking whatever was in the way, the dog's red ball, polka-dotted like a mushroom, the elegant slippers Kostje had given him, the newspaper, the wooden measuring tape, the blunt pencil, the red ball of wool that appeared from somewhere because my mother knits, hey ho, until I collapsed at the rock bottom of existence and stayed there for the next three days. Incapable of parting with my life and the notions that I had already discarded, deadly miserable for no reason, incomprehensible to myself.

***

It's the morning of day four since he left, the autumnal sun is shining through the lace curtain, it seems I fell asleep sitting up, my head resting on my arm on the table. I stretch and yawn, life is hurting my bones, I'll go to the toilet first, and then it's your turn, I say to Tanga, who is also stretching and yawning, because that's how our bodies are, hers and mine, in that respect there's no difference. The toilet is in the hallway, and there are insects in the hallway, I realise as soon as I enter, some are already blackening my leg, biting, we've got no place else to go, my dog and I, the dining room is their next stop, a fortress conquered in advance.

We'll wind up on the street, I say aloud after peeing, just to make things clear, to make myself understand that I've reached the end, it's either the hall or the street. Obviously it's the hall, I'm not somebody who panics, I'm always calm and collected in a crisis, as I discovered during a tremor, when I pushed visitors paralysed with fear out of the house, even I was surprised by how firm I was.

I open the door and walk straight into the empire of the fleas, and they immediately jump onto me, blackening my legs, and I grab the phone, shove the plug into the wall and dial Information. What's the number for sending a telegram, I ask, my left hand swatting the fleas off my legs, hopping around as if that will help. Then I dial the number they give me, hello, I say, I want to send a telegram: *Mama, come back, the fleas are going to eat me alive*, says the message, short and to the point, and I put the receiver back on the hook, go into the dining room, and onto the balcony to wipe the parasites off me with a wet rag, inasmuch as that's possible, scratch the itching and wait – with the last bread cubes, the last drippings in the pan and the last bottle of wine, red of course, Pharos, twelve-and-a-half per cent alcohol, which doesn't make me drunk. The dog can poo on the balcony.

***

While I was clearing up the place after all the painting, I found letters in a drawer that we had written to each other when he was in the hospital in Rijeka, a stack some eight inches high, held together with a rubber band. What do I do with them, I asked myself, automatically removing the rubber band, so that they fell all over the floor. Addresses, postage stamps, franked stamps, Sofija Kralj Vidović, I see my name in his handwriting, tiny letters, slanting left; my handwriting is big and slants right, or it is straight, it changes. I can't resist opening one of them, my letter to him, not the reverse, I want to see what the person I used to be.

You wanted me even when you were having me burned at the stake, I read randomly, not recognizing my own words; what pleasure it gave him to send me to the stake while still wanting me, I can't get over it, as if it was an act of supreme dedication, sacrificing me even though it meant he would lose me, love even through death, I suppose that's how I explained it to myself, stupid as I was, not seeing that I was being sent to the stake, seeing only that he wanted me, and that this was why I was being sacrificed.

Unbelievable, I say aloud, putting the rubber band back on the letters, wondering what to do with them because I can't throw them into the rubbish. I'll burn them in the stove as soon as the heating season starts, if I remember, I think to myself. I find an empty shoebox in the hallway, stuffed the letters in there and put it in the storage compartment of my mother's sofa, along with the instalments of *The Witch of Grič,* balls of wool and moth-eaten clothes, where, for the time being, they can stay and collect dust.